SKY NEWS

BREAKING NEWS
SKY NEWS POLITICAL CORRESPONDENT
PETER SPENCER
11:55 VISIT skynews.com EMAIL US news@sky.com TEXT 84501

ABOUT THE AUTHOR

Peter Spencer was a Political Correspondent with Sky News for twenty years. Before that he did the same job for the same length of time for London Broadcasting. These days, in addition to ad hoc freelance television presenting, he writes a weekly political column in a men's lifestyle magazine. He's still trying to work out the difference between satire and reporting. That's if there is any.

PITFALLS OF POWER
PLOT ON THE LANDSCAPE

Peter Spencer

Matador
9 Priory Business Park,
Wistow Road, Kibworth Beauchamp,
Leicestershire. LE8 0RX
Tel: 0116 279 2299
Email: books@troubador.co.uk
Web: www.troubador.co.uk/matador
Twitter: @matadorbooks

ISBN 978 1800460 546

British Library Cataloguing in Publication Data.
A catalogue record for this book is available from the British Library.

Printed and bound in Great Britain by 4edge Limited
Typeset in 11pt Adobe Garamond Pro by Troubador Publishing Ltd, Leicester, UK

Matador is an imprint of Troubador Publishing Ltd

ACKNOWLEDGEMENTS ...

Grateful thanks to my friend, mentor and inspiration, the playwright Stephanie Dale – who's gone to so much trouble getting me to moderate my language.

Also to my granddaughters and their friends, who've taken fiendish delight in undoing all Stephanie's good work.

PART ONE

Decline and Fall

PROLOGUE

Percy saw something nasty in the woodshed.

Actually, it wasn't nasty at all. Only Mummy and Daddy doing the sort of thing mummies and daddies have to do to become mummies and daddies in the first place.

Has to be said though, Mummy was as clamorously appreciative as she was adventurous. And the sight of Daddy on his back using his tongue to staunch an open wound between her legs was not what he was used to.

But then he was only six. And, as kiddies are wont to be, a bit impressionable about things they don't understand.

Percy stared, transfixed, and fled in paroxysms of terror. He never dared say a word about it, couldn't even bring himself to picture it, but the image haunted him. Stuck, seemingly indelibly, in his mind. He didn't look at his mother too closely again, or any other woman, for half a lifetime.

Things weren't helped by a tragedy in the family.

A few years down the line, when little Percy wasn't so little any more and had finally clocked that stories about babies found behind gooseberry bushes weren't really true after all, Daddy died.

A quietly spoken, self-effacing, balding sort of chap, he'd

always done his best to keep everybody happy. Especially his wildly enthusiastic, energetic and very much younger wife.

Quite what this raven-haired beauty could ever see in him no one could quite figure out. Maybe it was to do with her being, well, not quite all there. Although, in her newly enfranchised state of widowhood, she rather gave up on motherhood, passed Percy on to her sister, Nora, and became all things to all men.

Her ninny was lubricious, delicious and amazingly resilient. All the blokes agreed, at least all those she could get her hands on.

Things got a bit out of hand, however, when the vicar became the answer to a maiden's prayers.

He loved the first lesson, but there was no second coming. Elderly female parishioners arriving early for evensong saw to that. 'I'll get defrocked for this,' he snarled, taking cover under a pew from the hail of prayer books.

Percy's mummy giggled. 'But you haven't got anything on anyway, silly.'

It got worse, as quavering lips chanted 'Crucify'.

'Bugger you, bitch. I want to rip your bloody guts out.' Swearing in church wasn't the vicar's thing, but right now god could fuck off.

So did she, naked as the day she was born but much sexier. By the time the ladies had given up the chase and returned to the church the vicar had got his act together.

'What you saw was an apparition sent by Satan to test my resolve not to fall into temptation.

'And yours,' he added darkly, 'to avoid the sin of envy.' A fire and brimstone man in the pulpit, he could knit his forehead so tightly his eyebrows met in the middle.

'Can't believe they fell for it, daft old biddies.' The vicar licked his lips later. The communion wine wasn't so bad mixed with gin.

Trouble was, they didn't fall for it. The police were called, and poor Mummy, still wearing nothing but her birthday suit,

4

was carted off and charged with gross indecency and attempted rape.

It was a bit unfair of the vicar to claim she'd come at him, so to speak, in a state of nature and left him in a state of perplexity. But then, as the Good Book says, thou shalt not commit adultery. Or at least not admit it.

When her case came before Crown Court the judge agreed with the psychiatrist she was a child in a woman's body, peered a little too appreciatively at it over his pince-nez and opted for protective custody, hoping this wasn't for the wrong reasons.

Not that she was interested in anything apart from the must-have rookie copper on the door. He clocked her staring at him, and was soon standing to attention in more ways than one. His police issue helmet covered the one he was born with.

She'd told her legal aid solicitor that playtime with the vicar seemed a lovely idea because he was a man of god and not like some of the others. 'I was a bit disappointed when he said he'd pull my insides out, though. And he called me a rude name, nasty old toad.'

The lawyer perked up for a second, but decided her tainted word against that of a pillar of the community wouldn't achieve anything, apart from finishing his career.

He gave up trying to explain this when Mummy leant over to pick up the dollies she always carried around when she was anxious and started singing to them.

'Raindrops on roses and whiskers on kittens. Bright copper kettles and warm woollen mittens. Pretty boys' naughty bits right up my minge, these are a few of my favourite things.'

'Are you mad, woman?' Sounded like a yes then when she undressed first Ken then Barbie and kissed them in unmentionable places. He sighed, took off his glasses and polished them wearily. The question had answered itself.

*

5

That was it for her then. No more love among the haystacks, or anywhere else. Only nasty ladies with faces like mouldy walnuts, making her take horrid tablets and telling her she was a disgrace to her sex.

'But I like sex,' she'd explain. This did not help.

From now on there'd be no more giving the fellers a dreamy smile and a hand job to get them started. Not that she'd have gone for any old dog, mind, though she did try it once with an Alsatian. He didn't stop wagging his tail for a month. The vet couldn't understand it.

She couldn't understand either why Percy hardly ever ventured out from Auntie Nora's to come and visit her in this miserable, sexless place. Somewhere in her muddled mind she sensed she might have let him down a bit. But now she missed him so much, and cried herself to sleep almost every night.

Actually, she knew all about crying. Half her schooldays were spent doing just that, at the back of the class, because she couldn't understand a word the teachers were saying and they couldn't be arsed to tell her. The girls loathed her because she prettier than them, as well as stupid, and the boys just didn't notice her.

They wouldn't, would they? She was only a girl after all. And a bit gangly back then.

Could be the male attention she got later mattered more to her than the sex itself. Though it happens she was born with a libido that, if marketed in tablet form, would make Viagra look like a stiff snort of bromide.

*

Word spread about her post-marital exploits, and of course the court case. And, over the years, Percy came in for loads of stick. Try as he might to shrug it off, he was smothered in shame. It dovetailed into the woodshed, etched deep in his subconscious.

So, what with one thing and another, his relations with the gentler gender became and remained strained. So much so that even as a grown man he was still one of the boys. This upset the ladies no end as he got better and better looking.

They'd ask friends his name, only to dab their eyes, and elsewhere, at the bad news. 'Afraid we call Percy Pussy, dear.'

The pretty young undergraduate with the elfin figure and bowler who came closest to getting her fill was also shafted by the woodshed, if not by anything else.

Vivienne, Viv only to nearest and dearest, nearly didn't go to Percy's Weimar Republic Cabaret-themed fancy dress party. She'd heard stories about alcohol abuse and drug taking. But the spotty third-year student who wanted to score talked her round.

In the elaborately made-over digs, her eyes opened unnaturally wide. She could have come as a frog if she'd turned as green as she felt. Posters of topless Lisa Minnelli lookalikes and the statue of a dominatrix riding a naked man screamed pure sleaze and impure thoughts.

But the sight of Percy did the trick. She'd finally found Love. 'Oh brave new world, that has such people in it,' she murmured. The kid with acne looked miserable and hated Percy.

Red hair billowed out of a black turban, and deep-toned make-up highlighted his chiselled features. The catsuit, diamante-studded belt and high-heeled boots emphasised a perfect figure, while the codpiece promised deep joy. Almost life-threateningly deep.

Percy was savvy enough to know the difference between gilding the lily and blowing it apart. It took four ecstasy tablets and three whopping lines of cocaine to get him out there.

Mummy always used to say 'Just be yourself, my lover'. That was all very well when, as a baby, he wanted no more in life than a tit to suck on. Not that he got that lucky, at least not for a very, very long time.

Meantime, teachers at the village school noticed he wasn't like the others. Never mind down below, it was happening up top.

'Will I gwow up to be a culi-nin-nin-ary gene... genie... ever-so-clever boy and wear a white hat like Daddy?' he'd asked Mummy when he was two. The family firm, Penislow Proper Pasties, was, like Percy at the time, small but perfectly formed. The locals loved Daddy's battered Ford Thames van wheezing up the lanes. Sometimes it would even go 'parp parp'.

The boy's horizons broadened in time. 'Fuck firing ovens in conservatories, I'm going to grow weed, industrial scale,' he told his mates in year six. By the time he was eighteen he was smoking the stuff, but four straight As had him wondering.

'Some are born great, some achieve greatness, and some have greatness thrust upon 'em,' he muttered. 'Some kind of post-Hegelian Darwinian synthesis.' A teacher standing nearby pretended to understand. The other kids decided Percy was a posturing wanker.

In time Percy took their point, but still wondered about his greatness. 'Search me,' he admitted to Auntie's rescue dog. 'Born a prole, die a prole, right? How many brain cells do you think us lot have between us?' The mongrel licked his bum then Percy's face...

Loads of bloody good washes and three years later he got a first at uni, then the distinction at Masters that earned him a scholarship for a doctorate. He wrote the thesis in clear, jargon-free English that exasperated his Ukrainian professor. 'You settle for dumbo-speak? You become bad thing like journalist, or join politburo.'

'What? And earn twice as much as you do, for half the work?' Percy was furious.

He'd got the hang of wearing the social equivalent of an anti-radiation protective suit, learned to sound like a cultured person and spent years reading all the right books, classic tome on one knee, dictionary on the other. But there was a line from Oscar Wilde that still got to him. 'Nowadays to be intelligible is to be found out'...

*

Same as Percy, Vivienne was worried on the night of the party. She did look boyish with her bobbed black hair tucked behind her small, neat ears. The more so with suspender tights showing off her strong little legs like that, while her just about A-cup breasts almost dissolved under the low-cut leotard. It took a small glass of sherry to clinch the argument.

An eager nineteen-year old, she was star-struck by these clever PhD students in their mid-twenties. But none came close to Percy, whose talk fluttered from high camp to low politics. A metaphor? Images of gods swooping down on enthusiastic virgins flicked through her mind, and she gave herself a severe talking to.

She was a good northern lass, but the elocution lessons her parents put her through as a kid meant you'd never know. They only wanted the best for her, though the effect was to mask that she was a sharp little cookie, practical and pragmatic as well as clever.

But she was only human. Dazzled in the headlights of fate, she couldn't take her eyes off Percy, a turn-on for any man. When he eventually strode across and gripped her forearms tightly she felt like a little bird, wings scorched and lower intestine behaving most oddly.

The boy with the skin condition skulked off to the loo, squeezed a couple of spots till they burst and had a wank. Didn't enjoy it much.

In a mock A-level essay Vivienne proved a sexually aroused girl doesn't really get a melting sensation in her lady garden. Her tutor splattered exclamation marks everywhere, underlined whole paragraphs and recommended in-depth research. Remembering the sex offenders register he rubbed out in-depth. He'd have rubbed his hands in glee now.

'Who's a pretty boy then?' Not an ideal chat-up line for a heterosexual woman, but Percy didn't know. Now that the drop of sherry had been topped up with five pints of lager and half a tumblerful of gin, Vivienne didn't care.

'Is that a pistol in your pocket, or are you just pleased to see me?'

Dutch courage? She was ready to sail up the Medway, conquer the East Indies, and shaft the Stuart dynasty.

In no time they were in the bedroom, where nothing was as it seemed. The fairy lights only flickered because of the dodgy wiring, and under fresh burgundy paint the crumbling masonry almost didn't hold up the prints of Karl Marx and half-naked flapper girls. Vivienne was pleased every one of them looked like her, apart from the bloke with the beard, obviously.

The riot of drapes overhanging what looked like a king-sized bed disguised what it was. An ill-suited pair of singles pressed together. Like the people about to get in it.

'Come to me, lover boy,' Vivienne whispered hoarsely. The throat infection she was getting over made her sound like the pubescent male Percy thought she was. Mistakes happen when you've just popped three more tabs and snorted for Colombia.

'Oh boy, Vivian, I want to plumb you to the bottom,' he sighed. An ambiguous choice of words.

'No peeking now, I'm not going to bed with a naughty boy,' Vivienne giggled. Not knowing that was exactly what Percy had in mind, she turned her back to throw caution and clothing to the winds. 'I've never got so close to a bloke in less than four months, let alone four hours.'

'I have, I'm afraid,' Percy sighed. 'Lots of times. But you're special, Vivian.' Once again Vivienne failed to take in exactly what was being said to her. The blissful expression on his face as he lay back was enough.

She turned to face him, partially cupping her breasts in her hands. 'There, lover boy, open your peepers. These are for starters. There's an opening coming.' Vivienne was naturally cautious, but her heart had melted. This was Her Man.

Percy too was bowled over, but in a different way. Confronted not with firm and familiar pectoral muscles but with what were unmistakeably a woman's breasts, he suddenly saw Lord Kitchener glowering down at him from those First World War recruitment ads. 'These nipples need you,' he muttered.

'Oh yes, yes,' pleaded Vivienne. 'These nipples need kneading.' Her lady garden was doing just what she's sworn wasn't possible, though Percy would not be going with the flow that night. He got a flashback to Auntie Nora, ever ready with a cliché. 'You never know till you've tried, dear.'

Off his face as he was, he guessed she didn't mean this sort of thing.

MDMA can make the impossible seem the best idea ever, and in spite of the codpiece Percy hadn't wanted to seem forward. But now, naked, erect and throbbing, he was trying to lay back and think of anything other than woodsheds.

Vivienne had always told herself she didn't care about looks, only the person's soul. But the rippling chest and taut stomach changed her mind. She trailed her fingers along the soft pubic line stretching to the navel. Up, then down, finally greeted by a one-member reception committee, showing its appreciation in the time-honoured way.

Percy looked at her closely. 'Your jaw's a trifle firm. Nose a bit short. Forehead rather high. Pah! Grit in the oyster. That mysterious smile. Those melting eyes. Too beautiful.'

There hadn't been much discussion of such things over breakfast when he was a kid, but he'd learned later from D.H. Lawrence people have a special glow for special people.

Doggedly keeping his mind on her face, he caressed one breast and felt a tautening in the centre of his palm. Safe so far. But down below? La différence! At the base of the gently rounded stomach was a silky triangle shielding stuff of his nightmares.

Viv gasped as Percy's fingers toyed with her salivating lips, her back arched and her legs parted to receive the slow descent, his tongue teasing out her secrets. She felt spasms in her pelvis, her juices flowed freely, and tears of joy leaked through her fluttering eyelids.

But then... the scales tipped.

A spot of acid might have swung it, but not having gone there Percy was going nowhere. His eyes snapped open and he sat up, head slumped in shame. His throbbing Shard became a modest single-story dwelling. Viv, soon to become Vivienne, wasn't happy.

'You see,' he stammered, 'I saw something nasty in the woodshed.'

'Why on earth do you say that?'

'Don't know, but it haunts me. Read it in book somewhere about crazy country people. Supposed to be funny, but I don't think so.

'Fact is, I'm a chap sort of chap. Don't really go in for girls. Or into them. Sorry about that.'

So it wasn't just stage fright, then. Viv was definitely Vivienne again, and snarling. 'You fucking wanker. Now you fucking tell me. Hate you. Hate you. Hate you.' She hardly ever used the F word, but she'd never been so humiliated or disappointed either.

As she struggled to find something to cover herself, staggering between wall and bed, the lights went out and the pictures tumbled to the floor. She steadied herself with the drapes, before they too went the same way as the Jazz Age and the overthrow of capitalism.

Hearing the commotion, Percy's mates sniggered at what fun the happy couple must be having, but paused when they heard the front door slam, its ill-fitting window shattering on the doorstep, then stopped when they sniffed the air.

The Bashar brothers, friends from the Middle East who'd been welcomed by the university because overseas students always brought in a fortune one way or another, had a brief conflab in their cut-glass English public school accents. 'Jolly poor show, what? Better call the rozzers?'

'Tally ho, number's 999, old boy.'

The place was on fire, no surprise given the state of the electrics. Not that Percy noticed. He tried to punish his penis by biting the end off. But, as certain drugs bend minds but not spines, he pinched it instead, then burst into tears. The pain didn't help.

Two days later he was still nursing the wound as well as second-degree burns, while Vivienne was doing the same with her broken heart. 'He's a beast. A brute. A monster. Got me in the sack then told me he was bloody well gay,' she sobbed.

Her flatmate was a sturdy, shaven-headed young woman who cut a dash with her tattoos that said on the one hand 'don't' and on the other 'screw men'. She toyed with trying to get in where Percy didn't, but knew she was hearing a definite 'no'. Pity, she'd fancied Viv for months.

'The course of true love never did run smooth, jigglypuff,' she murmured. 'You'll probably end up marrying him.'

'Yeah yeah, pigs might fly to Pluto,' Vivienne snorted. 'He'll land in Downing Street, and we'll live happily ever after.'

Only later did she discover Percy wasn't living anywhere at that moment, the blaze having consumed his entire flat, and most of the two adjoining properties.

CHAPTER ONE

Percy wasn't struck on his new accommodation, even though the place looked like a palace. If they've any idea where they are, punters at The Priory know they're on the naughty step.

'Think yourself lucky your auntie got you insured,' Viv scolded. 'God knows how she found the money, but she obviously knows you better than you do. As I found out, to my cost.'

Percy winced. He couldn't get over her being there. 'How can you be so good? To me of all people? Still, if you take out the drink and drugs, mental instability and sexual psychosis I'm quite a catch.' His self-effacing grin was infuriatingly seductive.

Viv caressed his hand and considered his face. And his body, in spite of herself. Another good talking to beckoned, the moment she got off the hospital grounds. Getting off with him wasn't going to happen any time soon.

During the weeks after the party she'd had many a heart-to-heart with her surprisingly thoughtful flatmate, Jacky as a child, now only answering to Jack, and discovered she wasn't the only one who'd been shafted in the wrong way. She even toyed with trying toys on Jack, to get her own back on Percy.

'No way, Bambi-lovey. I'm up for missionary work, but you'll never convert,' Jack told her, with a rueful smile.

'So what am I supposed to do?' Viv's voice quivered with more than one kind of frustration. She sensed what was coming next meant never coming at all.

'For god's sake go and see *le bâtard*, excuse my French,' Jack insisted. 'Say it with flowers if you must, though best not give him Flame of the Forest. He might not get the joke.'

The local rag had gone big on the fire and Viv was convinced it was all her fault when she learned Percy was in The Priory. Besides, much as she'd hated him, she knew he was the one for her. She went to the West Wing with an armful of nice safe pink roses.

'My dear, an efflorescence! Veritable plenitude of munificence!' Percy always hid behind long words when he was embarrassed, but Viv wasn't having it. In any sense, unfortunately, though there were alternative approaches.

She wasn't counting on a *soixante-neuf*, but polarities were being reversed. Viv spotted behind Percy's charisma, charm and brilliance a vulnerability and self-destructive silliness. A tendency, as her down-to-earth mum would have said, to bite off more than he could chew.

When he mentioned what he'd tried to do to himself after she left on that anything but fucking night she nodded grimly to herself. But couldn't help but smile at the same time.

Percy had tried to carry on as normal after the party which destroyed property and took lives. Four budgies, two goldfish and a tortoise, belonging to the old bloke upstairs. He was lucky, getting so bladdered at the pub he'd fallen into a manhole and spent the night there.

'Lost me bleedin' denshures,' he grumbled when Percy visited him in hospital. 'And what abaht me free flying ducks? Gave me place a bit of class. Up the bleedin' Swanee nah, same as me Reichsmarks. Wanted them, in case the Boche comes back.'

Before the delayed shock set in and he was carted off to The Priory, Percy made a hundred quid donation to the RSPCA and went to see the old man several times.

'Really sorry about the cracked ribs, and the Reichsmarks.' Percy meant it. 'Got loads of French francs though. Could be more useful. The Frogs have more form than the Huns.'

*

Now that Percy was on the receiving end of visits he was guarded. Viv was a girl, he got that all right, but not much else. What did she want? She didn't let on at first, asking him loads of questions instead. Turned out he loved telling stories, even against himself.

'The fireman wanted to know why I hadn't tried to douse the flames in the bedroom. Didn't realise I was quoting Lord Byron when I told him I thought I'd died and gone to hell, and did a runner when I said I never could resist a man in uniform.' That grin again. Bastard.

Viv was fascinated by Percy's brain, and what he did with it. It made up for what he didn't do with his... best not think about it. She was a smart cookie, but didn't know much more than she'd been taught at school and uni. Percy seemed to know everything.

The more she listened, the longer she held his eyes in hers, the more he felt himself falling for her.

'My dear, who needs hanky-panky? An acquaintance that begins with a fire, a breakdown and the death of four budgies, two goldfish and a tortoise is sure to develop into a real friendship. It starts in the right manner.' Viv smiled. She'd no idea most of his gags were adapted from gay authors.

He did, however, try to be honest about who he was. 'Didn't like train sets when I was a kid. Preferred dollies. You could dress them up. Anyway, girls weren't as silly as boys.

'Had a wooden dagger though. Used it on a big fat slob I caught torturing a mouse. Didn't cut it, pardon my language. He put my lights out. Could have been worse. Imagine if I'd been a fly, I'd have really got it.'

Viv obviously wasn't getting it, so Percy explained. 'Thing is, flies have five eyes to punch, instead of just two. Love seeing him these days, still stacking shelves at Tesco's. A man can't be too careful in his choice of enemies.

'Had a special mate though. Rodney Rumpledore. Came from my village. Might be my uncle.'

'Might be? Don't you know?'

'The lads who missed out on Passchendaele in Flanders lucked out on passion in Cornwall. And the boys in the trenches didn't know their babies should've been born nine months after home leave, not weeks or years later. Back then, stuff like that wasn't taught at school.

'But Rodney definitely did risk his life and save mine when I was proving how brilliant I was by climbing down a redundant pit shaft.'

It struck Viv all Percy was doing was proving how bloody stupid he could be. But she didn't interrupt.

'Seems only yesterday old Rodders was calling out "What'm you bleddy doin' down there? How'm I goin' t' bleddy fish 'ee out?" He'd heard me squealing for help, rushed to the rescue and knew exactly what he'd have to do. Didn't fancy it much. Don't blame him.

'I made it worse, telling him we'm bleddy tinners and there'm a Cornishman at the bottom of every mine in the world. My little jokes, always bubbling to the surface. Funny that, seeing how far I was below it.

'"Bleddy Cornishmen at the bottom of every bleddy hole be beggared," he shouted. "Not much use if ee'm a bleddy corpse."

'I heard him spit several times, but he abseiled down and got me in a fireman's lift back up to the flat, safe grass. The sunny uplands. Could have cried. Well I did, actually.'

Viv went to The Priory most evenings and the unlikely romance now definitely cutting both ways did Percy more good than all the shrinks and drugs put together. They celebrated his discharge by moving in together, after a visit to the lovely auntie who'd seen him through his adolescence.

He was sentimental about her, in a tentative way.

'Dear Auntie Nora, ignore 'er at your peril, I always say. You can picture me, can't you, in my hempen homespun youth, all set for the life of a horny-handed son of toil?'

'Snobby sod,' Viv snorted. 'You were as out of place in a council house as a giraffe in a birdcage. And you know it.'

Even when he was being idiotic Percy oozed culture and sophistication, while his dad, as he described him, had been so salt of the earth you could have bagged him up and sold him at Lidl.

'He was a Wesleyan socialist, my dear, but was always more interested in profits than prophets. Little wonder, poor sod, after all his hideously badly paid years in service.'

Viv thought about this. And about the apparition she'd first clapped eyes on at that party. In her head she couldn't get it straight. Any more than he could, manner of speaking.

She was also eternally curious about Mummy. But all she could get out of him on that subject was 'Mum's the word', which wasn't very helpful.

Truth be told, he was heartbroken as a kid when she got locked away and made no effort to stay in contact. He wasn't to know that, until she finally gave up, she'd written him masses of desperately loving and appallingly badly spelt letters.

Unfortunately, as she'd addressed them to 'My Sweeet and Luvly boy, care of Lord Whatsisname in the grate big bewtiful howse', the postie didn't stand much of a chance.

So, as he passed through puberty and discovered his little winkle wasn't just for doing wee wees through, he locked away the pain alongside the woodshed in his emotional attic. The inscription engraved on the key read 'Really really don't trust girls'.

*

Viv's parents were as puzzled as she was when they too eventually came face to face with Auntie Nora.

'Can't think where I am,' her father grumbled. 'I teach geography for god's sake, supposed to know where everything is.' Her mother, an accountant, sighed. 'Yes dear, things really should add up.'

Percy wasn't surprised when Viv told him what they'd said.

'Sometimes wonder if I was smuggled into the maternity ward in a warming pan, like in the olden days. Anne Boleyn would've lived longer if someone had popped a baby boy into her bed.' This was veering off the subject, but Viv found it reassuring. Percy was still Percy, whoever he was.

'Anyway, I'll get my doctorate in a few months and the local TV station guys are gagging for me. They like the narrative of turning a nobody into a star, patronising provincial bastards. But it'll get me started.

'I was born to perform. When I was Macbeth in the school play Auntie Nora was scared of me for weeks. But make-believe makes more on telly. Oh and one day I'm going to be Prime Minister. Bollocks to it can't be done. With you at my side I can do anything.'

It struck Viv Percy's 'anythings' tended towards life-threateningly dangerous. But his enthusiasm was infectious. So once again she didn't interrupt.

'Ever since I first looked upon your wonderful and incomparable beauty, I have dared to love you wildly, passionately, devotedly, hopelessly.' Though Viv was sure she'd heard that line before, somewhere, she was already choking back tears.

'I want you to be my First Lady. I regret children are out of the question, but would you mind awfully marrying me?

'You can't help being a girl and I can't help being rubbish in the bits department. Do whatever you please, it's only fair, but we're made for one another. Just stick around and try and put up with me. It's all I ask.'

A big ask? Not in Viv's mind. Jack's battery operated plastic arsenal had convinced her natural urges could be fittingly contained. She hoped Percy would at least be discreet.

This was not weakness on her part, she was devoted to him. Besides, a promise of a lifelong commitment, ten-a-penny from a bloke angling for a quick shag, is invaluable when that's the last thing he wants. Anyway, maybe they could get that bit right as well. One day...

CHAPTER TWO

Today, some twenty-five years later, it's all come true. Percy's been erect and throbbing everywhere, except in bed, though he's been a devoted husband, and unexpectedly restrained with male admirers. Viv's passion for him has mellowed but deepened over time, so his vagina phobia wasn't an impediment to a marriage of true minds after all.

And one other thing. They recently moved in to Number Ten Downing Street.

The only downside is Percy's hating the job. Sitting at his desk in the flat upstairs, Viv slumbering in the next room, he thinks how often she's mentioned her mum's advice about biting and chewing. There's more of that coming, and it's going to hurt.

Coiled spring isn't in it. Fang is more AK-47, bayonet glittering in the moonlight. Eyes narrowed, pulse quickened, body tensed. Killing in cold blood is like sex when you're seducing a complete stranger in a railway carriage. No more conscience for the dagger than the erect penis. He strikes and the victim succumbs, without a murmur.

As you do when you're a shoelace.

But Doctor Percy Penislow PC PhD MP is roaring like a lion. He hadn't noticed the little psycho, and after leaping in terror at this unprovoked assault on his foot he tips half a cup of coffee over his trousers and the rest into his computer.

Undoing his flies and uncovering the already reddening area of leg, he's feeling hateful. 'You're the one that's supposed to be scalded. You're the fucking cat.'

Watching the Apple Mac screen fade to black, taking with it the hours' work he's just spent fiddling around with tomorrow's big speech to the Confederation of British Industry, he decides the original draft was probably just as good. Have to be now.

Anyway, as he's not on till after lunch the overpaid Tory slobs will be too well oiled to take it in, and media interest will be zero unless he collapses at the lectern or moons at the cameras.

Fang's not fussed either. Bored with writhing, scratching and snapping, he sits up and has a good wash. Total war? What war? Percy sees the funny side, collapses into his clapped-out swivel chair and laughs till tears run down his face and he tumbles over backwards.

The cream-coloured carpet, cleaned in honour of Percy's arrival, is soaking up four half-drunk cups of coffee and a hardly touched bottle of red wine, gurgling into huge and indelible stains.

Muttering his displeasure in yet more unparliamentary terms, the Prime Minister picks up the now nearly empty bottle, tries to mop up the mess with his trousers, then lunges for the brandy. Throughout his brief time in office he's ended most days too tired to hold a glass, let alone drink out of it. But this is different.

The decanter's wide base suggests it once belonged to a sailor. Probably a pirate, as it came from Penzance. He respects Cornish traditions like smuggling and wrecking, in spite of Labour's crackdown on tax evasion and violent crime.

As he half-fills his enormous balloon, inscribed 'Percy Penislow – County Free Fall Stunt Champion', he thinks back to the insane moment he agreed to jump out of a hot-air balloon for charity. Auntie Nora told him to go before he went and he did. And again on the way down. More than once.

'What doesn't kill you makes you stronger. Friedrich Nietzsche,' was his take. Nora did not approve. The name sounded German. Probably a Nazi, then. But she'd given up trying to understand Percy before he'd even started secondary school.

He's often struggled himself, but it seems logical now to dip his fingers into the drink and offer them to Fang for a taste test, praying it won't cause another episode. 'I'm an artful dodger,' he informs his new drinking partner. 'More of a third way than third Reich kind of guy.'

The animal licks the hand of peace, claws agonisingly up his unclothed leg onto his lap, and seems to enjoy being caressed behind the ears. Just like a normal cat. Percy risks a confidence. 'Uneasy lies the head that wears a crown.'

He doesn't expect the Shakespearean reference to his own situation to be understood, but has second thoughts when Fang leaps onto the desk and savages the now redundant computer mouse.

'Mouse? Mouse? Does the brute understand words?' As the second serious slurp works its soothing magic, Percy thinks he's being purred at sympathetically.

'Supposed to be an aphrodisiac, right? Power. Supposed to put you in touch with your inner superhero, right? Batman, Beelzebub, Mrs Beaton, right? Or Lenny the Lion,' he adds, remembering he's talking to a cat, albeit a smaller one.

'It's one fucking crisis after another. Fucking Brexit. Fucking coronavirus. Economy utterly fucked, my lot scrapping as hard as the Tories. It's like a kid's join-the-dots puzzle. Except you don't end up with a nice little flightless bird, cat, but a ghastly three-headed dog. Sticking its tongues out at you.'

Another huge glug, rather an ungentlemanly belch, for which he apologises to no one in particular, and Percy remembers he hasn't eaten for eight hours. 'Imagine you're in a tank, Fang, surrounded by crazed guerrillas with machine guns, aircraft, artillery. You'd need eyes to the front, to the sides and up your bottom for god's sake.'

Fang yawns and looks bored.

*

Percy twitches his willy, like when he was in trouble with Miss at nursery school, which is how he's feeling, and tells himself a few home truths. *What did you expect, village oik? Toffs have actually been to the Sistine Chapel, and feel like they went to school with the Medici brothers. All our sort have is the chapel up the road and the bloke in the Post Office.*

That problem again. Nagging insecurity burnt in like Catholic guilt, there to stay. He knows he's clever, always got an answer to everyone and everything; even Viv took a while to decode him. But never mind the others, he knows better.

At least she's still with him. Amazing after he made such a prick of himself, or rather didn't, when they met. Kissing her framed photo he keeps on his desk, he downs another twenty or so units, carefully aims the Dunhill at his ciggie then closes it quickly. He hasn't forgotten his bedroom getting foggy and the end of four budgies, two goldfish and a tortoise.

The end's looking nigh for him too, in spite of his best efforts. As he passes out, his brandy sploshes onto the sodden carpet, his ciggie lands in it and doesn't go out.

Only the racket from the smoke detector saves Percy from becoming Britain's second shortest-serving leader ever. This thought occurs to him just as Viv bursts into the room. 'Doing my besht, dear, but Lady Jane Grey schrewed up after only nine days. That'sh a hard act to follow.'

But Viv's in Vivienne mode. 'Bugger history, if that's who you want to be you're on your own.' She hunts out the fire extinguisher and glares at him. 'Getting to be a habit, this. Once is understandable, twice is carelessness.

'And it's not funny,' she snarls, catching the smirk on Percy's face. 'You deserve to be burnt at the stake. Not that you need any help in that direction.'

CHAPTER THREE

Percy doesn't need the help of the London Fire Brigade, the London Ambulance Service and the Army either. But when the Cabinet Secretary tells the Metropolitan Police Commissioner and the Chief of the Defence Staff that Number Ten's a raging inferno, alarm bells tend to ring.

Sir Bernard Brenstorme OBE was odd from the word go, being born upside down and back to front. His nanny was accused of inappropriate behaviour and unfairly sacked after he'd shut his winkle in a door. At the age of eight he accidentally blinded his fencing teacher. Later, his prep school was quarantined for a week after he'd reported an outbreak of bubonic plague.

It wasn't reopened till someone realised the housemaster, who still used a typewriter, often smeared his face with carbon paper ink.

But he's got a brilliant and forensic intelligence. So in spite of his weirdness, perhaps because of it, he's always shone in the civil service. Until recently. If he'd had a wife she'd have spotted the signs of his rare and premature form of Alzheimer's disease. But as he hasn't he just carries on, doing madder and madder things.

Tonight is like the prep school incident but bigger, as no one spots there's a loony on the loose. Trouble starts when the

Downing Street coppers, who open up for ambulances and police cars, say no to the tanks. Their mistake. Challenger 2s? Gates? No contest.

Whitehall becomes a war zone. Fleet Street is in meltdown, Twitter crashes and Percy will shortly try to strangle Sir Bernard.

Word spreads. Global arms dealers burst into song, and when the White House learns Britain's facing a military coup the President decides now's a good time to teach the limeys a lesson and scrambles the USAF. There's even a call from an old colonial outpost in the South Pacific.

'It's for you.' Without another word Vivienne hands the phone to her husband, who's amazed to hear the distant, crackling voice of the Prime Minister of Tuvalu fervently hoping the guards at Buckingham Palace with their wonderful hats will save the day.

Assuming this is a prank call from some idiot radio station Percy laughs, suggests he do one and hangs up. The Prime Minister of Tuvalu lodges a formal complaint with His Excellency the Secretary-General of the Commonwealth.

Minutes later there's a soft tap at the door and the Cabinet Secretary presents his compliments. Discreetly ignoring the Prime Minister's near-nakedness from the waist down, he explains what steps he has taken, and recommends a peek out of the window.

'You did this? You protozoan fucking throwback.' Percy has instantly sobered up. Arms outstretched, he charges. But, not noticing the snoring cat in his path, he trips over and falls flat on his face. Sir Bernard bends down to help the Prime Minister, who tries to eat his face.

'I say. I say, now look here, that's a bit thick you know.' Sir Bernard is a 1950s kind of guy. He wears a clockwork fob watch, gave up on television when they introduced colour and hasn't trusted policemen since they stopped driving in Wolseleys.

Leaving Percy gibbering uncontrollably in the bedroom, Vivienne takes control of the situation. 'Your actions were disproportionate, Sir Bernard, kindly undo them.' Her gorgon Medusa's death stare suggests that mightn't be such a bad idea.

After several frantic hours on the telephone he manages to persuade the US Department of Defense that military intervention would be undesirable, but can't get the Prime Minister of Tuvalu to see reason. Brenstorme wishes he could send in a gunboat.

*

As luck would have it, a member of the England Squad is filmed that night having it off with his golden retriever. When the footage goes viral, the governance of the United Kingdom ceases to be an issue.

By morning workmen have more or less bent back into shape the gates supposedly guarding Downing Street, and the British public neither knows nor cares about the pulverised ramp a short distance back that halts all uninvited vehicles except tanks.

But the failure of the rumoured coup does trouble those in the know. Shares in arms firms plummet, and the Presidents of Russia, France and the European Commission recork the fizz. The German Chancellor stops goose-stepping round Berlin yelling, 'Leck mich am Arsch, Britische Brexit Schweinehunde,' and starts to cry.

Percy's meeting with Sir Bernard is also pretty miserable. 'Bloody nincompoop, you've got the brains of a jellyfish. You're as much use as an umbrella in the Sahara. Well, what've you got to say for yourself?'

'Actually, Prime Minister, parts of the Sahara have up to four inches of rain a year, when it does come down it's torrential, and—'

Percy cuts him short. 'Sod the Sahara, you deserve to be scalped.' Apparently keen to get started, Fang pounces on Brenstorme, snatches his toupee and scurries off with it.

'It'd have taken a heart of stone not to laugh out loud,' Percy tells Viv later. 'He's my bestie beastie.'

Viv, still very much Vivienne, is not amused. 'I've stood by you through thick and thin, but you can be so stupid I want to bite your balls off. Make no difference to me anyway.'

Percy squirms and says nothing. But he calls Rodney, now Lord, Rumpledore, as his old mate's always had the best of intentions. Shame the road to hell was paved for him.

He started well, rescuing Percy from that mine. And topped it by standing up to the rich bastards who'd have done very nicely out of a planned American airbase while the locals would have got bugger all.

Apart from losing a lovely spot for the older ones to walk their dogs by day, or for the younger ones to shag one another by night, they'd have been stuck with oversexed, overpaid Yanks ravishing everyone alive. Perhaps even checking out the graveyards.

Rodney's part of Cornwall repaid his efforts by electing him to Parliament, on a huge swing. Huge salary too, next to the pennies he made from his little farm. The pretty milkmaid he was dating promptly told him she was expecting his baby.

Yesss! He wanted nothing more than her, and a son.

Percy remembers what a catch Rodney was before she got her claws in, and how he tried to warn the silly sod. 'She's a feral bitch on the make, can't 'ee bleddy see that?' Rodney didn't knock his block off because all he could see was the best tits in town.

He saw the light, though, the night he tied the knot. The missus announced the pregnancy had been a false alarm, and she had a headache. A bad one, as it turned out. Lasted fifty years.

Heartbroken but old-fashioned about divorce, Rodney settled for the odd fling. Later he hit the bottle and reinvented himself as a cross between a sly old fox and a silly old fart.

The gay fraternity in the parliamentary press corps found his *Carry on Matron* humour amusing and pretended to like him. It would have broken his heart to learn it was him not his jokes they were laughing at. Getting him pissed was like giving a spliff to a chimpanzee.

*

They were tickled when he tried to make out he was being smart in trying to get some country bumpkin kid he knew into the lobby. 'No bleddy skin off me nose, mark me bleddy words, I'll get me back scratched back. My Percy, 'ee'm a bleddy catch to be snatched.'

'Oh dear darling Rosie, she's just a babe.' Rodney wasn't sure about the nickname Rosie, or much else about these guys, but had a feeling Percy's mugshot might be a trump card.

'Mmmm. She is a babe, isn't she?' The Chairman of the Lobby stroked his immaculately trimmed goatee beard. 'Good face for current affairs, or any sort.' He smirked. 'Can see why you want to give him a leg-over. Oops, sorry dear, leg up.'

Percy got an invite to drinkies in the press bar and ended up climbing down a rope ladder from the press gallery into the chamber. It was full of MPs, but he clambered back in time. Just.

Viv was appalled at where this frightful behaviour led. When one of the big networks advertised for a political correspondent and Percy applied, other candidates might as well have tried to sell their toenail clippings to beggars. The poofter political editor saw to that.

'Bit of fun, and a spot of lubrication, always helps a chap on the way up,' Percy giggled. Viv tried not to think too specifically about that.

Years later, when Rodney was made a peer, he wangled it that Percy got his seat in the Commons. 'Getting they selection committee party to choose you as candidate weren't no bleddy corruption,' he insisted. 'Just a case of merit.'

'And a case of Bollinger Special Cuvee?' They both sniggered.

Rodney guessed what might have happened the night there was a security alert in Downing Street, and isn't surprised to hear from him.

'You see, Purrsi,' he mutters, 'they scientist party, they'm got no idea what most of that there grey matter actually do. Well I can tell'ee. It lay a'slumbering, like, ready to come to life if a feller gets to be gaffer. Because he'm be bleddy needin' it then.'

It's exactly what Dad would have said if he'd lived long enough. In the event, apart from Auntie Nora, Rodney's the only real link with Percy's childhood since the Penislow Proper Pasties oven blew up and left him, for a while at least, in Mummy's hopeless hands. Little wonder he's not fond of fires.

Sounding posh can feel like a straitjacket, while Rodney's unreconstructed Cornishness is a reassuring skeleton in his cultural cupboard. Poor sod even looks like a bag of bones, still wearing shirts bought when his neck was four sizes larger.

He's alive and gibbering today though, especially about the devil drink. Percy feels purged by the good ticking off, and comforted by this opportunity to revert to the vernacular of his early years.

'You'm bleddy right me 'ansum,' he admits. 'I'll watch me bleddy step in future.'

Rodney hopes he will, but wishes he'd just told the lad straight. 'Do as I say, not as I bleddy do.' He takes another swig from his hip flask and tears at the remains of his wispy white hair, making it look even more like a kid had a crack at it while he was asleep.

CHAPTER FOUR

Since Percy got to be PM, Rodney's refused to be wined and dined by anyone who might try to use him for access to his old mate. And he's stuck by it.

But he had no problem with the two Arabs he bumped into in a West End pub when Labour was still in opposition. In fact, he came over all unnecessary with delight.

'Well poke me bum with a rusty bargepole! You'm bleddy mates of his from they there university? Always wished the boy was mine. You'm making me go all sloppy.'

His thinking, as it turned out, was much the same. Sloppy as buggery. These guys had sought him out deliberately to find a weak link in Percy's armour, and he fell into the trap. It was as wide as the mineshaft he'd rescued Percy from all those years ago.

'No one got no bleddy money, see, in they there local parties. Not enough to scratch their arse with.'

The slimy sods couldn't believe their luck. And couldn't wait to make full unfair use of it.

'My dear fellow, surely we can help? Percy's such a fine fellow. Frightfully busy fighting the beastly government, leave it with us.'

Rodney grinned. 'You'm the bank manager from heaven, splash the cash and bugger the overdraft.'

Hours later, stuffed full of food and booze, he'd passed on the sort code and account number at the bank used by what was once his local party – and is now Percy's.

In the morning he didn't remember much about anything. A couple of fellows called Bash, or Blabber, or Bladdered or something and that was about it.

Fragments came back like pound coins or rubber johnnies buried in the sofa. But the truth didn't really dawn on him till he dropped by his old constituency office for a chinwag and stumbled on something between a celebration and a riot. You couldn't miss the song, and Rodney sung the child's version. 'The people's flag is palest pink, Mum washed it in the kitchen sink.'

But when he opened the door and got the full blast, he heard something different. 'The working class can kiss my arse, I've got the foreman's job at last.'

The aptly titled vice-chair, a retired colonel who'd been slung out of the Tory party for texting photos of his willy to the vicar's wife, lurched up to him. Pulling aside his paper Mickey Mouse mask he hummed a line from the old song 'We're in the money', offered Rodney a plastic beaker full of wine and a vol au vent, and started dropping hints.

'Life in the parish ish crowded with inshident.'

Yeah yeah, filthy talk about the vicar's wife, not to mention the unmentionable vicar and that business with Percy's mummy all those years back, Rodney had heard it all before. But the money bit was different, very much the wrong sort of rusty bargepole moment.

'Huge standing order, old boy, offshore bank. Foreign wallah must have set it up, no idea who, or how he got our details. Don't know, don't care. Calls for a song, what?'

Giggling like a schoolboy, the vice-chair lurched onto a table and raised his voice. 'Let's hear it, comrades. You can tell old Joe I'm off the dole, he can stick his red flag up his 'ole.'

Rodney hated him. And himself. Accepting donations from overseas was against the law; the sort of corruption that could bring down a government and it was all his fault. He must fess up.

But he looked at the peeling paintwork, knackered computers and net curtains you wouldn't clean the bog with, and changed his mind.

Pulling the Colonel to one side, he tapped the side of his nose and crinkled his eyelids. 'God gives to they 'oo ask, see. But don't let on, they'm all be bleddy wanting some.' As confessions go, this was up there with Cain telling god he wasn't his brother's keeper.

Sitting in the outside loo when he got home, Rodney thought hard. *That Percy, he'm a bit wet behind the ears, best keep me voice down. Keep him in the dark. Hearts never bleed over what the eye don't see.* Then he saw there was no paper. 'Bummer,' he muttered, choosing the right word for once.

*

Stumbling back into the garden a wiser if not cleaner man, he made a decision. *Bleddy think ahead in future. No more taking bleddy chances with Percy.*

He didn't, until the next time, though there was no way he could know he was being tricked again. Labour was after all still in opposition, and, anyway, what could possibly be more innocent than a couple of Chinese researchers inviting him for a chat about his committee work, over a bite at Gordon Ramsay's? He was only nervous because they probably knew more about his subject than he did.

A snifter before he set off seemed the best way of clearing his head. Bad move. He got there as defenceless as a paper lantern fighting off dragons.

With the geeky glasses and leather elbow patches, his hosts were the picture of the earnest students they'd been before the China Nuclear Engineering Group Corporation financed their doctorates. And sent them to Harvard to learn the wicked ways of the Western world.

One of the first, dispiriting, things they discovered was the Western way of treating them as vaguely inferior, on account of how they looked. The worst offenders were generally the stupidest people. Annoying, but unsurprising.

The temptation to say "Fuck you, honky" was great, but they were too busy to square up to every old school redneck in the New World. So many fights, so little time. They did say it, mind, but in code. Every time they called one another Fyok Yu and Hon Ki they sensed sweet revenge. The nicknames stuck.

At the same time they quickly found they could weaponize caricature Chinese voices. Box clever by acting dumb. Worked a treat at Gordon Ramsay's with poor, pissed Rodney.

'Great honour to dine with famous chair of honourable House of Lords' Energy and Environment sub-committee,' Fyok Yu announced with a bow.

Doing his best not to seem patronising, Rodney risked a joke. 'Only took the job because jollies sewer le continong beat the caravan at Bognor and the bleddy missus.'

Fyok Yu pretended he didn't understand and picked his brains about wind power in Wallonia and biomass in Macedonia before easing round to the real agenda. Now that the Chinese were exporting nuclear knowhow, surely the Brits could slip in some spent uranium?

Recognising this might be a slightly tricky sell, they put it in what they hoped was sufficiently idiotic terms, stressing their country's contrition for the unfortunate misunderstanding over coronavirus.

They exchanged a lightning glance, a shared prayer the ploy

had worked and grinned outwardly from ear to ear but fretted inwardly, as Rodney didn't seem too sure.

'Apples don't just grow on trees, you know,' he mumbled, then paused as his befuddled mind strayed to his orchard in Cornwall. He farted uncertainly.

*

Fyok Yu and Hon Ki glanced around the restaurant and at one another, wondering whether their guest was having a catatonic fit. When you're well gone a two-second pause for thought can last several minutes.

Eventually Rodney came to, sort of. 'They green beggers and they bleddy papers, they'd go bleddy nuclear.' Neatly chosen words, if unintended.

'Course it could be done on the QT. Snouts in swilly bits. Ministers and folding stuff? Grunters in shit.' Fyok Yu and Hon Ki were struggling with Rodney's peculiar language and slurred speech, but his next words were encouraging.

'Wouldn't want to dig they bleddy Tories out of a hole. But if they went down this one they'd be well shafted.'

Looking from one grinning face to the other, Rodney tried and failed to count them and leant forward precariously. 'Four heads'm better'n two, my lovers.' They watched the finger to the nose routine, wondering what it meant.

'There be some bleddy beggar, 'ee'm proper at fixing things. Getting ministers to do all sorts they bleddy shouldn't. Turn water into bleddy gold, 'ee can.' Getting hold of his fourth double Courvoisier at last, he spilled the beans, and the brandy, all down his front.

CHAPTER FIVE

It was a sensation at the time. A dodgy lobbyist who'd appeared before the Lords committee Rodney was chairing tricked a minister into tweaking government policy in a way that created one billionaire and bankrupted the entire competition.

The findings were excoriating. 'This Machiavellian malefactor is a common criminal who must be prosecuted, and all victims are entitled to financial redress.' Not that they got a brass farthing, any more than Rodney wrote the report himself.

Poor sod wasn't even literate enough for books like *Winnie the Pooh*. Though he wouldn't have denied he was a bear of very little brain, bothered by long words.

He was gamekeeper then. Fyok Yu and Hon Ki were filling him with booze and food to get him to turn poacher now. After the election the polls all said Percy would win, this common criminal was just the man they needed.

Trouble was, he'd disappeared in mysterious circumstances. Their hope was he was still kicking around somewhere, and Rodney could help find him.

The man got bird, though he repented behind bars and joined the priesthood. Couldn't resist it, after the prison chaplain had him on bended knee, plus several other positions, and made heavenly promises.

'Endless supplies of choirboys, my child. But you can always top them up with nuns, if your tastes are catholic.'

They weren't. He was as bent as a nine-bob note, in both meanings of the phrase. But the chaplain's laissez-faire attitude emboldened him, and in no time he was carrying on with business as usual in the slammer. A win-win situation with knobs on, as the screws, likewise, were bent in both senses.

But all good things come to an end. In his case, sadly, when he apparently drowned off the beach at Margate while on parole, leaving nothing but his passport, a pair of frilly Y-fronts and two tubes of K-Y jelly.

With no sign anywhere of a body, suspicions were bound to linger. Not that that troubled many in Fleet Street. The *Express* boldly stated he was in heaven blackmailing Princess Diana, the *Sun* had him shagging a topless angel and the *Star* announced he'd been eaten by an alien hamster-like creature with even bigger tits.

Scoop-hungry freelance snappers nonetheless scoured the world for sightings, compromising clergymen from Marrakesh to Maidenhead, plus an entire synod on Hampstead Heath.

One of the Sunday rags actually did some proper checking, and carried authoritative pieces suggesting he'd become a parish priest somewhere, under an assumed identity. But the paper's proprietor, who was buggering the religious affairs correspondent who was also buggering a diocesan bishop, ordered the editor to drop the subject.

However, Fyok Yu and Hon Ki had spotted the story at the time and researched it thoroughly after their meeting with Rodney. Discovering that the trail seemed to have gone cold, they approached the chief investigative reporter and offered him a hefty fee upfront to find the man.

The chap was chuffed to bits, and resolved to waste no time.

Only, convinced he'd locate the tosser in a jiffy on the net, he hunted high and low instead for the E-type Jaguar he'd always wanted and could now afford.

Retro cars cool, retro journalism boring.

He got a shock eventually, when Google told him there were more than fifty thousand churches in the United Kingdom. Be like looking for a needle in a haystack. As it happened, the one he was after did have a huge pointy steeple and bales of straw all round it, but he wasn't to know that. Or where the fuck it was, for that matter.

When he finally gave up Fyok Yu and Hon Ki torched the motor but let him off with two broken ribs and permanently impaired eyesight, on the grounds that Rodney might be worth another go.

*

This time they struck lucky. Another hugely expensive dinner, expressions of extreme interest in Brits behaving badly and promises of a substantial financial thank you from the Chinese authorities, and he agreed to help.

Once again, the booze got the better of him. He stumbled out of the restaurant with the down payment in used fivers wedged in his back pocket and not the faintest idea where or how to start looking.

But, when he had a good grumble about it next morning, the missus, miraculously, came to the rescue. It was the first time in twenty years she'd taken in a word he'd said, but, then again, it was the first time in twenty years he'd ever said anything that interested her.

Fact is, the woman was as fascinated by crime fiction as she was bored by politics. She hadn't the foggiest if her husband was a Monster Raving Liberal or Notional Socialist, but The Case of the Vanishing Vicar thrilled her.

The once slender young milkmaid, now morphed into a fat old bag, was suddenly austere and alert. Adjusting an imaginary deerstalker, she demanded a description of the lobbyist's manual endowment which had intrigued everybody throughout his appearances before the committee.

She then knitted a pair of digitally enhanced gloves and put them on eBay, muttering 'Elementary, my dear Watson' when the sole bidder gave her the address of his church.

Telling Rodney to deliver them in person, she discreetly followed him. The bald vicar with the droopy moustache and monocle seemed nothing like the clean-shaven, long-haired lobbyist who'd appeared before his committee, until he crossed himself.

The thumb count was normal, but each hand had five fingers. Yes, five. Yes, weird.

*

When the missus returned to the church on her tod, her Inverness cape, curly pipe and magnifying glass looked as weird as any six-digit hand. But a little old lady with a white stick and a guide dog was happy to prattle on about Reverend Chancer's vergers, all former prison officers, and his Roller.

Back again next day, this time with a huge Suffragette-style hat and a heavy silver-topped cane, she confronted the Vicar. And seconds later made it clear patience wasn't her thing.

'You'm that bleddy bastard what played bleddy tricks in they bleddy Parliament, then bleddy buggered your way into a bleddy dog collar.'

Every time she said 'bleddy' she lashed out either at the monocle and eyeball behind it, or the other one.

The former lobbyist quickly saw if he didn't play ball he wouldn't see anything in future and came clean. In return for a vow of silence, he shelled out a fat enough wad for the vicious old cow to bribe the council into giving her the allotment she'd been after for years.

As it happens, the cash the missus had already got Rodney to hand over after his second Chinese chinwag was more than enough anyway. But better too much than too little, she reasoned.

Impeccable logic, surely, always worked with the sherry trifle and double cream.

*

The promise the missus had extracted from Rodney not to say what he knew was easily fixed. At his third and final Gordon Ramsay dinner, he simply wrote it down instead.

As he scribbled on a napkin the address of a church, in Essex as it happens, the glint of triumph in Fyok Yu and Hon Ki's eyes could have lit up Blackpool Tower. Possibly even the Twin Towers, if Al-Qaeda hadn't got there first.

Their rage with the journo who'd let them down melted, and they quickly ordered on Amazon a headstone for the puppy that went the same way as the Jaguar.

Next, after decanting the old fool into a cab they gave one another a high-five, dumped the geeky glasses, sports jackets and phoney Chinese accents and got tanked up at Groucho's.

*

Slumped in the back seat, Rodney noticed the driver was female when she gave him her usual patter with harmless old men. 'Where to, handsome stranger?'

'Houses of bleddy Parrrlourmaid, maid, where all members be well 'ung,' he giggled, chuffed at what she'd said. Reminded him of when they were all on his case. Nowadays he felt lucky if a woman just patted him on the cheek and felt sorry for him.

Back in his office he worried that giving those low-lifes the low-down on a criminal mastermind clever enough to screw governments might have been a mistake. He did want to sink the Tories, but had he missed something?

Next morning, after about a gallon of coffee in the greasy spoon on Horseferry Road that opens early, he worked out what it was. The bleddy election. If Labour won it they'd be the ones in the firing line.

He glanced at the banner headline on the copy of the *Mirror* someone had left. 'Percy's Poll Surge. 'Ere We Go, Comrades.' Rodney closed his eyes.

He fiddled with the lucky ball of binder string he always carried around, had a pee and paid. A couple of guys in spivvy suits sniggered as he passed their table. When he turned into Millbank he realised his flies were undone and a bit of his shirt was sticking out. It looked rather rude.

*

Normally Rodney just laughed when smartarse faceless fucks treated him like dirt. But something inside him snapped. He was quivering with fury, once more the plucky young Cornishman who'd take on the world.

He didn't dare actually square up to faceless fucks, but there were hundreds of them just down the road and he'd show them all right. Even their office was faceless, but boy would they get a shock.

Seconds later he was outside MI5's unmarked premises with its masses of discreet CCTV cameras. He shielded his face with one arm, slipped the shirt in and his pecker out and waved it around to give them a hard time. Or at least harder than he could have managed.

Rodney's Revenge, as he saw it, turned out to be a cock-up in more ways than one. After the bloke on the screens had wasted a fortune at Specsavers, an elderly female colleague told him his eyes weren't playing tricks on him.

She refused to say what made her so sure about the dirty dog's identity, but discreetly filed a report on the incident.

For weeks Rodney worried he might get arrested for public indecency. But, as winter melted away and spring flowers blossomed, nothing seemed to happen.

So he slipped the incident into the least-said-soonest-mended file. Like if you'd been sick over the devoted couple's curtains at their golden wedding and not let on.

At Labour's victory party on election night he told Percy all about it, well nearly all, and enjoyed being pinched on the cheek and told he was a loony old git.

Seemed a shame to spoil the moment by mentioning the Chinese chappies. He'd no idea what the word meant, but had a nasty feeling in the pit of his stomach that he'd been shanghaied.

*

He certainly had been, and Fyok Yu and Hon Ki made good use of the information they'd got out of him. Locating the church on Google Maps they researched the county, to be sure of creating the right impression.

Turning up in a sixteen-seat Hummer limousine, they were reassured they'd pitched it right by the vicar's response.

'Strewth.'

Though Reverend Chancer was born just on the London side of the Essex border, he seemed to fit awfully well with the online dictionary definitions of the local culture. 'Loud, large, feral, brash, materialistic.'

This was everything Fyok Yu and Hon Ki had been brought up to despise, as their lecturers at China's prestigious Peking University had told them never to deal with dishonourable persons.

Confusingly, they were then taught at Harvard that, because business is business, Western arms sales to genocidal kleptocratic dictators were a moral duty.

Ushered into the Reverend Chancer's lavishly appointed vestry and puzzled by the peculiar shiny things on the desk their host kept playing with, they watched in silence as he placed all his fingers in the solid gold holy water font and blessed them for their faith in him.

When they explained what they wanted him to do, but insisted he hang on till after the election, he raised his eyes to heaven and went through the motions of praying.

'Are farver, wot art in 'eaven, give us dis day are daily bread. When yer bleedin' ready, yer stoopid bleeder. Wo'evvah. God gives to geezers wot wait.'

He was even less impressed with his visitors' planned strategy for when Labour took the reins of government. Before getting him to force Percy by underhand means to soak up their nuclear garbage, they were going to ask politely if he wouldn't mind doing it voluntarily.

Charlie Chancer didn't do history, but the drugs trade was different.

He pointed out that when the Chinese authorities politely asked Queen Victoria to stop flooding their country with opium, the Brits sent in more. And gunboats. 'And all dem Chinese junks, dey got junked, right?'

Though Fyok Yu and Hon Ki knew he was right, head office had quoted a Chinese proverb. 'To subdue the enemy without fighting is the supreme excellence.'

'Bloody proverbs,' Fyok Yu grumbled. 'He who hesitates is lost, I say.'

'Then again, you should always look before you leap,' Hon Ki murmured with a smirk..

Fyok Yu acknowledged there's a counter to every argument, and weighed up whether to laugh at his friend's joke or kill him.

CHAPTER SIX

A couple of months later Fyok Yu and Hon Ki prove their Beijing bosses wrong, in what turns out to be a bad day for everybody, especially Percy.

He'd already got off to a particularly nasty start, awaking with a jolt from a horrible nightmare. All bloodshot eyes and Dracula teeth, the opposition leader had just stepped through the dispatch box and prodded him several times on the lower forehead.

He lashed out, knocking the cat off the bed. This struck Fang as ungrateful, as only a moment earlier he'd been checking Percy was still alive by dabbing him between the eyes.

Only one thing for it then. He sprang back and did it again, this time with his claws out.

Flailing around as one does when in danger of being blinded, Percy knocked the alarm clock on the floor. Stepping on it as he clambered out of bed, he broke the glass, cut his foot and couldn't find a fucking plaster.

Despairingly, he sellotaped one of Viv's tampons to his toe, but it didn't really work.

Then there's his overflowing in-tray before he even gets to the morning's scheduled Downing Street summit. Fang, in a better mood now, spreads his body across every official document he can reach, and with one swoop of his paw sends the new wireless computer mouse ricocheting across the room.

Miraculously, it still works. Percy celebrates by ordering a clock on Amazon that plays the sounds of kittens mewing. It makes him smile, unlike his briefing paper on 'The Future of the Non-Fossil-Fuel and Renewable Energy Sector'.

'Piece of piss, working out how to keep the lights on by lunchtime,' he grumbles. 'Tide power, worked for King Canute.'

*

At precisely that moment, a few yards away in Whitehall, Rodney is having a panic attack at the sight of two vaguely familiar-looking Chinese guys headed for Downing Street. He shambles into the Red Lion and scratches his head till it really does look like a turnip.

Maybe he's wrong. In their Armani suits and slimline glasses slick marketing managers peer over to intimidate people, Fyok Yu and Hon Ki don't look like wide-eyed research students.

Though they glance in Rodney's direction, they don't recognise him. He's more ancient history than the Han, Tang and Shang dynasties. They're up against Percy now. Percy, and time.

As they're shown into Number Ten, Fyok Yu curses Western ways. 'He rule now. Maybe deposed in five years.' Hon Ki agrees. 'Dumb system, democracy.'

Indeed, Percy doesn't say very much. Forcing himself to gaze at every speaker, he stifles yawn after yawn and occasionally massages his wrist, rotating his arm and glancing down as if assessing an injury.

Discouragingly, his watch seems to have stopped, and holding the position long enough to check the second hand would give the game away.

Towards the end of the session Fyok Yu and Hon Ki make their presentation. Looking as dull as dead fish and sounding like the shipping forecast on a perfect summer's day they drone on about balances, returns, resources and income streams. Suddenly Percy clocks they're talking about dumping spent nuclear fuel at the Breezethwaite reprocessing centre. It's tucked away up north, but very much open for business.

He was only little at the time, but can see his dad now, waving the *Daily Mirror* around, banging the kitchen table with his fist, and bellowing the headline 'The World's Nuclear Dustbin'. And this is worse. Masses of new stuff, from the second-largest country in the world.

Already Percy can hear the Yankee schmucks running Breezethwaite telling him not to buck the markets. They're a private company and the man in Whitehall can go screw.

If England's green and pleasant land is suddenly overrun with two-headed sheep and one-eyed frogs they can always scuttle off back home to Houston. Well, screw them too.

The nation's strapped for cash. Has been ever since it stopped repaying moneylenders by chopping them up or chucking them out. Worse now thanks to the double whammy of Brexit and the coronavirus pandemic. Unlike efficiency savings and crackdowns on tax evasion, the take on this little scam would be real.

It's also a really bad idea. Percy scowls at himself for even thinking about it and one or two colleagues look at him anxiously. But his expression changes, to one of grim determination.

He remembers Jim Callaghan's response to the offer of a massive bribe to save his tottering administration. 'The British Government is not up for auction.' Looking Fyok Yu and Hon Ki in the eye, he adopts the same tone of voice.

'Stick your uranium up your anus.'

Sir Bernard Brenstorme twitches, stabbing the green baize cloth covering the table with the nib of his fountain pen.

'I'll believe almost anything of a Prime Minister given to self-immolation, indecent exposure and attempted homicide,' he tells his secretary later. 'But bad manners are beyond a bit thick.

'Best get MI5 to run checks on the man, to root out evidence of insanity within the family. And MI6. Always possible the blighter's not even one of us. Never mind not really British, the Cornish are barely human.'

He can't draft instant memos to the spymasters because his pen doesn't work any more, but he will. 'Prime Ministers are only passing through,' he reminds himself. 'The sooner the better when they're common people from council schools.'

He could never understand why Harold Wilson wasn't hanged as a Soviet spy.

*

The two Chinese gentlemen are as shocked as Sir Bernard by what Percy said to them. For a second their deadpan faces wear the sort of expression you'd expect from the Mona Lisa if a young man had crept up and goosed her.

In an instant they've reverted to inscrutability, but with a just about discernible difference. Fang would recognise the gleam in their eye as full fair warning to all shoelaces.

Unlike some of his betters, Percy never learned to play prick up the pig, but poker at infants' school taught him to spot the look that says 'We got flick knives and you ain't.' He feels a knot in the pit of his stomach, and tidies the papers in front of him. They're upside down. Bugger.

He's already thinking about his next meeting, a Foreign Office briefing about the Arab trade delegation he must treat as new best friends at Chequers this weekend. Human rights? Blood money?

Sod them, he thinks, as he thanks everyone warmly for

coming, patting people on the arm with his right hand, fumbling for his fags with the left.

As they step into the street Fyok Yu and Hon Ki brush their sleeves with their silk hankies, and add swearwords to yet another Chinese saying. 'War not determine who is right, but who is left.' Indoors, Percy yawns and forgets to cover his mouth. Not his style, but no one's looking.

Elsewhere in the building, Sir Bernard is already getting to work, occasionally lifting his toupee to scratch his head. 'Dear Director General... ?' Too formal. 'Now look here old boy... ?' Not quite. He'll get there.

Unbeknown to him, MI5 already has a file open on Percy, thanks to Rodney's penis parade outside the Millbank headquarters. The PM's possible family links with the old man are well known. So he's suspected of guilt by association, at very least of extreme eccentricity.

The incident would only have raised a few titters if it hadn't been for the mature lady operative's confidential note. She was interrogated by the Director General, who couldn't understand how she could make such a positive identification when she couldn't see the man's face. He didn't spot the obvious, or the funny side.

A discreet word then with all that's apparently left of Percy's family. Auntie Nora's long gone, but there's still a little old lady living in all-female secure accommodation somewhere west of the Tamar. He won't find out till he gets there that Mummy's years of incarceration have exacerbated her symptoms of pathological if dormant nymphomania.

After going without for nearly half a century she'll give a zing to the expression head to head.

*

In the late morning sunshine the Downing Street rose garden

is at its loveliest, and the newly mown grass gives it a special perfume. Percy breathes deeply and luxuriates in it till he takes his first puff. He wishes he could obliterate the Chinese threat that easily, and the FCO bloke.

Picturing a schoolmaster with mortarboard, gown and cane he pokes his eye out with the butt end of the fourth fag.

In the event, Our Man on the Middle East desk is young, keen and always placing one hand on his chest while patting it with the other. Percy finds his speech impediment irritating after a while. 'If you must say sorry is there any chance you could put it another way?'

The lad does it again within seconds.

However, he has failed to spot a last-minute change in the guest-list. The oil minister from a small Middle Eastern state is unable to attend due to legal procedures.

After confessing under torture to possession of a bottle of temperance wine and bestiality with the neighbours' oxen, he's to be crucified. After eight thousand lashes, castration and evisceration.

Though the merciful king has granted the second half of the sentences be carried out first, it's pretty clear a stand-in's needed.

Step forward the Bashar brothers. Though they aren't officially members of the government, they are related to the monarch, and happy to play their part in affairs of state. Arguably they already have, by stitching up their uncle in the oil ministry.

*

Come the Saturday, Percy drops the fixed smile in the doorway of Chequers and beams at the sight of them, though he can't understand why his wife has suddenly vanished. She reappears wearing a wig, and glasses with bouncy spring-loaded eyeballs dug out from the dressing-up box.

Viv felt she didn't show herself at her best on the night of Percy's Weimar Republic party, the last time she saw the Bashars. She can hardly see anything now, but they can.

'Exquisite beauty, visible personification of absolute perfection, you look quite the first lady, if we dare make so bold on so relatively slight an acquaintance so relatively long ago.' Though they're speaking in unison, the brothers aren't being as insincere as they sound. If she'd turned up for sale on the Dark Web they'd have snapped her up at any price.

They've learned the British trick of saying one thing while thinking another, or there's no telling what Viv might have done. As it is she's just mortified at being rumbled. Percy continues to gawp at the weirdo, wondering who the fuck it is.

Eventually he recognises the dress and shoes, giggles vaguely and bungs the wig on his own head, pretending he thinks it's really funny. So the ice is broken, as well as the glasses Viv's chucked on the ground.

Unlike Percy, the Bashars are on the front foot. They were baffled at school why anyone would hunt animals and not eat them. But they got the point of the double-barrelled shotgun, and if illegally funding Percy's local party only wings him, the second shot will bring him down.

The jaunt they've got in mind for him at their lovely place in the sun is the cheese in a mousetrap. Once he's bitten on that he won't be able to refuse a few juicy oil contracts. 'Jolly shame and all that, blackmailing such a capital fellow,' the elder Bashar admits.

His brother grins. 'Blackmail? Black gold, surely?'

They're acting from the purest of motives, putting king and country first. Fluctuations in the market have brought many of their royal relatives almost to their knees, only five palaces and three yachts each.

'Annoying we're out of pocket over that bottle of temperance wine we lent our dear late lamented uncle, though. The chief of police will never return it,' the younger Bashar grumbles.

'Beastly corruption, it's everywhere these days,' his brother sighs.

CHAPTER SEVEN

Percy's top-hole comedy act over dinner helps the Bashars forget their money worries. He flicks cigar ash everywhere, sticks out his stomach and jawbone, snatches up a decanter, peers into it and lisps.

'This is not the end.' Pause. 'It is not even the beginning of the end.' Pause. 'But it is, perhaps, the end of the beginning.'

Guests whose nations sided with Hitler in 1939 don't think it's funny, but the Bashars do. They batter the table with their silver-topped canes, clamber onto it and perform a Highland jig. When it collapses they take a tumble, smashing several chairs and a sideboard.

An expensive night then. Percy doesn't cheer up till the Bashars mention their private island, over a farewell pint in the pub. 'Spiffing villa. Catering thrown in, brilliant air con, and an Olympic-sized pool. Right up your street, what?'

Bashar Major, his title at public school, pauses to draw on the eighteen-inch platinum cigarette holder Alfred Dunhill gave his grandfather. 'All the bloody booze you can get down you, and Turkish bongs to blow your brains out. Just the ticket, don't you know?'

'We can probably rustle up a spot of cricket on the green too.

The locals won't be all that good at it, but they're good sports, manner of speaking.'

He flicks his white silk scarf across his shoulder and smiles, so taken with Percy's look of delight he doesn't notice Viv's in earshot when he has a quiet word with Bashar Minor. 'Tickety-boo, dear boy, trout's tickled.'

The limo's still purring up the drive when she turns on Percy and tells him what she's just heard. 'What the hell did he mean by that?'

She's scared, but Percy makes out he isn't. 'Just their funny way of putting things. My old flatmates would never shaft me.'

'Never? They went home to a despotic mediaeval autocracy. People change, you know.'

Percy frowns at her. She's even prettier than when they first met, but a damned sight smarter. Her forehead's still unlined, but the naiveté is long gone. He wonders how her pert little breasts are holding up these days…

Pulling himself together, he promises to check out the Bashars with the Foreign Office chappie. It won't help, any more than killing him next time he says 'Fwightfully sowwy, Pwime Minister'.

*

The meeting starts better than expected. The lad manages to put his first apology differently. 'Wegwettable oversight my end, Pwime Minister, more wigour in future. I pwomise.'

Percy studies his face, wondering when in his short life he managed to squeeze in a PhD. Perhaps he took his GCSEs at infants' school.

To make up for his mistake over the Chequers guest list, the young man's done his homework on the Bashars. They aren't ministers of government, so their offer's above board. 'No more a bweach of pwotocol than Tony Blair's stay at Cliff Wichard's wesidence in the Cawibbean.'

He's earned his coffee and biscuits, though it's not long before Percy wishes he'd just drink up and clear off, instead of going on and on about the bloody Bashars.

'They are members of the woyal family, but all they do is gamble and get wich,' he announces. 'They hardly even know any politicians, apart from your fwiend Wodney Wumpledore.'

'What!' Percy rather lets himself down by spitting out a mouthful of light refreshments. Fang flees and Our Man on the Middle Eastern Desk gets his hanky out, wiping first the table then his face. He's out of the door in no time, saying he's fwightfully sowwy.

Percy feels like a seabird in an oil slick. He's got nothing really to go on, but the anxiety reminds him of times in the past when he'd had difficulty peeing. Off to the clap clinic then. Again.

A discreet word with the whips' office and he learns Rodney's been going on in the bars about his new best friends. 'They Bashars saw me right in Soho. A right proper nosh-up. And they like brothers to the boss.' Made him right proud, apparently, knowing all the right people. Though to Percy right is exactly how it doesn't feel.

He means to call him up but doesn't get round to it for the usual reason. 'So many bloody distractions, can't think how anyone in government even manages to tie their shoelaces.' Hearing the magic word, Fang lashes out at them.

*

Percy's so busy running away from the cat it takes him a moment to register what the *World at One* has just reported. A Tory leadership contest. It's been on the cards ever since Tiddledick lost the election, the only surprise is it took so long.

'Means no more to me than the teenage kid next door

having a noisy shag in the garden,' Percy tells Viv later. She's not impressed.

'Don't lie. You're fascinated by the guy.' Percy mutters something about women knowing too much for their own good, but switches tack when she gives him the Vivienne look.

'Don't know where I'd be without you, lovely one. Supposed to be girlies who spot everything except the obvious, but it's the other way round really.

'Never liked to admit it, but I have sometimes wondered if he's a little too particular about his appearance, and whether his complexion's a shade too pink. Behind that Tory toff tosh, d'you think he's a bit of a softie?'

'Men!' Viv snorts. 'It's bloody obvious. You're peas in a pod. And you'll miss him if he goes.'

Though Percy prides himself on his gay man's girlie intuition he feels no better than a builder with his bum hanging out.

'Sod it, Viv, I'm only a bloke. Can't help it.' She pats him sympathetically on the arm, but doesn't say anything. Still, she values intensely the time he still manages to make for her, and the fact that he takes what she says seriously.

And of course she's right, as usual.

Tiddledick is indeed desperately fragile. He felt limp from the moment he lost the election, and the challenge reminds him it's a clean fight with your opponents, but dirty with your own side. It takes all his wife's ingenuity to keep his pecker up...

With her long fringe and pointy chin and ears, Fanny Tiddledick looks so like her favourite pet her friends call her Horse-Face. And she's a speedy filly. At the hunt ball where she met Ponsomby, she pinned him down on a full-sized billiard table, practically in sight of everyone.

'Room for an open leg policy,' she giggled.

'Prefer closed doors,' Ponsomby muttered. But Fanny didn't care. She once asked Mummy, at church, why she had a beard on her ninny.

Daddy's background in the SAS gave her a taste for danger as well as discipline. When Tiddledick eventually rose to the occasion, she smiled. 'Goodie goodie, privates on parade. Prezent... ums!'

He managed it a fair few times during the leadership struggle, thanks to Fanny's joss sticks. She always knew they'd come in handy on a rainy day, and right now it was pissing it down.

Ponsomby's religious education chimed with her brothers' stories about lavvies with no doors and levitating sheets in the dorm, and their sniggering confidence that flogging doesn't just mean corporal punishment.

He remembered the queer feeling he got from those wandering, reverend fingers in the one-on-one study sessions with the padre. The room reeked of incense, and one night he confessed to Fanny he still had a fetish about it. This was duly noted, though she made light of it at the time.

'What was it Daddy used to say? Who shares wins? Something like that.'

Percy and Viv would have cried if they knew how the Tiddledicks' counselling sessions compared to theirs. A straight fight between a painting by Michelangelo and a battering ram.

*

Sky News is first with Ponsomby's surprise win. Percy glances at his head of communications, Biff McNasty. 'We'd a bin bleddy buggered if it a went the other bleddy way,' he says softly.

'You're not wrong there,' Biff mutters. 'T'other bastard would have ripped your feckin' eyeballs out and shat in the sockets, just for the craic.'

The funny voice routine is the two Celts' private joke, though Biff's knack of going too far often spoils it. Percy carefully eases Fang's lips back to expose his teeth and make him look like a particularly nasty tiger.

'OK, Tiddledick's smarmy but a gent. The other guy's a cult, spelt with an N. But d'you have to rub it in?' Stupid question, he knows Biff can't help himself. Same as cult with an N, he fought his way from nowhere, in his case the Falls Road in Belfast.

Like Percy, Biff's tall and strongly built, with a lion's head of hair, speckled complexion and penetrating eyes. The difference is he still oozes teenage testosterone. He's manic about Arsenal and is always singing Irish rebel songs about armoured cars and tanks and guns.

At least he's nice to his parrot, Sir Roger, named after an Irish diplomat hanged by the British for treason.

The two men's partnership goes back to broadcasting, Percy preening before the camera, Biff snarling behind it. Typical TV producer, savaging the talent. Sometimes described as creative tension, it makes for a perfect political marriage.

Biff's three ex-wives, however, have long thanked Christ they're shot of the bastard. His love of the bottle and the powders didn't make them laugh, any more than his joke that with a da who loved the Brits and a ma who hated them, he was buggered from day one.

Actually, he's anything but, in either sense of the word. Which is why he can smell when something's afoot, and usually knows exactly what to do about it.

Though the Tory leadership contest's well and truly dominated the headlines there's been a story festering away for a while like symptoms of gonorrhoea, just below the surface. Chatter about a subtle shift in government policy on nuclear waste, a green light maybe to soaking up lots more stuff from overseas. Extra revenue? Good for Brexit Britain?

'It's as obvious as a shed of shite the fecking minister who signs it all off has been lobbied and tempted. He's testing the fecking water.' The menacing look on Biff's face gets Percy thinking.

'OK, OK, me 'ansum, I'll deal with it. Our beloved Secretary of State for Energy will hear from me. If he's up to no good he'll get one up the Khyber. At very least a discreetly probing memo, and perhaps a slap on the wrist.'

Biff snorts in exasperation. 'Bollocks to one up the fecking Khyber, get his testicles in a vice and stick electrodes up his prick. Worked for the British Army in Norn Iron, it can fecking work for us now.'

It's Percy's turn to be irritated. Though he tries not to show it.

'Certain allegations against the crown have never been fully substantiated. And, anyway, appropriately trained interrogators may be hard to come by nowadays.'

'You know your problem? You got the balls of a fecking amoeba.' Biff turns his back on Percy and switches on his computer.

That does it. Selecting the strongest rubber band in the desk tidy, and the sharpest pencil, Percy revives a skill he hasn't used since year nine. Biff's desk is at an angle to his, and his temple forms a perfect target.

A direct hit. Biff leaps out of his seat, grabs Percy by the hair and tries to headbutt him. They wrestle and shout. The words insubordination, sacking and attempted murder crop up several times. When they crash to the floor the security man downstairs looks up in alarm.

A huge pot of flowers toppling over on them works like a bucket of water on two scrapping dogs. 'OK, be Jaysus, I'm a fecking eejit at times,' Percy admits. The rubbish Irish is his way of saying sorry, as is Biff's useless Cornish. 'That Rasputin, ee'm bleddy cheerful next to me.'

After they've straightened the room up a bit, chucked the smashed up Apple Mac into the bin and coaxed Fang down from the top of a filing cabinet, they get the brandy out to celebrate the reshuffle which will probably start with the Energy Secretary.

By the time they're on the second bottle and Fang's slurped

his way into a calmer frame of mind they decide he should choose who gets the chop.

Percy digs out a stash of printer ink cartridges, places them one by one on the desk in front of the animal and above the now refilled flower vase, and names a name. Fang looks from one man to the other, has another lick at the saucer of brandy that's all for him, then delivers his verdict.

Plop, plop, plop. One by one, the entire Cabinet gets the dab. Biff finds it funnier and funnier. The cat's in tune with public opinion. Calls for a song.

Percy knows the words of Biff's opening number. Stealing an armoured car and giving it to the IRA suddenly seems a brilliant idea. The English have pissed the Cornish off enough times too.

The Protection Command officer below hates what he's hearing. He's proud of his dad's military service record in Northern Ireland, especially the bits with rusty pliers and terrorists' toenails. The line about the peelers not being able to catch the bastard is the last straw.

He bashes the ceiling with the butt of his sub-machine gun. Percy and Biff can't understand why whoever's doing the drumming is so crap at keeping time.

CHAPTER EIGHT

Next morning Fang looks awful, and Biff and Percy feel it. 'Don't think we're being a bit hard on the poor sod, do you?' Percy's never much liked his Energy Secretary, but feels everyone deserves a fair hearing. Biff doesn't. 'Put his fecking head in a vice, and screw yours on right while you're at it.'

'And screw you too.' But Percy says it with a smile, thinking about the benefits of the Good Friday agreement, and the cost of Apple Mac computers.

Half the morning is given over to a political Cabinet session, an attempt as always to boost party popularity while doing the right thing by the nation. 'Like scratching your back with a cut-throat razor.' Biff tells the story as it is.

As the Welsh Secretary bores on, an hour into the meeting, Percy asks himself serious questions. *Was Fang right to drown the lot of them? Or was he avenging his ancestors? Does he have nightmares about tiny kittens and water butts?*

He's dragged back to reality by a screaming siren sound from his mobile. A text from Biff, sent on the smartphone only used in emergencies. 'Energy Sec dipping it. Reptiles on our case.'

It's the moment between the crisis of the convertible breaking down in a safari park, and the catastrophe of being eaten by lions. Everything goes slo-mo. Percy trembles as he picks up and replaces the cap on the Victorian fountain pen Viv gave him last Christmas.

'Gotta go now. Got a problem.' Though he speaks softly, almost to himself, he sounds like a Sunday School teacher telling a bunch of eight-year-olds she fancies a shag.

*

The Chief Whip opens the inquest. 'OK, I'm supposed to know the size of every nodule on every prick in the party. But I can't superglue their fucking zips up.' He runs his hands through his greasy hair. Percy doesn't like to think what his fingers smell like.

Titus Armlocke is a funny little weasel, hardly an ounce of flesh on him, fizzing and popping like overdone butter in the microwave. Percy can see him on the red benches in forty years, still the same gunge under his fingernails. Not reclassified as a National Treasure.

'Fucking pathetic,' Armlocke continues. 'Fucking a hooker while his wife's having twins. Family values campaigner? Lay preacher? Bible-bashing, bird-bashing hypocrite. Tabs will be on him like frogs fucking a lump of wood. Fuck his two-handed fucking pork-sword.'

The veins are standing out on the Chief Whip's temples like the funnels on the *Titanic*. His fingers twitch as though he's just taken a bullet in the stomach. An intern at the back of the room, a former medical student, suspects he's having a stroke.

Percy tries a spot of Zen. 'If you can keep your head while all about you are losing theirs, you're in with a chance. So what you're only acting?

'Think about the Conservative administration of the 1990s. Fun and games back then puts this into the shade. Even John Major got a slice of the action. Probably steadied his nerves at the time.'

Trouble is, this is different. And, reluctantly, eventually, he admits it.

'We're not just looking at a minister on the job, alas, but a slime-bag on the make. Our Archibald Haddock, Energy Secretary until about ten minutes ago, seems to have been getting a bit of quid pro quo. Or rather willy up pro. In return for a bit of slippy-dippy on nuclear waste import policy.'

Biff nods vigorously like someone with an unpleasant nervous condition.

'Boring little fat men like Haddock don't just stumble on beautiful Puerto Rican prostitutes at respectable trade fairs in New York. Someone did the honours for him, to get something back.'

As Percy lists the unsourced nuclear garbage stories in the papers it becomes more and more obvious he's right. And Armlocke gets into more and more of a state.

'D'you reckon torturers in the Spanish Inquisition felt this bad about people's heresies?' Even now Percy can't resist winding Armlocke up, humourless git that he is.

'Look on the bright side, Titus, they could hardly say this is going to hurt me more than it hurts you.'

*

Haddock is more than hurt. Bad enough being caught with his trousers down, being filmed turned the knife. Hardly sexy, showing his bits with his shoes and socks on.

In the uncensored single frames easily found on the web, the dusky looking naked lady on the huge bed fascinates men and women alike. But no porn movie director would have touched the man's shoddy posture and pot belly. And his thingy's small even when it's big.

Norman Wisdom carried the standard for the little guy. Haddock doesn't.

His resignation, already emailed from the hotel, has been curtly accepted along with a summons to Number Ten, via the Cabinet Office entrance on Whitehall to dodge the snappers. Twenty-four hours ago they'd never heard of him. Now he's gold dust, even with his kit on.

Biff usually just sneers when briefing the scribblers in the scruffy-looking press gallery. But this time, more or less pinioned against the battered table, he tries blokeishness.

It doesn't work. The question's endlessly repeated. 'Is the man corrupt, as well as oversexed?' He has to pretend their guess is as good as his. 'How did he get a looker like that to shag him, even for cash?' Biff winks and says the poor cow's probably sight-impaired.

Reading their filthy minds, he feels like telling them to go off and have a wank, and eventually stalks out, promising himself one thing.

'When I get the little fat shit on the fecking rack they'll hear his fecking screams right up Tottenham Court Road.'

Carpeted, humiliated and haggard, Haddock has a go at hand-wringing about his marriage and career. It means no more than his obviously sincere wish he could cut the little feller off, though Biff smiles at the description.

In time he fesses up. The nuclear waste pitch meant big bucks, plus the sexy little sweetener. So, yes, he spent several nights with the lady and, yes, at this point the screams would have been hitting the junction with Euston Road, he did boast about who he was.

The cracking of Biff's knuckles sound like a burst of machine-gun fire. Haddock hides under the table, expecting to be beaten to a pulp. Biff settles for kicking him in the gut, which is as shapeless and yielding as a sack of blancmange. Fang eventually gives up trying to bite it.

Biff and Percy forget he's even there as they try to figure out why the blackmailers would squander their precious footage when they've got the bloke under the cosh.

'It's like a tapeworm killing off the host just when it's nice and warm in his large intestine,' Percy mutters.

'Haddock's could fit in fecking colonies of them,' Biff snarls.

Percy finally remembers the one man kooky enough to make sense of it all and reaches for the phone. A couple of hundred yards away, the Director General of MI5 is astonished to hear that familiar cultured voice with a hint of West Country burr.

The peculiar questions about Haddock bear out his theory that Percy's a nutter, but it'd be more than his job's worth to just say so and put the phone down.

'Only one possible explanation, Prime Minister. Two armies in the field. Haddock caught in crossfire. Faction A got him in the sack and filmed it, gaining the high ground. Faction B neutralised the footage by leaking it.'

It sounds plausible, but Colonel Blimpsky-Korsakov hasn't finished. 'No sympathy for the fat rat. Pacifist swine. He'd have the nation's defences down. Like his trousers.'

The Colonel's parents fled to Britain when Hitler invaded Russia in 1941. He's always secretly admired Nazi efficiency, which is why he goes out of his way to sound more British than British.

'Roger and out,' he snaps, and the dial tone gurgles over the speakerphone. Percy replaces the receiver, looks at Biff and raises an eyebrow.

'Wake up, fecking eejit,' says the Irishman. 'The fascist screwball was trying to tell you there are two sets of lobbyists on Haddock's case. One lot wouldn't let the other get the competitive edge, whatever the cost.'

Percy leans back in his chair and places his elegant fingertips together as though he's a world-famous forensic analyst.

'When all other possibilities have been eliminated, the least improbable has to be the one.'

Biff thinks what a pompous prick Percy can be, though Lady Rumpledore would have told him he was bleddy right there.

They're interrupted by a whimpering from under the desk. 'But I thought she liked me...' Percy thinks of that terrible first night with Viv and suddenly feels sorry for the man. Biff doesn't. Armlocke can't say, as the only loves in his life have staples in their tummies.

Between sobs, Haddock tells of the odd-looking missionary with the moustache and the monocle who convinced him his half-sister was gagging to know him. In his dreams he was Prince Charming wooing Cinderella, not Mr Slimy ravishing Julie Andrews.

It seems obvious the lady will sell her story to the highest bidder and expose the minister's corruption as brutally as his bits. But it doesn't turn out that way, as the very next day she gets knocked down and killed by a hit-and-run driver.

Percy first learns about it on a factory visit in the North East. Glancing apologetically down at his smartphone, he reads a text from Biff and simply stops hearing the white-coated executive who's telling him loads of things he's not interested in.

There'll be no kiss and tell tale after all, then. Of course it's a relief, but Percy's ashamed of feeling it. When a second text comes through he's appalled. 'There's a fecking god in heaven! Fecking love'im! Couldn't have done a better fecking job myself!'

What's happened fits Blimpsky-Korsakov's theory. The first mob has surely covered its tracks by eliminating the potential source of potentially incriminating evidence.

The cops don't dig that deeply as the stolen Cadillac involved was abandoned nearby leaving no clues apart from a person-shaped dent in the bonnet. Probably a kid on drugs. Case closed. And the senior detective sent by the Met to double check confines his activities to a thorough investigation of Manhattan's strip joints, and comes home with a smile on his face. And not much else.

The New York media are more interested, but only in the local angle. They establish the dead woman was forced into prostitution because her bastard ex-husband left her solely responsible for her mother's cripplingly expensive end-of-life care, and the baby. Plus three cats.

Because the cats are Siamese and the woman's beautiful, the Big Apple takes the story to its sentimental heart. They call her Mata Hairy, for one reason and another.

Biff thinks it's funny at first, but late that night it gets to him. His filthy basement flat, in what friends call the 'disappointing' end of Islington, is full of unwashed underwear and empty bottles. He feels shit about himself, and needs help.

Alcohol doesn't calm him like it does Percy. He's just broken his only clean glass and the sink's brimming with dirty crockery. A chipped brown coffee mug will have to do. Perhaps he should eat something, but there's nothing in the fridge. More whiskey then.

After opening the birdcage he bashes the badly dented table top with the base of his mug in time to the songs he's turned up to full volume. This time 'The H-Block Song' and 'The Sniper's Promise' don't do the trick.

He looks at Sir Roger; the Irish martyr he's named after died for his country's freedom. A noble cause. Today he's been crowing over some poor cow murdered because of a greedy fat bloke with a small cock. He asks himself the obvious question. 'How low can a man go?'

'Brits out, Brits out, Brits out.' The parrot's incorrect answer only makes him feel lonelier. He knows he's an intelligent and under it all a compassionate man. But when his blood's up he's the erect penis with no conscience, Darth Vader minus silly hat.

'No wonder my fecking wives fecking left me. Fecking gobshite like me, I'd have fecking left myself.' He slumps on his ripped horsehair-stuffed sofa and passes out. Using his master's hair for leverage, Sir Roger clambers onto his head and gets it right this time.

'Fecking gobshite. Fecking gobshite. Fecking gobshite.'

CHAPTER NINE

Percy spends the next day fending off the same questions. Who paid the lady? Why the entrapment? Blackmail gone wrong? Who else was in on it? What's the government hiding? Why doesn't he resign?

He longs to say what he really thinks, just to see the faces of the reporters and the sound engineers staring at their headphones. Three little words. 'Just fuck off.'

'D'you think it's possible to bite your tongue clean off, surgically remove it, like Charles The First's head?' he asks Viv.

'Best not, could come in useful one day.' The wistful tone makes him think of her silky triangle. He hopes he's misunderstood.

Sir Bernard Brenstorme can see Percy's problem and tries to be helpful. 'Joseph Stalin's network of Gulag camps accommodated about twenty million people between 1929 and 1953. A final solution to the problem of unwanted journalists, surely?'

Percy laughs and suggests shipping them off to Tuvalu. 'Ah but, Prime Minister, the Penal Servitude act of 1857 renders that solution judicially obsolete I'm afraid. On the other hand...'

'And no one has the stomach for hanging, drawing and

quartering these days. Never did, either before or during the procedure, let alone after,' Percy cuts in.

'From an anatomical point of view this is not surprising. The human intestine is twenty feet in length. If you stretched out all the blood vessels in the body they'd be about sixty thousand miles long. That's enough to go round the world twice. And another thing...'

At this point Percy stops listening, though the day doesn't stop being weird.

Late that night, he tells Viv all about it. 'My next meeting was with a bunch of druids fretting about a car park right next to an ancient burial site.

'I felt like Harold Macmillan, the day he had to politely listen to complaints about a railway arch at Euston minutes after a top-secret briefing that there were Soviet missiles in Cuba.

'Got a feeling I pitched it wrong at the end, when I promised to consider their concerns carefully and agreed motor cars should be allowed to rest in peace.'

Viv smiles indulgently, and asks what happened next.

'They started fiddling with their ceremonial daggers. Funny, that.'

Not for the first time, his wife raises her eyes skywards. She's grateful, as ever, for the shared confidence, though they're fewer and further apart these days, she's appalled at its sequel.

*

'The hacks wouldn't bloody let up when I went on to a secondary school in constituency. Tried a fag behind the bike sheds. Didn't help.

'And, shame to say, lost my rag a bit when I stepped back into the classroom. I know, I know, was supposed to say something uplifting to the kids, but didn't quite come out like that.'

Viv's eyes return to earth. 'So what did you say, exactly?'

'Er, er, asked if they'd ever thought where the main ingredients of an English breakfast come from?

'Course they bloody hadn't, so I told them. Hens and pigs. And asked if they knew the difference. That the hen is involved and the pig is committed.

'Would have left it at that if they hadn't started looking bored and fiddling with their fucking smartphones. That sort of did it.'

By now Percy's in full performance mode. He's Macbeth again, spitting fury at anything in range.

'You know what I said? I said I'm the fucking pig, sizzling in the fucking pan, and I hope I'll give them all fucking dysentery.'

'You. Said. That? In those words?' One look at Percy's bowed head and Viv's eyes have gone skywards again. Into orbit. Actually, like one of those space travel horror movies, when the satellite's got disconnected and the astronaut's going to slowly starve to death.

'Pity these little shits aren't old enough to vote,' Percy continues thoughtfully. 'Several of them tried to give me a high-five as I stomped out of the room, and started chanting Per-Cy, Per-Cy, Per-Cy.

'Before I went in the headmistress told me she loves my style. *Guardian* reader, you know. Gotta feeling that might have changed somewhat.'

Percy's in a better humour now he's got it off his chest. Viv isn't. The look bordering on anguish in her eyes suggests he'd best shut the fuck up. Now. Though there is more to tell. Or would have been.

The scribblers may have cleared off but the TV cameras were still perched on their sticks, and he was Popeye with a ton of spinach in him.

As he marched across the playground the headmistress followed at what she hoped was a safe distance, and gawped at the weapons he snatched up en route. A sports shoe in each hand and a ruler gripped between his teeth.

Biff spotted the signs. He's allowed to tell people he'll blow their fecking kneecaps off, the boss isn't. Jerking his thumb at the driver to fire up the Jaguar, he intercepted Percy at the school gate and stamped on his ankle.

Busy chatting about the footie, the cameramen missed the shot of Percy being dragged into the car by the left ear. All they got was some bloody schoolmarm retrieving stuff from a puddle and shouting at them. 'From now on it's the *Telegraph* for me. The Torygraph! Got that?'

All they knew was they were getting a right earful. And when one of the sound engineers suggested she 'Cheer up, luv' she strode up to him and actually spat in his eye.

At this point, for once, Percy got lucky. Breaking news that the England Squad bloke's golden retriever might be pregnant blotted out that story completely. And by the time normal service gets resumed, more or less, the political correspondents are once again chuntering away about Haddock.

Some are mates of Percy's from the old days, but he'd love to sneak up to the live point with a Gatling gun. Rat-a-tat, and it's back to the studio for the sport. 'Sorry, folks, no news from Westminster today, no one to tell it.'

At least the mainstream media isn't buying the conspiracy theory about the Mata Hairy woman having been murdered. Of course it's all over Facebook and Twitter, but mostly from people who swear Elvis is shagging Queen Victoria in Epsom and Hitler's in a Führerbunker on the moon.

*

'When sorrows come, they come not single spies. But in battalions.' Percy likes quoting Shakespeare to Fang, even though the cat never seems particularly interested

The dipping/bribing crisis has masked it, but he's got something more serious on his mind. In the past he'd end an

71

exhausting day dumping on Viv over a couple of bevvies. But all too often he gets to the flat so late she's already in bed, and he's so knackered he just wants to close his eyes.

An occupational hazard, the burdens of office squeezing out a person's private life, but that's no consolation.

It's just as bad for Viv. Though her own job helps keep her sane she's troubled at how the sight of one particular copper puts a spring in her step. Time to do something, to prevent things getting out of hand.

The kitchen's the one part of the flat that isn't a bit pokey, so she makes a dinner date with her own husband and does a full Greek from scratch. Marinaded lamb shanks, mixed salad and meze, rounded off with baklava cheesecake. She's sure she bought cream, but can't find it.

As usual Percy's late, and seems more interested in the booze. But it helps loosen his tongue, and he's got a lot to get off his chest. Especially about Biff.

'The text about that woman was just for starters, it got worse, much worse. When I saw him later he looked me in the eye and thanked god she was fucking dead. No pity. And I just stood there. Should have decked the bastard.'

Percy looks across the table at her, imploring. 'God help me, have I lost it?'

She doesn't know which of them she's crying for. Tears smear her mascara, making her look like the kind of giant panda its mother would reject. All she knows is the old intimacy hasn't quite gone.

As he kneels in front of her she ruffles his hair and feels a tautening around her nipples and moistening between her thighs. A waste, but she can't help it. Glancing down at Fang, she notices he's grown a white moustache.

Eventually Percy eases himself back into his chair and Viv sits up properly. She's sorry the moment's passed but relieved her knees and back will soon stop aching.

Wondering why her husband's smirking she slips out to the loo, glances in horror at her reflection in the mirror, and does a hasty repair job.

Returning to the table, Viv pours herself another glass of Retsina and makes Percy feel a lot better about himself. 'You were numb, desensitised, but now the pain's kicking in. So you're not lost, just a bit shrunk, poor love. Goes with the job, I'm afraid.'

Percy digests her words, as happy as Fang when he spotted the cream and ran off with it.

He's accepted 'difficult choices' means shafting one lot to get another off your back, not that any politician will say so, any more than admitting they occasionally scratch their bums. But that's not it.

What happened that day's taken things to a new level. He shudders to think how he felt about the woman's death. At least Viv's forgiven him, though, and he really wishes he could shag her. But his mood changes when he spots the little pools of sick Fang's left all over the place, and by morning he's an ostrich again. Problem? What problem?

Viv asks herself about others in her predicament. *Did Maggie give Denis a good rogering after overseas jaunts, to put a smile on his face? You never know. No one saw John Major coming, apart from Edwina, obviously. Lucky girl.* She's only human, of course she feels sorry for herself sometimes.

*

Brenstorme too sometimes feels let down by Percy, especially when he's sharing invaluable legal and biological insights. But, not one to give up easily, he gives Blimpsky-Korsakov a call. Seems, though, to no avail.

'Hard cheese, old boy. No can put agent in every newsroom in Fleet Street, entire media mole budget already allocated.

Bloody BBC. Trots to a man, or woman, if you can tell 'em apart. Which you can't. Dirty pervs.

'But while you're on, strictly on the QT, PM IQ in hand.' It won't be the only thing in hand when he finally meets nutty Mummy, something to not look forward to. Meantime, he returns to Sir Bernard's question about annoying journalists.

'Ever thought of concentration camps? Worked with the Boer. Shame bloody blacks won in the end, filthy dogs. You'll think of something. Must rush. Secrets to keep, suspects to torture. Roger and out.'

Sir Bernard sighs. Blimpsky-Korsakov can be as puzzling as Percy. But then he hits on a plan. A stiff letter to editors telling them to stop being beastly to the Prime Minister, with the stick of closure by sinister means, and the carrot of drinks at Number Ten.

Having signed the letters 'PP PM', Sir Bernard's looking forward to Percy reading the cringing replies and telling him how brilliant he is.

*

The first email is from the editor of the *Sun*. 'Piss-up at yours? I should coco! Whaddaya call your gaff? Last-chance fucking saloon? PS: BYO? I'll bring a bucket of shit, just for you.'

'Any idea what this means?' Utterly baffled, Percy wonders if Sir Bernard knows anything.

'Er, well you see, Prime Minister, er—'

'Interfering sub-moron,' Percy cuts in. 'Brains of a fucking ant. Fuck you, fuckhead.'

Brenstorme is rather hurt.

But Percy turns adversity to advantage. If the Haddock stories can't be spiked, the drinks can. He pictures the *Sun* editor doubled up before his limo even makes the Embankment, shitting himself to death and asphyxiating the driver half way to Canary Wharf.

He'll deserve it after what he said when Percy asked him, relatively politely, to ease off a bit. 'Dream on, asswipe, we'll have Haddock's for brekkie. Everyone knows the slime-bag was on the take, two-faced fat fuckhead.'

Percy's plan, not to rise to the bait but wait for the sweet taste of revenge, quickly goes wrong. Biff has to deploy the crunched foot and wrenched ear routine several times, finally dragging him out into the rose garden.

At this point, frothing at the mouth, the Prime Minister of Great Britain and Northern Ireland breaks most of the outdoor toys belonging to the Chancellor of the Exchequer's ten-year-old son and rips up an entire flowerbed.

Eventually, Biff hits him over the head with a mallet, knocking him out.

CHAPTER TEN

The party continues, minus host. If it had been held anywhere else Percy would have been trashed on Twitter, the government destroyed in minutes, with the Prime Minister of Tuvalu on the blower again. But Downing Street security demands all visitors hand over their mobile phones on the way in.

Also, Brenstorme has finally done something useful.

Percy's plan to poison the editors he hates most has already failed, as he left the super-strength Doo-doo Voodoo tablets he got on the internet in the flat, and Fang ate them. But Sir Bernard's idea was better anyway.

After their conversation of the previous day, Blimpsky-Korsakov remembered his oppo at MI6 telling him liquid cannabis often helped in tricky negotiations with 'friends and allies', particularly the French. So he'd sent Sir Bernard a flask of the stuff pronto.

As a result, no one gives a monkey's wank when Percy loses the plot. Defacing pictures of his predecessors is far more fun. The party really gets going when the *Sun* editor salsa dances with the proprietor of the *Morning Star*, and senior executives of rival papers debag them.

Hearing the racket, Biff leaves the still unconscious Percy slumped over a garden table and takes a peep. They're all half naked now and bellowing at the tops of their voices, to the tune of 'The Red Flag', 'Let's fake the news and fuck the facts, our readers are all fucking twats'.

The police, who had been fiddling with the safety catches on their sub-machine guns, have started sniggering. And when the party finally breaks up they don't even try to work out which nutter should get which iPhone.

*

As Percy comes to, helped by a slug of brandy tipped down his throat by Biff and a dab of cocaine rubbed onto his gums, he thinks there's been a security breach. Looking at the wrecked trampoline, churned up ground and smashed quad bike he tells Biff to get on to it.

Informed he got there first he starts remembering things, though not how he came to lose consciousness. Biff pretends he hasn't a clue, helps Percy to his feet and guides him indoors.

Here the only sound is the occasional muttered swearword from policemen wiping glasses, moustaches and swastikas off the faces of former Prime Ministers. A cleaner asks Percy what she should do with the six pairs of trousers, eighteen ties and nine shoes retrieved so far.

He's got no idea. Nor can he work out what is that vile stench when he finally totters up to the flat, or why his sleeping wife looks like Pinocchio. Eventually he spots she's got a clothes peg on her nose and can see why when he gets to his own bedroom.

There are nasty brown smears all over his white pillow, and Fang is nowhere to be found.

Percy retreats to the sofa, picking up two large lumps of Blu-tack en route. They'll have to do, as he can't find any more clothes pegs. He suddenly remembers he left those tablets he'd meant to give the editor of the *Sun* in plain view on the work surface. Fuck Fang.

The cat was paying for his greed in no time, but feels better now, and lighter. Hearing Percy turning the key in the lock he grabs his chance to get away from the smell and races off to the lobby, where he claws the doorman savagely in the bottom. As the man leaps to his feet and his ticker gives out, Fang springs onto the seat and gets a spot of kip at last.

*

In the morning Percy and Biff can't work it out. The red tops are still salivating over the footballer's disgusting behaviour, helpfully providing their readers with pull-out sections on the ovulation, gestation and procreation of golden retrievers. But about last night's shindig there's nothing. Diddley-squat. Likewise the websites, blogosphere and Twitter.

They find out why when Sir Bernard drops by. He doesn't seem to have anything in particular to say, but his best toupee is a sure sign he thinks he's got something right for a change. In his weird way, he's preening.

'Right, me old darling, spit it out, what have you done this time?' Percy's abrupt query throws him slightly, but he's here to enjoy himself. After carefully clearing his throat several times and minutely examining his expensively manicured fingernails he gets out his gold pocket watch, as though he hasn't really got time for this.

'Mark my words, gentlemen, Brenstorme never leaves a stone unturned,' he begins.

'And Wilde's boyfriend said critics never leave a turn unstoned,' Percy interrupts.

Sir Bernard glares at him, yes, actually glares at him, which Percy thinks is a bloody cheek. 'Art any more than a steward?' he demands haughtily. 'Dost thou think because thou art virtuous there shall be no more cakes and ale?'

This really does put Sir Bernard off his stride. Unlike Fang, he has read a bit of Shakespeare, and knows perfectly well when he's being insulted. But this is his moment of glory, and no one, not even Percy, drat him, is going to spoil it.

'If you'll forgive me, Prime Minister,' he resumes in an injured tone. 'There are one or two facts I'd like to place before you. You may find it worth your while curbing your, ahem, impetuosity.'

Percy glances at Biff, with a look that says 'One or two facts buggery, but he'll have to bloody burble it out or we'll be here all bloody night'. He then folds his arms like a good boy at school and gives Sir Bernard a look that tries to say 'Pray proceed, oh lord and master'.

'I believe I mentioned difficulties with punitive transportation,' Sir Bernard murmurs with a half-smile intended to indicate he's a patient and kindly man. Percy nods, trying not to look bored.

'In addition, I have thoroughly researched the methodology employed by Stalin's secret police, and the Stasi in East Germany. Also Mao Zedong's suggestion a hundred flowers should bloom, to enable his security forces to identify and eliminate dissidents.'

Percy grips the arms of his chair so tightly his knuckles turn white, but keeps up the rapt expression.

'All of which leads me,' Sir Bernard continues, 'to my conversations with our friend Colonel Blimpsky-Korsakov. It was he who supplied the cannabis that saw off your foes at the party.'

Pause for applause, then deep shock as Percy leaps up, clasps his face and kisses him on both cheeks. 'I say, I say, steady on old boy,' he splutters. 'The housemaster would have given you six of the best for that, you know.' Still, he's rather pleased at the way it's gone.

Biff laughs hysterically, bangs his desk with both fists and bashes his forehead against it. In view of unaccountable bruising Percy doesn't follow suit. But he does catch Fang mid-flight to save the toupee from getting chewed to bits.

The cat is so angry he arches his back and heaves and strains to leave one last visiting card. Annoyingly, after last night he's got nothing left.

*

Next day Fang's motions return to normal, the flowerbeds are restocked and the Chancellor of the Exchequer's son gets new bits of junk in place of the old ones. The Cabinet is reshuffled, in much the same way. Goodbye Archibald Haddock, whoever he was. Hello Sir Percival Spectacle, whoever he is.

And, a few weeks down the line, struggling with his new brief but hoping he'll get the hang of it before he gets the boot, Sir Percival is peering down his nose at his computer. Makes him look arrogant, though for a Privy Counsellor and QC he's rather a sweetie.

It's tough having a beak like the Eiffel Tower and eyeballs that only focus when you're squinting along it. *Private Eye* once placed his photo next to an image of a pterodactyl and questioned which was which. He wonders how he ever got elected. The same as Andrew Marr with the big ears, he supposes, at least people knew who you are.

He's quite looking forward to tonight, however. When a glamorous young lady from the Associated Press told him American readers are interested in the UK's take on global warming he was flattered. Now he's found the lavvies in his new department and survived energy and climate change questions in the Commons he's learned delivery is key, not knowledge.

In the event the reporter, who's barely half his age, asks nothing difficult and seems fascinated by what he says, not how he looks. Gives him a lovely warm feeling inside. Widowed now for sixteen years, Spectacle doesn't expect to find a new love. He gave up hope when he drew a blank on a dating site for the partially sighted.

So it's understandable that when the lady puts away her notebook he gets the sherry out, discreetly dims the lights and draws his armchair cosily closer to her. Feels like the doctor just told him he's not on death's door, but good for another fifty years.

He becomes waggish with his guest, even risks touching her arm once or twice, while she in return becomes ever more attentive. But when she comes back from the loo, having clearly removed her bra, he's uneasy, and not just because his trousers feel too tight.

Her close-fitting dress shows off her breasts to advantage, and the outline of her nipples under the thin, silky fabric leaves little to the imagination. He wishes he could see better.

But he's not an idiot. Haddock's fall from grace proved looking a gift horse in the mouth can be a good idea. He's brimming with desire, but not to make a tit of himself.

On the pretext that he too needs the loo he slips into his office, and does a lightning Google check on his tablet for UK staff members of the Associated Press. Her name isn't there. He feels like a kid who's just been told Christmas has been cancelled till he's ninety.

His willy slugs it out with his brain. Maybe she's only just joined, maybe the website's out of date, maybe she's standing in for someone on maternity leave. Yerright. Maybe the earth is flat, and the moon is made of green cheese.

He's deflated in more than one sense, though at least he can now actually have a pee. Afterwards he whips up his fly like a slaughterman. Dear little lambkin's one-way ticket to the dinner plate.

Downstairs again, he doesn't sit down. 'Time to go now, my dear, must get on, you know,' he says coldly. She makes her eyes well up, but when he holds up her coat and shakes it at her like a matador she knows the game is up.

'Plain girls cry, pretty girls go shopping,' she says over her shoulder as she slides into her little pink sports car. At the next red light she switches off the miniature tape recorder hidden in her pen and pops her tiny camera back in its case.

Though the pay will be the same she's sorry the evening ended like this. Cynthia Payne's pervy brothel was before her time, but she loved the stories about it. And with Spectacle it'd be like having it off with an aardvark. 'Never hurt anyone,' she giggles.

CHAPTER ELEVEN

Marianne is cheery, industrious and thorough, a credit to the escort agency which pays for her swish apartment in the posh part of Islington. 'So handy for the Almeida, darlings,' she jokes with her theatre friends. When anyone jokes back she must have a sugar daddy, she winks and says there's safety in numbers.

At her drama school near where she lived in the East End the students had to toss themselves off in front of the class. She loved it. Later, playing Juliet, she gave the bedtime scene so much welly the director booked a bigger venue and extended the run. The bloke playing Romeo thought he'd died and gone to heaven.

As she finally gets past the Angel she thinks how pleased her cats will be she's home early. Peaches and Cream adore poached salmon, so they can celebrate together. Then she'll get her lovely little Jiggle balls out, and all three pussies will purr themselves to sleep.

The Reverend Chancer, who'd hired her to entrap Spectacle, duly pays up. 'God, grant me da serenity to accept the fings wot I can't change and da courage to change the fings wot I can,' he grumbles. Meaning if he can't shaft the new top man in the department a junior minister or the Permanent Secretary will have to do.

Marianne guesses what he has in mind and smiles sweetly. 'A business doing pleasure with you, dearie. A grand a go's better than a slap in the face with a wet kipper.' She giggles, he grunts. But says he'll be in touch.

*

Sir Percival Spectacle's evening ends very differently from Marianne's. He closes the front door, flicks off the welcoming light and scowls. The Prime Minister needn't know, got enough on his plate as it is. Besides, no harm's been done, more's the pity.

The delicate grace of his stucco-fronted Georgian house is a reminder of everything he hasn't got. And with the lights turned up the drawing room's not cosy any more. It hasn't been touched since Lady Spectacle's day, and looks dated and tired. Percival knows the feeling.

He glares at the ample sofa that looks like it's laughing at him, fiddles with his disappointed little winkle, and gives the gilt-framed oil painting of his father a V-sign.

All hooked nose and hatred in his barrister's wig, he looks vile. Percival curses the old bastard for passing on that hooter, and for separating him from his mother before his balls dropped. It broke her heart seeing him packed off to boarding school, but Pater was determined to have her to himself again, at least during term time.

The other boys at Winchester pissed themselves at the sight of him, and again when he blubbed during a film society screening of *The Lord of the Flies*. Years later he learned of a news editor at the *Mail* with his problem. The hacks used to refer to him as the nose editor.

*

The summer recess is approaching and Spectacle's emptying his departmental drawers, as ministers do. Westminster's getting demob happy, even the press pack acting like Bloody Mary after a good spate of burnings.

But Reverend Chancer is fretting about where to strike next, while Percy wonders why he hasn't done it already.

'Maybe whoever was behind the Haddock affair's given up running people over and driven himself over a cliff instead.' Percy can but hope. Biff doesn't bother. 'More likely he's genital herpes during a quiet phase, waiting to burst out again next time love is in the air.'

And then there's the problem of the summer holiday. Percy knows he'll be wrong wherever he goes, but provided the Russians don't annex Scotland while his finger's off the nuclear button, the story shouldn't do too much damage. The Bashars' island it is then.

Yet he still can't quite get that stuff about the trout being tickled out of his mind, any more than his uni chums wining and dining old Rumpledore. *Should have checked that out myself*, he thinks. *Still, Viv'll be pleased.*

She is, the more so when she discovers Sergeant Chalky White will be in charge of security.

It troubles her, that flutter in her heart when Percy mentions his name. She's always been loyal, but loneliness is starting to eat her. The wonderful Greek night was like a dribble of methadone for a heroin addict after a quarter of a century on the wagon. Not quite it.

*

Sergeant White doesn't fit the professional stereotype. Off duty, you'd guess he's a lecturer, a musician, maybe a writer. Not a copper. For a start he's got normal feet.

He talks normal as well, none of that maddening mix of cockney and officialese. And he likes opera. Viv can't think what he's doing in the force and Percy can't think what to do about him. Cram in more time and attention for his wife? Or leg it so she can part hers?

As they were never more than friends, Percy knows his jealousy is ridiculous. But it's intense.

The fifteen emails that have just popped up in his inbox distract him. Likewise two phones ringing at once. The Foreign Secretary's fretting about civil war in Slovenia, and the Sergeant-at-arms is moaning about the same thing closer to home. Armlocke and Haddock have had another punch-up in the Members' Lobby.

Brenstorme tiptoes in with yet another red box and does a runner when Percy snatches up a paperweight the size of a hand grenade. He puts it down again as he needs both hands to cup his head in. Another twelve emails have just appeared.

'Not surprising leaders do dumb things,' Percy tells Fang. 'That much pressure it's odd they haven't blown the world up. Still, never say never in politics.' Lighting another fag he reaches for the brandy decanter. The cat starts purring. He's a party animal.

*

The party starts all right, as Percy just ticks everything in his fucking red box, but goes downhill when he asks Fang about the really important things. What to buy Viv for her birthday, which falls in the middle of the holiday, and what the hell he's going to wear.

'A Turkish island in summer? So what it's private? That never stopped the paparazzi. And I go red in the sun, then peel like an onion. Great.'

Percy needs answers, but when he absent-mindedly fondles the cat's paws in a way he can't bear the response is bloody. 'Hate you, bastard.' A natural reaction, though the cat's narrowed eyes and twitching tail suggest the feeling's mutual.

Come departure day, however, the question of Percy's dress code nearly becomes academic, as a national rail shutdown looks like screwing everyone's holiday, including his.

He's spent hours glued to the phone, in Downing Street, in the car, even in the bloody lavvy at the airport. Gone is the public façade of calm. Red spots appear on his cheekbones and the nape of his neck.

The strike doesn't get called off till minutes before last call on Percy's flight, and it takes a thousand air miles and eight double brandies to get the spots down. But at least Viv's remembered the Nicorette patches. When she gives him one he's so grateful he wishes he could return the favour, in a sense.

As he steps out of the plane into the searing heat that makes the ground wobble, his mind goes the same way. The release of tension feels like hiccups stopping after fifteen years.

'Funny old world,' he mutters, thinking of Maggie at her last Cabinet meeting, and almost takes a tumble on the aircraft steps.

Within hours his brain's fluttered off to the moon. The perfumed air doesn't help. Herbs and spices mingle with the backdrop of pine resin. Feels like a vibrating love egg up his nose.

The snap-your-nipples-off air conditioning in the villa makes it feel as homely as the Moscow underground. Gold fittings, gilded surfaces, excessive furniture and terrifying gadgetry add up to something between a swish shopping mall and a James Bond movie set.

Percy's first go at turning a light on generates a blast of Wagner's Ring Cycle from a concealed ghetto blaster. When he tries to turn it off, hard porn appears on a huge TV screen.

Viv is fascinated and appalled, and during that night's banquet, one up on a takeaway doner kebab, she lets rip. 'OK they don't torture their people, much, but they rob them blind. What's the average income in their country? Infant mortality?

Child poverty? Don't suppose they live long enough to worry about dementia care.'

Percy takes a huge slug of the velvet-smooth cognac that seems to gush from the well of heaven, and sighs. 'Shod it, Viv, it'sh hard enough at home. At least this is one mesh I don't have to clear up.' He knows that's an appalling answer, and expects a bollocking.

All he gets is a glare. Viv craves to be noticed, human, breathing, farting even, in a ladylike way, instead of being increasingly blanked.

Her birthday present's another sore point. Cartier watches cost, but it felt impersonal. She'd have much preferred an interesting find on eBay, at a tenth of the price. In fact Percy was trying to say sorry for being such a rubbish husband and got defensive when she obviously didn't get it. It was a horrible evening.

It hurts like hell, all of it. And, Viv's ashamed to admit, she wants to hurt him back. Maybe that's where the policeman comes in.

Sergeant White could not have behaved more properly, but that just makes it all the more obvious to Viv he's placed her on a pedestal. She likes the feeling.

*

The Bashars' outdoor air conditioning is just one more ridiculous extravagance, but a guilty pleasure for Viv, glowing on a lounger and only partially shielded from the sun by a silken canopy. Suddenly, she fancies a chat with that policeman, and by chance his timing is perfect.

He approaches Viv with a message for Percy. When she says he's popped upstairs for a siesta he replies it's not urgent and he'll come back. 'Sure,' says Viv, 'but first you must try some of this freshly squeezed lemon juice. Thirsty work, protecting prime ministers.'

He gives in gracefully, sits down and does the honours. But in refilling Viv's glass he tips half the contents of the jug over the top half her dress, making it totally see-through. In that heat, naturally, she isn't wearing a bra.

Of course he can't mop her up while looking the other way. He's a crack shot with a semi-automatic, but too on target with the silk napkin. It's embarrassing when he's accidentally massaging her breasts, but Viv doesn't mind. 'Discretion is the better part of fervour,' she jokes, then blushes like a little girl.

She's poles apart from Marianne, but wasn't cut out to be a nun. OK, it was by accident, but it made a nice change to have someone else kneading her nipples…

CHAPTER TWELVE

Mustafa is the villa's youngest waiter, treated by everyone as a glorified mosquito. The ornate uniform only adds to his shyness, especially the fez that's more Tommy Cooper than Kemal Ataturk. Small wonder he worships Sergeant White, he's always kind to him.

Imagine his horror as he approaches the table to find his hero violating the English milady, who's more beautiful and important than all the kings and queens of England put together.

He must defend her honour! He must fight the demon to the death! But what with? Gallipoli flashes through his mind, but all he's got is a tray of fruit, cheese, coffee and little Turkish cakes. Hardly a machine gun and a stash of explosives, but it'll have to do.

Baring his teeth, yelling as bloodcurdlingly as he can, he charges.

Sergeant White doesn't have time to get his gun out before the boy's upon him, knocking him over the edge of the balcony into the rosemary bushes below. Though, his professional training kicking in, he takes Mustafa with him.

No way he can neutralise the psycho because the kid's

unarmed. So he falls back on the standard-issue hold, and old-fashioned patter. "Ello, 'ello, 'ello, what's all this then?'

Viv works it out in a flash and bursts out laughing, just as a tousle-headed Percy stumbles into view. There's his erotically exposed wife apparently in a state of hysteria, while the man charged with keeping him alive is in what looks like a homosexual clinch with a mannequin.

Viv puts her hand over her mouth like a kid told off for blowing a raspberry in class, and Sergeant White stands to attention and salutes. Mustafa's in floods of tears.

Picking up the boy's fez, Percy adopts a benevolent if bemused tone. 'Something in the air, my dears? Or are we holed up in Sodom, perhaps, or Gomorrah? Just curious, you understand.'

'Well you see… What happened was…' But it's no good, Viv can't stop giggling. Eventually Percy sits down and suggests she change into something drier. Mustafa bows low. 'I come back. Bring more refreshments. Not attack again. I repent.'

Ten minutes later he places a restocked tray before the now sedately seated threesome and places his hand on his heart. 'Sword before. Ploughshare now. Praise god.' He kneels down and loves it when Sergeant White pats his head. Less so at what he says next.

'Let go of my knees now, dear chap, or I'll have to shoot you.'

As the boy leaps to his feet, hands up and face contorted in terror, Percy gently tells him the man was only joking and he really should join them in a nice cup of tea.

Of course the kid doesn't dare accept the invitation. Instead he clicks his heels and gallantly mimics Sergeant White's wonderful salute. Also, before scuttling off again, he makes another announcement. 'This best moment of my life. I treasure till day I die.'

Left to themselves, they debate how they can help him, and opt for a college course to get him a career to make his mum proud. 'If she says no, we could always kidnap him,' Percy suggests. 'He could teach Fang some manners, and in return get tips in assertiveness.'

The conversation turns to the message Sergeant White was supposed to be passing on from Bashar Major. 'Dear Percy and Viv in residence? Good-oh, mission accomplished.' As the handset at the other end didn't get replaced correctly, he also overheard a few words exchanged between the brothers. 'Teed up a treat old fellow'... 'Top hole dear chap.'

Neither the PM nor the sophisticated policeman know quite what to make of that. Though, after a lifetime's exposure to double-dealing creeps, Mustapha could have told them. The Bashars were checking they'd got Percy where they wanted him. In the shit.

Percy would have been appalled if he'd heard the rest of the Bashars' conversation in the Nineteenth Hole, a copy of an English golf club bar in the basement of their favourite palace. Annoying there's no natural light there, but drinking alcohol is after all a capital offence in their country.

'Now we've led the dear chap to the gallows, better get the noose out,' says Bashar Major, sipping his G and T and winking at the gilt-framed photo of Albert Pierrepoint on the wall.

'Whacko,' replies his brother. 'Let's up the payments to his constituency party. Every little helps, as they say at Tesco's.'

'Tess? Coes? Who's she?'

'Silly billy. It's where poor people go instead of Harrods.'

*

Not knowing any of this, apart from existence of shops other than Harrods, Percy focussed on giving Sergeant White instead of the Bashars the third degree.

'Let's begin at the beginning, Sergeant White, why do people call you Chalky?'

'Simple, Prime Minister, all Whites in the service are called Chalky. Afraid my esteemed profession is noted neither for its literacy, nor its imagination.'

Percy does a double take, but he's used to thinking on his feet. 'OK, so what's your real name?'

'Well, Monty, actually.'

'Right, from now on, Monty, I'm Percy. At least in private. Got that?'

'As you wish, Prime... er, sorry, Percy,' Monty says with an effort. Percy had in mind to trample on the guy, but instead is finding him interesting and uncomfortably attractive. Viv's just glad she's properly covered. Erect nipples would hardly do in mixed company.

The interrogation reveals Monty hates his CV. His South London comprehensive was a warzone where no one looked beyond a career in organised crime, and his mother's early death from cancer dashed his hopes of becoming a forensic scientist.

'Dad was unemployed, and with four younger sisters I needed a job further down the ladder, fast. The police service would have been a career, if it hadn't been for my idiot principles.

'Blowing the whistle on a bent senior officer is right in principle but wrong in practice if you're a rookie. The bastard was good at getting his own back on snitches.

'On the beat in Tottenham, where the "filth" are only good for a kick in the whatsits, I wished I'd looked the other way. It particularly got to me giving evidence at inquests and being patronised as dozy Mr Plod by people no cleverer than me.

'I sat by the river and waited, and at last a body floated by. The dodgy Super got up to his tricks once too often, and had the book thrown at him.'

'So you got a transfer to SO1 Specialist Protection Branch, and promotion?' Percy dislikes but understands the system, and Monty smiles. 'Hardly Met Commissioner Sir Montague White

OBE, but it could be worse. Can't think of a nicer chap I'd want to take someone out for.'

Percy smiles too. He can see why Viv likes this guy. In his mid-forties, tall and slim with greying hair that makes him look distinguished, he's bloody sexy. *Now now*, Percy thinks to himself, *behave yourself*.

There's a cooling breeze when Mustafa appears with a tray of booze. He's still ever so polite, but his fez is at a jaunty angle. When Viv says how nice he looks he manages, just, not to cry.

*

The sun begins its slow descent towards the horizon, eventually lighting the sea with what looks like a stairway to heaven. Percy, who's liking Monty more and more, steers the conversation from police work to his other interests.

'Literature, art and, well, opera, I'm afraid.' This comes with the self-effacing smile Viv always loved about Percy.

Not noticing her hands starting to tremble, Percy tells how he played Don Giovanni in a student production. 'Modern dress, done for laughs. The director got me to leave the stage in one scene and reappear smothered in cocaine.

'By the end of the run I was binning the talc and having much more fun with the real thing,' he blurts out, forgetting that he's talking to a serving police officer.

'You have a right to silence, but I must caution you anything you say may be taken down in evidence and used against you.'

Percy panics, then remembers the death threat to the kid. 'Bastard,' he mutters with a grin. Day turns to night and the butler serves dinner. Viv looks from one man to the other but can't make sense of anything as she's getting tiddly.

At times like this Percy's still the man she married. But Monty's a different kettle of fish, as Fang would put it. She thinks of a particular film star's take on marital fidelity. 'Why go out for a hamburger when you can have a steak at home?' But which is which?

She feels like a shipwrecked sailor after a month without food getting the hang of cannibalism. It takes a succulent, meaty person looking peaky to get the mouth watering, but Viv's juices are flowing. Her college lecturer would have said it's only natural.

Listening to the men swopping famous writers' smutty jokes, she soaks up the atmosphere and her panties, and gravely slips in a quote from Lord Byron. 'What men call gallantry and gods adultery is much more common where the climate's sultry.'

Percy stares across at her and pulls himself to his feet. Monty tenses, hoping this won't turn into what his colleagues quaintly term 'a domestic'.

He needn't have worried. Percy's only worries are that his wife isn't being frivolous enough, and that nature's calling. Monty eyes Viv uncertainly. His heart leaps at the possibility she's just made a pass at him, but sinks at the thought of where it could lead. Back to Tottenham.

On the scale of bladdered-ness, Viv's six out of ten, Percy is nine, while Monty's carefully positioned no higher than three. He's sober enough to give his conscience the kind of seeing-to in the cells the lads at the station enjoyed.

During the evening he's bonded with Percy, and would hate to do the dirty on him. Against that it's become obvious that if Viv has gaps that need filling, one way or the other, her husband's not the man for the job.

Percy's gags are textbook gay. Particularly the one from Oscar Wilde, that he'd never play croquet because it involved unbecoming postures.

In the downstairs gents' lavvies, the size of the centre court at Wimbledon, Percy wonders how the hell to flush the urinal.

After the first solid knob turned on all fifteen showers, and the second activated a voice saying over and over 'Gentlemen, please wash your hands', he decides the fucking bog can sort itself out. Also, it's time to hit the sack.

As Percy totters towards the table, Viv's notices the small dark patch in the front of his trousers. Time and again she's warned him he needs a couple of extra shakes if he's wearing light-coloured fabrics. He's always forgetting, which she finds loveable.

But there's different sorts of love. Marianne always loved the scene in the Cynthia Payne movie when police barge in on an old man shagging a girl a quarter of his age, and he says he's waited so long he's not stopping now for anyone. Viv suddenly feels the same.

*

'Nightie night, shildren, need a shpot of shuteye. Don't shoo do anything I wouldn't.' Drawing on past experience Viv tells her husband not to have a last fag before getting his head down. 'The Bashars probably have their own private fire brigade, but let's not put it to the test, eh?'

'Heard thish joke once. German comedian. About hish lot losing both world wars. You know what he shed? Shird time lucky.' Percy stumbles off, muttering something about Catholic conspiracies and Pudding Lane.

Monty stares at Viv anxiously. 'Not losing the plot is he?'

'No. The Great Fire of London might be a bit much, even for him, but remember what happened in Downing Street? That was his second go. His old flat went up in smoke too, though that was partly my fault.'

96

CHAPTER THIRTEEN

'Ah. Didn't know. *Tout s'explique, Madame.*' For some reason Monty speaking French tips the balance. Viv leans across and kisses him full on the lips.

That does it. Too late trying to stiffen his resolve when his willy's already halfway there. Her tongue between his lips knocks Tottenham for six. Plus he's been a widower for six years and hadn't had the heart to do it since.

She's waited four times as long, so it's her whole body trembling now.

As she slides onto his lap and feels his fingers caressing her inner thighs the cascade begins. She thinks of the underlining and exclamation marks all over that essay, and can almost hear the tutor saying 'Told you so'.

Here is not the place. They rise from the seat, head for the pool and descend onto a huge embroidered cloth, which melts into the shapes of their bodies. One classy mattress.

Unfortunately for them there's an elaborate system of sensors, intended to save would-be swimmers the trouble of pressing a button to uncover the water. The camera lenses are angled to ensure it happens automatically when there's movement nearby.

Very soon there's a great deal of movement on the canopy,

which rhythmically slides a short distance in and out in harmony with their bodies. Adds to the fun, like on a night sleeper.

'It's ardour on the Orient Express,' Viv sighs. This time she doesn't blush.

But sensitive electronic equipment doesn't like being repeatedly turned on and off. The circuitry eventually fuses, giving out a dense cloud of blue smoke and fully retracting the cover.

The lovers know nothing of this until the vanishing canopy finally drops them in it, in both senses. An unexpected dunking dampens ardour, especially when it's followed by flashing lights, alarm bells, wailing sirens and snarling dogs.

Viv does not enjoy the irony of having caused the sort of havoc she told Percy not to, and Monty finds nothing funny about soaking his mistress twice in the same day. Three times, actually, counting her… Well, no way he's going into that now.

The priority, apart from not drowning, is not being caught in flagrante by the firefighters, medics and storm troopers suddenly appearing from nowhere. Viv thanks god a pit bull terrier found her lost knickers in time and ate them.

Monty struggles to act the part of elite London police officer when he's soaked to the skin and suffering from coitus interruptus stress disorder. Viv feels more fallen woman than first lady.

However, the Bashars are fond of pool parties, so fishing out half-naked people is something their emergency services are used to. They offer Viv mouth-to-mouth resuscitation, and are disappointed by her reply. 'That won't be necessary, thank you very much.'

When Monty points to the smouldering junction box, the General Officer Commanding Villa Bashar Special Forces tilts back his armour-plated fez and grunts. He cocks his high-velocity machine gun and fires one short burst. No more flashing lights, no more alarm bells.

At this he twirls his waxed moustache and turns on his heel.

Alone again, Viv and Monty hold one another close, humiliated and ashamed, then trudge back to the villa, a respectable distance apart. A rotten night's sleep beckons, though Monty will have to clean his Glock 26 first, so the chlorine won't jam the works.

'The pistol's place is in the pocket, except in the line of duty,' he murmurs. Viv nods sadly.

*

'Did someone let off fireworks when I had my head down?' Percy, looking more than usually worse for wear, is wondering next morning about the popping noise that briefly woke him in the night.

'Probably a damp squib,' murmurs Viv in a crestfallen way. They both fall silent.

She supposes she got something out of her system, though Monty didn't get anything into it. Means she can't be pregnant then, for what that's worth. Loving oneself is all right in theory, but right now she wants to scratch her own eyes out.

Percy has a hunch what might have happened, and blames himself. 'If you don't feed the beast it's only a matter of time before it starts hunting its own food,' he snarls at himself.

The dog in a manger thing's not his style. He hopes she'll come back to him, little knowing she already has. In future she'll keep her head down, and everyone else's.

Monty, meanwhile, feels jerked out of a nightmare in which he was drowning, only to find he's safe, but lonely, in his own bed. Feels like the wrong sort of wet dream.

For the next few days he and Viv are like kids made to stand in the corner for playing rude games in the lavvy. A look and a hand-squeeze is as much as they dare.

On the flight home, Percy finally tries to broach the subject.

He shuffles his legs under the seat in front in a vague attempt to get comfortable and clears his throat. 'You remember that night with Monty when I got a bit pissed, my dear?' he begins.

Viv tenses. Remember? Could she ever forget?

'I just wanted to tell you...' One glance at her frozen expression and he's desperate for a change of direction, preferably starting from somewhere else.

'Remember when we landed on the island and I tripped on the steps?'

Viv frowns. 'Yes, but what's your point?'

'Thing is, I was in my cups then as well. And the top button on my fucking trousers had fallen off. I was holding the buggers up. So much for the conquering hero.'

Viv's face relaxes, thinking it's so like a bloke to tell silly jokes instead of admitting to his face the other bloke's a good bloke. In spite of everything she's a good bloke.

Feels like Satan being told by God he wasn't such a wrong'un after all. She tidies the magazines, empty coffee cups and sandwich wrappings on the little table above her knees.

'You were in good company, my dear. Sir Alec Douglas-Home once spent an entire flight to China muttering the word Peking to himself. Just so he wouldn't offend the reception committee by forgetting where he was.'

Percy pretends he'd never heard that story, laughs heartily and tells himself it's the best he could hope for. *If she must get her rocks off elsewhere it won't change the sleeping arrangements in the flat. At least we're still friends.*

For Viv too it's a bittersweet moment. No hamburgers in the diner, that's decided, even though there's no juicy steak at home. To hide her tears, she closes her eyes and pretends to sleep. Percy isn't fooled, and lays a hand comfortingly on her arm. They both feel better.

*

The bubble bursts the minute they drag their baggage into the Heathrow arrivals lounge.

Instead of the usual clutter of hysterically waving relatives dying to hear what a lovely time they've had, there is Biff, face like thunder. 'Good trip?' Not that he gives a shit.

'Fuck that. What's happened now?'

Apart from weathering the first seriously tropical storm of his marriage, Percy did manage to relax on holiday, but now he glances miserably at Viv. 'Feel like a deep-sea diver flung up from a thousand feet below. Got the bends, badly.'

The leather seating inside the bombproof Jaguar has a distinctive smell. Percy sniffs it hatefully. 'Like cancer coming out of remission,' he mutters.

As Biff tells him there's been a robbery at the Department of Energy and Climate change, rubbing his hands together, Percy remembers how Gordon Brown used to stab the back of the official car's front seat with a marker pen. He feels like doing the same to Biff, with a sword.

As he doesn't have one handy he makes do with the red box. Placing it on the floor beneath his feet, he raises his knees and stamps on it with all his might.

Biff takes the hint and backs off a bit. 'Jaysus, it's not the end of the fecking world. Just a worry the heist took place in the Minister of State's private office. It's her personal computer that's gone.'

*

Belinda Blusterham is a strappingly forceful woman of middle age with strappingly forceful steel-grey hair. It's expensively fluffed up then lacquered down to a smooth finish, making her look like a hero from the Trojan war, with his helmet on.

She's charm on legs with top civil servants and fellow ministers at the department, but vile to the underlings in her office. Word has got around, and Biff's convinced this was an inside job.

'Reciprocal fecking justice, like Oliver fecking Cromwell,' he grunts. 'Deserved being dug up and hanged, after his war crimes in Ireland.'

Percy knows Biff often throws things at the brute's statue outside Parliament when he thinks the cops aren't looking. 'At least the sod has the decency to be dead,' he mutters. 'Wish the same could be said of the bastard giving us grief now.'

Neither he nor Biff has any idea who the suspect is and can't even be sure he exists, but they'd both guessed whoever was behind the Archibald Haddock sting would have another go. The former Energy Secretary's number two is a logical target.

*

Fifty miles away, Reverend Chancer is happily proving they're right. Raising Belinda Blusterham's computer to his lips, he kisses it like a holy relic. Not quite the grail, but a fair old lump of Our Saviour's cross.

Tracking down a suitable burglar was surprisingly easy. He had a few jars in the scruffy pub by the department where junior staff hung out and listened in on their chatter. One of them, who obviously worked in Blusterham's private office, kept twittering on at the little spiv who often met her there about how much she hated the woman.

Chancer followed the man home and offered him a grand if he'd get his girlfriend to do the job. She was nervous, but so touched when he offered her fifty quid that she memorised the combination on the wall safe and was careful to wear gloves when she opened it.

Quite exciting when it came to it. Like having a shag on a clifftop.

Seated in the swanky wing of his rambling vicarage his

parishioners never see, he swivels round in his swanky executive chair several times, throws several of his swanky executive toys in the air and thanks god in all his mercy.

'Da Vatican may be more up west than my drum,' he tells his solid gold statuette of the music hall singer nicknamed Champagne Charlie, 'but my gear cost just as much. Right? Right.'

It doesn't take long to hack into the Apple Mac, and hallelujah! There's all the correspondence relating to the purchase of the ten-bedroomed chateau in San Tropez she thought she'd picked up for the price of a semi in Skeggie.

'Try explaining dat to m'lud from the dock,' he sniggers to himself. 'All above board? You know you're under oaf? A judge's way of saying the ovvah one's got bells on it.'

CHAPTER FOURTEEN

The Reverend Charlie Chancer kicks his legs in the air and breaks into song. 'Champagne Charlie is my name, Champagne Charlie is my name, Champagne Charlie is my name by golly, and rogueing 'n' stealing is a game.'

His voice is husky but melodic, though he can't help shouting those last few words.

'And woss wrong wi' dat?' He snatches up his statuette and glares into its tiny golden eyes. 'Am I not a criminal mastermind parr-excellornce? Eh? Ain't my foolproof scams craim der-lar fuckin' craim?' He accepts the Haddock job went a bit wrong, and that smug-arsed git Spectacle was a tosser, 'But I can't miss wi' dat busty bitch Blusterham, nah can I?'

Seems he's right. He paid next to nothing for the ten-bedroomed ruin in France, had the walls cunningly patched up, got an ace photographer to make the place look brilliant, and forged a couple of glowing surveyors' reports.

Blusterham coughed up twice what Chancer paid for the place, thinking she got a bargain, but knowing it was a backhander.

In return she promised 'flexibility' in government policy on nuclear waste imports. Yes, yes, she finally agreed, that means she will sign off the Chinese shipments he has in mind. All this in emails sent from the computer Charlie now has in his hands.

He was amazed she fell into his trap without making even the most obvious checks. 'Stoopid fuckin' cah,' he told his statuette. 'If I were a voting man, which fank da lord I'm not sir, I'd put me notes on de ovver mob any day.'

This can only go one way. She'll be too open to blackmail to break her promise to Chancer, or to complain the chateau's not all it was cracked up to be. Cracks being the operative word.

Charlie Chancer's natural cunning and greed would have made him millions perfectly legally in the investment banking sector. But it happens he went to the same school as Montague White, and going straight never occurred to him.

Fyok Yu and Hon Ki get where he's coming from. Though they're committed members of the Chinese Communist Party they've always thought Mao's Little Red Book was a load of bollocks.

*

Percy's priority is to keep it quiet if at all possible. If Blusterham's been nobbled he'll have to sack her, and people will want to know why. But when he and Biff get her in for a discreet chat she insists there's nothing more sinister on the computer than boring household accounts.

A fridge magnet in her vulgar mock Tudor kitchen in her vulgar mock Georgian house in a vulgar mock posh South London suburb has good advice on it. 'Sincerity is all you need in politics. Fake that and you're made.'

Pouring herself half a pint of crème de menthe when she gets home that night she curses herself for her carelessness and stupidity, and prays the prole who knocked off her MacBook Air can't read, or at least can't be arsed to go through her stuff.

She only got in on a by-election a year ago, but Percy fast-tracked her into government as he thought her background in corporate finance would be handy for the nuclear industry.

It obviously needed cash, and spent fuel imports would bring in loads. So what if Chancer's proposal included, ahem, a small consideration? Never a problem in the City.

She puts on 'Top Tunes from the Classics', chucks her bowl of mock turtle soup at her maid and snarls at her. 'Get your scrawny Albanian arse out of here or I'll burn your passport.' Because her papers aren't quite in order, the glorified slave meekly lowers her eyes and obeys.

Blusterham kicks her pedigree Afghan hound instead.

*

Chancer can see Blusterham will need to tread carefully if she's under suspicion, so he's hatched a plan B to jolly things along. The Permanent Secretary at Energy and Climate Change, the department's Sir Humphrey, is the perfect target.

He actually is called Sir Humphrey. Snodbury. Oxbridge man, rowing blue and college 12-bore champion. Total bore in every respect, actually, but there's got to be an in somewhere.

There is. Snodbury's son Heathcliff, living way beyond his means at Daddy's old college.

Remembering his day job, Chancer slips on his cassock. The former deputy governor where he did his bird has come up with a beauty of a sermon. The punters love it when he thunders on about the avarice and venality of the world and the meek inheriting the earth.

'Lord now lettest thou thy servant depart in peace according to thy word.' Chancer sends them home in his best clergyman's voice, then mutters to himself 'Bunch of fucking losers'.

*

Sir Humphrey Snodbury's head is a perfect sphere. From behind he looks like a ruler on legs with a ping-pong ball perched on top. And the bald patch in his perfectly trimmed sandy-coloured hair could have been marked with a child's compass.

He wears his Royal Artillery tie like a war wound even though he was never under fire from anyone.

At cocktail parties he hints there was something hush-hush about his service days. Johnny Foreigner wasn't having the hell blown out of him because he was having his throat quietly slit in a ditch somewhere. 'Can't say any more, loose talk costs lives.'

Young Heathcliff is his father without the brains, and was only accepted by the college because he was captain of the school hockey team and an ace athlete. He has got Mummy's golden locks, good looks and charm, but he knows it.

Chancer looks at a smug selfie he's posted on Facebook with two pretty girls kissing him and sheds tears for the lad, same as a crocodile when it's about to bite someone's legs off.

The kid's practically a wheelchair case already. When he's not partying more to his own heart's content than the bank's, he's in the boozer by his digs fretting about his overdraft.

His upbringing tells him help is always at hand, so he's not surprised to see the odd-looking clergyman with the monocle and droopy moustache who's sidled up. 'I dashed well need a guardian angel,' he announces.

Chancer winks and says: 'Afraid Gabriel's washin' 'is wings today, but Mephistopheles is free.' Risky, but it gets the ball rolling.

He does the old triple G and T for the lad, fizzy water with ice and a slice for himself routine, and it's so easy he feels like he's swinging the lead. Heathcliff says he's an entrepreneur, but moans his suppliers are grumpy about late payment and have baseball bats.

'So he's buying snort to sell, stuffin' it up 'is nose, and wondering why 'e's gettin' grief. I'd give'im fuckin' grief and all,'

Chancer mutters to himself. The pretty young Spanish barman has his eye on them, wondering what's going on. Chancer notices.

Heathcliff likes the sound of the Parable of the Talents. The god-botherer's going to help him trade his way out of trouble! He pockets the two grand, and heads for the door with a spring in his step and a twitch in his nostrils.

As he slips off his dog collar and touches up his rouge in the loo, Chancer clasps his many fingers together at the thought of the fun he'll have with Sir Humphrey. Returning to the bar he grins at the pretty little Spaniard, who pouts at him divinely.

Two triple brandies for starters then, and a celebratory shag after closing time. Ah, men, amen…

*

Three weeks later Heathcliff's in the slammer feeling sorry for himself, while Daddy would have been tearing his hair out if he'd had enough to get hold of.

Chancer's email is blunt. '*Your son is at real risk of being murdered, being done for drug dealing and getting sent down from uni. Only I can save him.*' As he sits at his computer waiting for the reply Chancer fondles his pet rat, Caligula. Like Biff, he has his soft side.

Snodbury is snotty. '*No son of mine blah blah. Something amiss surely? Who are you to pervert the course of justice anyway?*' And so on and so on.

Chancer hits him back with the gospel according to Saint Tony. '*Didn't the great Blair always preach that if it works, do it? Oh, and btw, your own career might be at risk.*'

Abrupt change of tone from Snodbury. It's agreed Heathcliff's creditors will be paid off, and all charges will be dropped, somehow. In return, Snodbury promises to give due consideration to the matter of nuclear waste imports. No promises, mind.

Reverend Chancer can't believe how limp these stiffs are when it comes to it. 'No better dan da fuckin' likes of us,' he tells Caligula. 'A couple of grand for da dealers and a ton for da dozy tart in da Crown Prosecution Service and it's sorted.'

Indeed it is. Sir Humphrey invites him to lunch at the Reform Club, and Reverend Chancer clasps his favourite executive toy so tightly that he snaps it. Pity. He'd always liked that solid silver ball scratcher.

Chancer pretends he fully understands he can't possibly be recompensed in any way for his trouble, and lets the pompous prat prattle on. At least the food's OK.

'Afraid it's no go, old boy. Must keep up standards, or where would it end? The other ranks would be stuffing their faces off the regimental silver platters. Wouldn't do, y'know.'

He gets to the point at last over coffee and liqueurs. 'Of course senior officers like me don't tell sergeants how to drill the men. Our department is strategy. Nuts and bolts? Good heavens no. We just see the job gets done.'

'The hooray Henry's a fuckin' blind eye merchant,' Chancer whispers to Caligula, who's been in his inside breast pocket throughout the meal. "Ee'll clear da nuclear shipments and make aht 'ee don't know nuffink abaht it.'

Chancer's gloating. Between them, Snodbury and Blusterham will have Breezethwaite awash with the stuff.

He opens a bottle of fizz and pours out a saucerful for Caligula, who laps it up then collapses in a coma.

The following day the rat's a bit groggy, and the Director General of MI5 will be too when he finally gets round to checking the Prime Minister's mental health.

CHAPTER FIFTEEN

Colonel Blimpsky-Korsakov is a conscientious man of late middle age with a pince-nez, colourful socks and a kiss-curl that's always falling over his forehead. Only by sticking out his lower lip and blowing hard can he see where he's going.

He's going to combine the business of seeing the old lady with pleasure, as he's got fond memories of childhood hols in Cornwall. Capturing and interrogating seagulls was the best bit, they always squawked under torture.

Blimpsky-Korsakov squeezes a miniature rack into his suitcase for old times' sake, as well as his sub-machine gun and a bouquet for Percy's dotty mater.

But she's well prepared too. The warden telling her to expect a gentleman visitor triggered something in her befuddled old brain. After feeling like a dead person for longer than she can remember she was suddenly gagging for one last breath of life.

First, she flushed her tablets down the bog, then begged to be allowed to go to Boots. When the lady and her minder weren't looking, she scooped up loads of hideously colourful make-up.

Next, she went through her collection of secret treasures. None of the sexy lingerie from her glory days anywhere near fits any more, and she's forgotten Agent Provocateur even exists.

But she's got a little penknife and several pairs of bright pink bloomers. Easily adapted to suit any occasion.

She's been having such fun limbering up that five dogs, three sheep and a tortoise have run for their lives. Mummy hasn't had a wink of sleep in almost a week. Though she can still just about walk she's in some pain. But it vanishes when the man appears.

'Hello, dearie, welcome to my parlour.' The quavering voice and glistening, beckoning finger tell Blimpsky-Korsakov he's come to the right place, and he's pleased to be invited in. That'll change when he finds out how far in.

He experimented with hallucinogenic drugs at uni, and wonders now if he's having a psychotic flashback. So many colours, so many wrinkles, so many chins. And bloomers wrapped round the head like a turban don't really work.

A big blow, his kiss-curl rises and he can see the bush billowing through the other pair.

'My name is Korsakov. Blimpsky-Korsakov.' The Director General of MI5 used this line many times during his earlier spell with MI6 and pulled with it plenty of times. But pulling and being pulled, he's about to find out, are very different things.

Years ago he'd have fallen for Mummy's coquettish smile and fluttering eyelashes, not now they're lost under a rainbow of lipstick and a tidal wave of mascara. But she's going to get her man, whether he likes it or not.

He tries to beat her off with the bunch of roses. A bunch of fives would have been better but a gentleman doesn't hit a lady when she's down. Besides, he doesn't realise why she's down.

He does when she rips open his zip and dribbles so enthusiastically her dentures fall out, which saves him getting his manhood bitten off. Taking to his heels is impossible as his trousers are wrapped round them. Wobbling backwards, he loses balance and knocks himself out on the marble-topped sideboard.

Crouching over him, Mummy's very taken with the yellow

polka dot socks, and promises them to herself when she's finished sucking him off. She can't believe what a lovely day this is turning out to be.

By now there's quite a crowd gathered in the doorway. The warden had discreetly followed the gentleman visitor, with crazy old people and young medical staff not far behind. Everyone is so fascinated that no one thinks to help him.

Clipboard and pen ever at the ready, the warden makes notes. She never really believed the stories about the old lady, but now finds her a most interesting case study. The loonies cackle hysterically, while the medics can't wait to see if a blacked out bloke can still get a hard on.

Eventually Mummy's dragged off her prey, discreetly bashed over the head and then sedated more according to standard practice. Game over for her then, unlike the Colonel.

*

The warden was so worried about who this secretive and still unconscious bloke really was that she phones the hotel where he claimed he was staying. When the receptionist recognises the description from the hairstyle, she calls the police.

Rummaging through the mystery man's personal belongings, the rookie constable with the goofy glasses doesn't notice the rack, bucket and spade or socks, but can't miss the machine gun. He alerts the Regional Crime Squad, armed officers are instantly deployed and the next thing the Director General of MI5 sees is a load of burly men in black.

Good honest criminal, or psychopathic terrorist? They pistol-whip him, to be on the safe side.

When he comes to again, this time in the local cottage hospital but still flanked by goons, Blimpsky-Korsakov can see one thing clearly. The Prime Minister's mater's bonkers.

Thanks to coagulated blood on his forehead keeping his

kiss-curl away from his eyes the Colonel can now also see his guards aren't the result of too many tabs back in the day but thuggish bobbies. Time to take control then.

'Assaulting a senior officer in the field is mutiny. Mutiny is treason. Think yourself lucky the penalty is life, not death.' His brittle delivery works wonders on the hangers and floggers gawping at him.

'Phone. Mine. Now.' He holds out his hand. As the suspect is within his legal rights, and probably wants to ring a dozy country solicitor who can be worked over later, the Sergeant obeys. Blimpsky-Korsakov keys in a number, switches to speaker and smiles grimly.

'Where the hell are you, Korsakov? Been trying to get you for days.' Irritable though it is, the voice is unmistakably that of the Home Secretary. The effect is electric. Shock, then panic.

'I never 'it 'im, it was you,' several of them bleat at once.

'Dem wounds was self-inflicted,' the Sergeant grunts. 'Got dat, lads?'

Although the Home Secretary's always found Blimpsky-Korsakov a pompous prick he can see a locate and rescue operation will be a useful exercise for the boys.

Forty minutes later the goons are still blaming one another when they hear screaming sirens and shattering glass. The carbine-toting anti-terror cops kick their way in, bellowing 'Armed police', as if that wasn't obvious. Also it wasn't strictly necessary to break the windows instead of walking through the door, but it's great theatre.

No TV cameras? Shame.

Cuffed up and marched out, the goons assume they're for the high jump. But when their case makes it to court m'lud accepts their claim that the victim got into a masochistic frenzy while in custody and beat himself up. They're free to go.

Back in the robing room the judge rips off his wig and punches the air with his fist. MI5 put him under surveillance when he was a CND activist in his twenties, and the look on Blimpsky-Korsakov's face as he delivered the not guilty verdict settled that old score nicely.

*

Though he was out cold throughout most of his ordeal, the Colonel does remember the Sergeant flicking his kiss-curl back, bashing his forehead and bellowing, 'The fucker's a fucking arse-bandit, lads, fucking give 'im one.'

Blimpsky-Korsakov was on his back, but he's not taking that lying down.

The old contact he calls in Berlin is at the airport within hours and home again that night, job done. The Sergeant's naked body is discovered on Hampstead Heath a few days later. Weirdly, there's a truncheon stuck up his bottom. No dabs on it, apart from his own.

The *Daily Star* splashes on the inquest verdict of death by misadventure under the headline 'Playing Cops'n'Knobbers!'

That night the Colonel has a jar in El Vinos with the editor, another old pal. 'Never let the facts stand in the way of a good story,' sniggers the journalist. 'And never let the verdict stand in the way of a good outcome,' replies the spook. 'Old Stasi guys cost, but you get what you pay for.'

If the *Star* editor had half a brain he'd have put two and two together. But he hasn't, so he didn't.

The half of Brenstorme's brain that still works, meanwhile, is sorely exercised by sore parts of his body, where Percy has thrown things at him or lashed out with rolled-up papers.

'Desperate times,' he mutters as he checks out replica suits of armour. However, even he can see clanking around Downing Street in steel plating might look a bit odd. A bulletproof vest under his shirt then, plus his fedora at all times. No one need know it's got a chain mail lining.

Percy stares at his bulked-out Cabinet Secretary and congratulates him on the dapper headgear. Brenstorme's a pain in the arse, but developing a serious eating disorder overnight? Of course he feels sorry for the man.

Biff doesn't. 'Now who's a bit thick then?' he sneers. Brenstorme looks puzzled, then rather hurt when the Irishman adds, 'Greedy gobshite.'

Percy and Biff gradually get used to the new look, though Fang hates the helmet as it means he can't rip the toupee off any more.

Monty sees through it all, as he's been around long enough to spot how much crazier Brenstorme's become. Wearing what's obviously body armour is part of the pattern and sporting the fedora indoors puts the tin lid on it. Come to think of it, it does look rather heavy...

*

'A policeman's lot is not a happy one.' Monty hums the song over and over again, not because he's that fussed about Brenstorme, but because he hates seeing Percy apparently going the same way. Making a fool of himself over some preening little intern, how barmy is that?

He's right in a sense, Percy is losing it. What happened during the holiday tore him apart and he's been wondering if the pain would go if he got his own end away. The fight with his conscience has gone on for weeks. It might have won if the boy hadn't been quite so pretty.

Holding Fang up close to his face, Percy demands answers. 'Am I just a horny old bugger or am I after revenge? Or comfort?' Fang considers the matter, stretches his head forward and licks the tip of his nose. Then bites it, savagely.

End of conversation. Percy wipes off small specks of blood and wonders how he'll explain his injury to anyone. Gored by a cat? Sounds ridiculous.

Everything makes sense to young Zorba though. With his PhD thesis nearly finished he's casting around for a proper, paid job, and fluttering his eyelashes at Percy seems an obvious shortcut. The old bloke's not too bad for his age, it's not like he'll be shagging a corpse.

His mistake is giving his boyfriend a bitchily funny account of how he's getting on.

*

Protecting Percy is more than Monty's job these days, it's his mission. On the off-chance he hacks into the kid's email account and the incriminating correspondence is all there. He can't believe his luck.

The evening it looks like things are about to happen, he clamps a hanky stuffed with chloroform over Zorba's mouth, straps him up with pink gaffer tape and heads for Percy's office.

Crouched over his desk, fantasising about a good rogering from fleet-footed Zorba, Percy is not pleased to see flat-footed plod.

'What the fuck do you want?' Ungracious, but Monty's not standing on ceremony either. Pulling his gun out of his shoulder holster he steps forward, aim unwavering. Percy freezes. It's no fun being about to die.

His life flashes before him. Dad. Viv. The village in Cornwall. Rodney. Auntie Nora. Mummy even. Shit, why that silly old bag? Still, she seems to figure.

Percy stares as Monty glides forward as though on miniature railway tracks. He raises his right arm and brings it down in a wide, swooping gesture.

This is it then, Percy bows his head. But in place of searing pain followed by nothingness, he feels… amazement. Instead of bashing his brains out Monty's swept all the clutter off the desk and flung a sheaf of papers in front of him.

Percy glances at them vaguely, but Monty motions with the gun he's to look more closely. When he does his eyes well up. He thinks of Haddock saying he thought the lady liked him, gets an overwhelming sense of shame and feels like rushing upstairs to Viv.

Holding his head in his hands, he shakes it at the bottle of whiskey and Glock 26 offered in place of a silver-handled revolver.

But then he changes his mind, usually a woman's privilege, but Percy's Percy after all. He draws the line at the shooter, but does lunge at the bottle. The first monumental swig is followed by a second. And a third.

It helps. After his complexion's lost its indigo glow he burps and smiles. 'Fuck's sake, bastard, men have died for less.'

CHAPTER SIXTEEN

The master-servant relationship between the two men is long gone. They're intimate friends now. So Monty's honour-bound to confess what was already obvious to Percy. That it wasn't actually fireworks making the bloody racket that night at the Bashars' island.

The next few moments are bad. Percy snatches up the phone and tells the Met Police Commissioner Sergeant White must be demoted and transferred back to Tottenham.

'What d'you mean I can't interfere in disciplinary matters? I bloody can.' The call goes on for ages.

Eventually Monty notices the number on the display is Percy's home number in Cornwall and realises he's not talking to anyone. They eye one another. Fang licks his lips in anticipation of a spot of real action, but is disappointed when Percy starts giggling. 'That'll teach you to pull a gun me, fuckface.'

So he's a good bloke then, after all, same as Viv. Whew. Time for a drink. Or, in Percy's case, yet another one.

When Monty finally stumbles out, on the implausible grounds he really must go and arrest someone, Percy gives in to the searing pain he knows he's no real right to feel.

After one last slurp he passes out. Fang climbs onto his head, purring contentedly and balancing improbably. Brenstorme, delivering yet more crap for Percy's urgent attention, would have taken his hat off to the creature if he'd dared.

Staggering up Whitehall, Monty also passes out, but a police motorcyclist recognises him, hauls him over the petrol tank and whips him off home. Half coming to, he starts singing in his glorious baritone. 'If my friends could see me now.' His mate tells him to shut the fuck up.

As Percy's emotions settle over the weeks he resigns himself to a life of passionate celibacy, same as Viv. They'll get a nice surprise in a while. So will Monty, any day now.

*

Coming home to his bijou little flat in Kentish Town and looking forward to his first afternoon off in months, Monty's astonished to see a woman sitting at his kitchen table. She's staring intently at a framed photo of him and his late wife.

'Er, pardon me for intruding. Can I help?' It's all he can think of to say.

The woman leaps to her feet. 'But I am evil woman, deserve torture and death for horrible wicked badness.' Monty assures her that's not quite the British way, and wonders how this crazy person got in.

Bakyt Sagdiyev came to Britain ten years ago to marry the man of her dreams, as she thought. But her Doctorate in nuclear physics from Kazakhstan's top university was no help in Hackney, so the bugger buggered off.

A top-up course would have solved her problem, but she couldn't afford it on her own, and took a job with a cleaning agency to get by.

Time passed and she got in a rut. But her scientist's curiosity refused to die and Monty's intrigued her for ages. There were two people in the picture but clearly he lived alone, with his serious books that looked like they'd been read and the classical CD collection to die for.

And now here he is, in the flesh. Rather nice flesh, actually. Feeling herself blush, she tries another gag. 'You not Jew, not come to torment me after end of world? Not turn into woman-hungry cockroach, crawl under door, eat me?'

Monty scratches his head, thinks of dialling 999, forgetting he's a policeman. Of course, it's Friday, the day his flat always gets cleaned. None of his business, but he'd no idea the agency employed such eccentric people.

He looks at her more closely; she's petite, trim and rather sexy. She reminds him of someone and he's curious. 'Coffee, madam? Least I can do.' What the hell, she's not going to rape him.

Sitting down opposite her at his elegant little Victorian pine table he recognises loneliness, displacement, disappointment in her tired but intelligent eyes. There's an awkward silence, then randomly she asks if he likes opera, knowing full well he does.

You couldn't shut either of them up if you tried.

'Thing is, discussing this stuff with my colleagues is like trying to cuddle a porcupine. Last time I had a conversation like this was with my boss, back in August.'

Monty sighs, thinking about what happened later.

He can't get it out of his head. And when Bakyt tells him for the fifth time her name is not Bucket, and with a hint of Slavic impatience defiantly whips off her headscarf he understands why.

Fluffing out her bobbed hair and smoothing it in a characteristic gesture, she's the forbidden fruit. Viv. Eerily, scarily, exquisitely Viv...

'When god closes a door he always leaves a window open somewhere,' he murmurs, then bites his lip, as quoting from *The Sound of Music* seems to lower the tone of the conversation.

By now Bakyt would forgive him almost anything, the

attraction's that strong. Monty's overlooked her fixation with Jews and cockroaches for the same reason, though he's not sorry when she tells him about Sacha Baron Cohen's movie *Borat*.

'I bring DVD. But only if noble gentleman invite slut cleaning whore back to house.'

They both laugh, it's obvious what's happening. Monty gets the wine out, orders food in, and in no time they're holding hands like lovers. Some hours later Bakyt makes a decision.

'Call me Bucket,' she whispers. 'Fill me any time you like.' She doesn't go home that night.

*

Next day Monty's floating about on Cloud Nine. Lucky no one tries to assassinate Percy, he'd probably have given the bloke a kiss instead of gunning him down.

During those exquisite dark hours he and Bucket made plans. She'll go to college, get that top-up degree and relaunch her career. It'll cost but she'll pay him back. 'Dirty unclean prostitute not steal wages not earned.' He keeps grinning at her crazy gags, they help him cope with having to go to piss-pool Blackpool for the Labour Party conference.

Percy irritates him next morning though, when he ducks into a fortune teller's tent during a walkabout on the front and tells him security can go fuck.

The Gypsy Rose Lee gig is a day job for the young drama student peering into the crystal ball she picked up for a tenner on eBay. She spots Percy's a poofter and a bit theatrical and gives him one of her favourite lines from *Macbeth*.

'No man that's born of woman shall e'er have power upon thee.'

A throwaway line, but it gets to him. During that weekend at Chequers the Bashars made jokes about their mother. 'Jolly old mater, too posh to push. Silly billy fashion victim.'

Shit, these guys were born by caesarean. Same as the bloke who killed Macbeth.

It's ridiculous. Percy isn't superstitious. But he's going to have a word with Rodney. Yes, yes, he meant to after what the kid from the Foreign Office told him. But now he really will.

*

Old Rodney's chuffed to bits at the call from Downing Street. Percy sounding him out to be a Knight of the Garter? Best Sunday suit then. Hasn't worn it since Dad popped his clogs. It stinks of mothballs. Good old Harpic. Pity he hasn't got a silk hanky to set it off.

The coppers on the gates are puzzled by the pong, and why this happy chappie's got a ball of binder string sticking out of his breast pocket. The bloke on the door's worried about him grinning from ear to ear and singing the Cornish national anthem.

Percy manages a bit of banter about the sheep-shagging back home, but Biff, glowering in the background, doesn't join in. Fang clocks the tension, positions himself out of range of unguided missiles, fists or bodies, and licks his lips.

After a couple of minutes Biff wades in. 'Out with it you fecking eejit, the craic with the Bashars?' Visions of Windsor Castle, beaming royals and the garter fade. Rodney fiddles with the ball of binder string and looks miserable.

Percy can't bring himself to give the poor sod who once saved his life the third degree, but Biff can. 'What d'ya fecking tell them, gobshite? Spit it out or it'll be yer fecking teeth. Not that y've got many.' Rodney turns to his old friend.

'It's like this, see, Purrsi. They'm proper folk, only wanting to see ye right, see. I be only trying to bleddy help, see. And the bleddy party, it be bleddy skint, see.'

'See? You stupid sod, you bet I fucking see.' Percy feels like everyone he ever loved has just stuck a stake through his heart. 'You dug me out of that fucking mineshaft just so you could drop me in a deeper one. How could you do that?'

By now Rodney's wringing his hands and sobbing. A tear lodges itself on the end of his nose. It looks like a tap that tries but never quite manages to drip.

Biff winds up the meeting in his usual delicate way. 'Get yer feckin' arse out of here before I feckin' stuff your feckin' legs up it.'

Officials only recognise Rodney by the mangled ball of binder string. The old man looks like he died years ago and has clambered out of his box for one last wail.

CHAPTER SEVENTEEN

Biff sums up the situation with brutal clarity. 'Your dear old pals have stitched you up, illegally funding your local party. And you've clinched it by accepting a gift in kind. Feckin' eejit, but there's no point crying over spilt milk.' Fang looks as though he strongly disagrees.

Percy doesn't, however. 'Yup, we might just survive this, so long as we do it quickly.'

'Do what quickly?'

'The right thing.'

'The right fecking thing? Too fecking right. Keep yer fecking gob shut, gobshite.' Biff wouldn't know how to sit on a fence if you cut off his legs and tied him to it.

'But… Watergate. It was the cover-up that did for Nixon.'

'He wouldn't have got fecking brownie points for fecking fessing up either.'

Biff wins the argument. The local party will close the bank account the Bashars' standing order's being paid into, and pray no one goes over the figures. Percy looks up to heaven.

Brenstorme, as usual, shows up exactly when he's not wanted. As he pops his head round the door again, this time with two armfuls of red boxes, Percy and Biff leap to their feet brandishing rolled up sheaves of official papers.

The saying 'hold on to your hat' has never rung truer.

Rodney, meanwhile, fails to chair a session of his select sub-committee, as he gets no further than the Red Lion at the bottom of Whitehall. Percy will never forgive him for his stupidity with the Bashars, and he doesn't even know about Hon Ki and Fyok Yu. Yet.

*

Ten doubles later Rodney really needs to talk to someone, and he mistakes the little poppet at the next table for a mate's research assistant. Young Sharon is easy on the eye, and does check things out, but little poppet she is not. Fleet Street prefers little snakes.

The editor of the sleazy rag she works for put her in the lobby for one reason. 'To dig da dirt on dem tossers wot fink dey can lord it over everyone. Especially da Labour lot, wiv all dat goody two-shoes crap. Make 'em bleed,' he added, rubbing his fat little hands together.

'I'll make it fast, make it tight and make it up,' she promised. He liked that. And the way she crossed her legs. And the mini-skirt.

She gives Rodney the same treatment when he staggers up and offers to stand her a drink because her exes were queried last week and she's a bit strapped. Besides, she's curious about that twine stuff he's fiddling with. 'How long's a piece of string, then, Granddad?'

The answer's rambling and barely coherent. But there's enough of a thread running through it, and enough references to someone called 'Purrsi' to get her turning on the miniature tape recorder in her denim jacket's breast pocket. Probably just a loony, but you never know.

Sharon's a pert little madam, blonde, sexy and dodgy, with a mind as sharp as razor wire. Her sentimental side, reserved for dear old Granny who was the much-loved Pearly Queen of Shoreditch before it went all posh, has no place in her professional life.

*

Back in her grubby cubby hole of an office she plays back the recording again and again and reckons the guy who broke Hitler's Enigma Code had it easy. But she's intrigued by his ramblings about suspect party funding. The weird stuff emanating from Beijing can wait.

She's interrupted by a colleague. Nobby Sleeseby leers at her and wonders if she'd like him to suck her tits. He's got stubbly hair, sticky out ears and warts, and is always looking out for short-sighted girls who prefer getting pissed to wearing their glasses at parties.

Her next visitor, Ernest Shurleynott, is the exact opposite. He's a dear old queen, a former academic and published poet who can't understand why he's been invited to work for the gutter press. A figleaf of literary respectability, he supposes.

At least it pays the bills, handy after that regrettable business over money all those years back, which never did much for his career.

He's taken a liking to Sharon, in spite of her vulgarity, probably because of it. She's the female equivalent of the bit of rough he usually goes for. And she loves a good gossip, same as him.

Sharon can't decide if he reminds her of Dad or Mum, or an actor in the old black and white movies they used to make her watch. But she likes his quaint gallantry and the fact he's definitely not on her case. She chatters away, missing out vital details of course, about her odd encounter in the Red Lion.

Ernest, who had a fling with Percy when they were at uni together, tries not to look too interested as his head screams scoop but his heart whispers love. The affair only ended when he got sent down for nicking drama society funds to help pay for dear mater's breast implants.

He eventually managed to blag his way into another college, and mater's new titties were spectacular, but the poor sod never quite got over losing Percy.

A quick call on the mobile, a few bars hummed of 'There may be trouble ahead', and he's invited to Chequers. Best avoid prying eyes.

Determined to travel incognito, Ernest borrows a friend's car, a noisy, smelly, crawling Trabant imported at huge and baffling expense from Hungary. He completes his disguise with a Russian fur hat, a lot of facial hair and dark glasses. Very KGB.

On the way he attracts more attention than that time he did a striptease on the Eiffel Tower.

The police stop him on suspicion of driving an illegal vehicle and of being a suspicious individual, and examine the mugshots on his driver's licence and security passes. He seems to have changed a bit.

They let him go but trail him in an unmarked vehicle, and inform Special Branch when he pulls up at Chequers. The file's passed on to MI5, and Colonel Blimpsky-Korsakov snorts.

'Prime Minister? Russki spy? Nutter not enough? Surveillance. Pronto.' He reaches for the phone…

*

The police are unhappy about opening the barriers even after they've been assured by the Prime Minister he is expecting a Mr Ernest Shurleynott. Percy will soon see their problem.

He remembers the footage of plucky little Trabants spluttering and farting through holes in the Berlin Wall. But the sight of this Cold War relic clambering out of one of them is a shock.

It strikes him as hilarious though, when he finally recognises the silly bugger. 'Greetings, comrade bum-chum, what is word from Black Lubyanka? Arski farski, as ever?'

'Not funny, me old darling, everything really is arse about face.' Ernest explains that, having slept his way to the bottom, he has to work with the likes of Sharon. 'Wouldn't know the Cabinet from an Ikea flat-pack, but she's a digger, and she's got something out of Rumpledore.

'Could be party funding, she's gnawing at it like a beaver on a tree trunk. Funny little mouth she's got, rather looks like a rodent, actually.

'Only good thing is she thinks the old git may be loopy, not as you notice in the Lords. Says he kept saying something weird about Chinese people.'

Percy's knowing grin freezes. He gets a flashback to that nuclear summit in Downing Street. Those guys trying to peddle radioactive garbage, what the hell were their names?

He's so grateful for the risk Ernest is running he gives him a big kiss on the lips. The poor chap hasn't got that lucky in years and gets a hard on.

Brandy is served and they get talking about the old days, and when it's time to go Ernest is so pissed he sticks his false moustache on his forehead and the beard across the bridge of his nose. He looks like a cross between a Viking in a face protector and a bison.

As he waves him off, Percy rings the police at the entrance, asking them to see his dear friend safely back to London. They escort him front and rear, blue lights flashing. Once again, Ernest worries he's drawing attention to himself.

After a pint of black coffee Percy summons Biff. The journey in his beat-up Mini is shorter and safer than that of the Trabant, whose brakes die outside Ernest's house. He panics, hits the accelerator and knocks the copper in front off his motorbike. His colleague pisses himself and they have a punch-up.

The old lady next door is deeply shocked.

Back at Chequers, Percy and Biff too almost come to blows. 'For god's sake, man, the vermin's on our trail. We've got to get our story out first. What else can we do?'

'Learn from Michael.'

'Michael? Michael who? Heseltine? Portillo? Not Foot, surely?'

'Collins, you fecking eejit. Drove the fecking Brits out of Ireland out by copying their tactics. Got us the Free State. Remember him?'

'Course I bloody do. He ordered the wholesale slaughter of British agents and informers. Bit harsh though, don't you think? Bit old school?'

Biff clenches and unclenches his fists several times, takes a deep breath, then looks at Percy as though he hasn't seen his marbles since the day he was born.

'Words of one syllable too long for you? Think banks. Not tanks. They play dirty, so do we.

'We need to be as sneaky as the Bashars. Closing the party's account with the dodgy donations was only for starters. Open loads more, friendly societies, building societies and a couple in Switzerland. Throw dust in the enemy's eyes.

'Beyond that, we can only pray to fecking Jaysus the old fart was too pissed to speak clearly, and the little bitch didn't have a tape recorder handy.'

'Amen to that,' says Percy. Though the 'fuck you honky' stuff is still playing on his mind.

*

Sharon's struggle to make sense of Rodney's ramblings is taking time, but she's not giving up, any more than nasty Nobby Sleeseby, who, unbeknown to her, is gnawing away at Belinda Blusterham's emails.

He wouldn't mind giving the old bag's knockers a go while he's at it. Licking his fat, slobbering lips, he fantasises about getting the Energy Minister to shag him in the hope of saving her skin, before he dobs her in it anyway. He'd have agreed with Noel Coward that work is so much more fun than fun, if he'd ever heard of him.

The fun started when he got a call out of the blue from a contact from way back, the little spiv who Chancer hired to get his girlfriend to nick Blusterham's laptop.

'I kept my side of da bargain,' he tells Nobby. 'I passed on da knocked-off gear to da weirdo vicar. But it seemed a shame not to plug in one o' dem gizmos wot stores ev'ry-fing there is on a computer while I 'ad it in me mitts. Two bucks better'n one, eh?

'Pain in the arse, ploddin' froo all dat boring household stuff, but ya never guess wot ah fahnd in de end. An email abaht a discahnt on some chateau somewhere, wo'evvah a fuckin' chateau is, and somefing abaht government policy being flexible.

'Smell a rat? I should fuckin' coco. Whole bleedin' colony of 'em when ah got a load o' da figures the old bag was on abaht and what she seemed to be offerin' in return.'

CHAPTER EIGHTEEN

Nobby wondered if his old mate had been hitting the crystal meth a bit hard, but then remembered he's an alligator. Ace at turning something that looks tasty into a ready meal.

Brought up in the slums of Whitechapel, Nobby was a proper little wide boy. He got away with everything till he got it off with his brother's girlfriend. In return he got grassed up and shipped off to Feltham Young Offenders' Institution.

The spiv was already doing time there and they hit it off like two fleas on a carcass, making a packet selling drugs to the screws. So it's just like old times. Sleeseby rubs his grubby little hands together. 'There's honour among thieves, my son, could be a four-figure sum in this.'

'Four-figure sum? Stick it up yer fuckin' jacksie.'

'OK, I'll try for five.' Nobby was always better at promising than delivering, in his professional as well as his personal life. Anyway, it's the paper's money not his.

When the deal's struck, Bellingham's finished. Especially as she has by now kept her promise to Chancer.

*

Assuming the lack of follow-up questions about the missing computer meant she was in the clear, she sent a memo to the Office for Nuclear Regulation man responsible for imports. It was a triumph of diplomacy, by her standards.

'*You're paid to do as you're told, not think. No questions about certain nuclear shipments. Straight to Breezethwaite with them, if you know what's good for you. PS: In case you can't spell or count, P45 stands for you're fired. Got that?*'

The junior civil servant was happy to oblige, but was puzzled when he received the same instruction from the Energy Department's Permanent Secretary. This too was curiously phrased. Not every day he was told to do something at the double or risk being put on a charge, court-martialled and shot.

*

Belinda Blusterham discovers she has a problem when her front door bell booms. Big Ben chimes. Ridiculously loud.

She recognises the ugly bastard in the porch with the warts on his cheeks and doesn't want to let him in, but he's too quick for her. Nobby Sleeseby's a past master at the old foot in the door routine and the patter that goes with it, though for once it's appropriate.

'Send not to know for whom the bell tolls, it tolls for thee.' Shurelynott taught him that line. He hasn't the foggiest what it means but likes it because it sounds scary...

The down-payment Sleeseby got out of the paper was big enough to buy him a peek at what the little spiv had on his gizmo. It confirmed Blusterham had accepted a substantial bribe in return for something, and he's at the tacky mock Georgian pile to nail her down.

Quoting a few telling lines from one of the emails, he reads the guilt in Blusterham's face and pushes past her into the house. Knowing what damage he could do to her, she tries charm.

To her amazement it seems to work, as he promises to go easy on the story in return for a bit of the other. He'd much sooner screw the foreign tart apparently reading stuff on her iPhone, but Blusterham must come first.

Actually, she doesn't come at all. They never do, as Nobby's a wham-bam-thank-you-ma'am kind of guy. The foreign tart's having a lovely time screwing him though, in her way. Far from reading stuff on the phone, she was using it to record everything.

She hated Blusterham from day one, when the fat cow told her the tomato-based pasta dish she'd cooked tasted too much of tomatoes, tipped the lot over the floor and told her to lick it up.

Besides, she hardly paid her anything, and made her sleep in a cupboard under the stairs.

No way she could fight back as she was technically an illegal. The English guy she'd married briefly was a bigamist, making her claim to British citizenship null and void. She'd have got away with it if he hadn't dumped her because she couldn't just walk into a top job.

Her story's like Bakyt's in another way. She's seriously brainy, fluent in most European languages. Tonight she's struck by the German word *Schadenfreude* and an old English saying, 'As you sow, so shall you reap.'

Outside the slightly open bedroom door she switches her iPhone to video mode and holds her nose, on account of Blusterham's lax personal hygiene. The whiff of scandal makes up for it, though. It'll finish her.

*

Things are going wrong for Colonel Blimpsky-Korsakov too, though he doesn't deserve it. After all, he did get Percy's nutty mummy a secret service commendation for returning his socks more or less intact, and made sure the Sergeant's widow got the truncheon back.

His mistake was checking the Prime Minister's credentials as a Russian spy.

He sends agents posing as workmen to bug Percy's phone lines, but the operation's so sensitive he briefs them separately so they won't even know about one another. Also, they must keep that bungling fool Brenstorme out of it.

Fat chance. The gas fitter, electrician and plumber immediately spot Sir Bernard's wearing armour and a helmet. After Fang's second go at flipping it off he got a chinstrap. That and his bulging eyes prove he's an interfering sod from Special Branch sent to snoop on them.

The mistrust is mutual. To Sir Bernard they look too clever to be of the labouring classes, might even be working for a foreign power. Besides, it's rumoured Percy had a peculiar visitor over the weekend. A Russian spy? He calls MI6.

Within an hour three odd-looking carpenters are padding around Number Ten in steel-tipped trainers. Their bulging holdalls look more like they're stuffed with clubs and guns than saws and hammers. The MI5 guys reckon they're every bit as dodgy as Brenstorme.

Uniformed police in Downing Street feel the vibe and start stalking all of them, discreetly releasing the safety catches on their pistols. The tension's too much even for fearless Fang, who takes refuge up a tree in St James's Park.

Sir Bernard nervously prods his chest, hoping the vest really is bulletproof. Lucky for him it is, because minutes later he accidentally turns the standoff into a firefight.

He only meant what he said to the secretary who offered him coffee without anything to stir it with that it was a bit jolly thick. But the MI6 men have heard him use these words so often they're convinced it's a code, possibly calling enemies of the state to arms.

Unaware that far from scuttling out of the lobby to betray her country the woman's actually off to find a spoon, they open fire. The MI5 men retaliate, and in no time the police join in.

Casualties mount. MI5 agent A takes one in the shoulder, MI6 operative B gets it in the leg and Margaret Thatcher's picture ends up with three slugs in the face. The secretary dies when a bullet enters her skull, and things get serious when MI6 officer C goes the same way.

Monty decides enough is enough, ties a white hanky to a selfie stick that's lying around and negotiates a truce. If nothing else to allow the various factions to bury their dead. But as the cleaners mop up the blood in Downing Street, more gets spilt in Millbank.

Colonel Blimpsky-Korsakov worries he'll have some explaining to do but doesn't get a chance. His oppo at MI6 is so outraged he fires himself out of his spangly green headquarters in a speedboat, just like James Bond.

In seconds he's crossed the river, where he bursts into Blimpsky-Korsakov's office and headbutts him. The kiss-curl is no protection.

*

Percy knows nothing as he's at a Quaker convention in Liverpool entitled 'Peace, Love and Understanding, Man'. In Downing Street next morning he can't understand why the women are wearing black armbands and chunks of masonry look like they've been gouged out.

Monty fills him in. Ministerial drivers are the savviest but the police still know miles more than the government. Understandably in the circumstances, Percy is not happy.

'So I'm a fucking spy then, thanks to fucking Brenstorme fucking meddling again?' At this point he's actually foaming at the mouth. 'I'll fucking kill him. Just watch me.'

Loyalties divided between duty and friend, Monty decides to

let Percy work the man over a bit, then step in. Listening outside Brenstorme's office to the bellows, squeals, thumps and crashes he glances at his expensive Omega watch.

He told himself off when he bought it, but the stopwatch function's coming in handy now.

When time's up he steps in, amazed at what an operator the Prime Minister is. Two computers are smashed, there's broken furniture everywhere, and Percy is kneeling over his gasping victim. No sign of the fedora or the toupee anywhere.

Monty disentangles Percy's fingers from Sir Bernard's throat and clears his own. 'Moderation in all things, there's a good chap.' The only response from either of them is a strangulated whimper. 'I say, this is a bit jolly—'

Sir Bernard's interrupted by Percy banging his head against the floor and shouting in his face. 'Where's fucking Fang? You fucking shafted him as well? You, you, you… cat-killer.'

He calms down when word comes through that the London Fire Brigade have rescued an animal answering Fang's description from up a tree in St James's Park, and will be dropping it off at the gate in a couple of ticks.

Caressing the cat as though he's just been rescued from the nine circles of hell, Percy's appalled when Monty gives him the full low-down. But at the sight of the Thatcher picture, singed by being shot at point-blank range, he can't resist rubbing it in.

'So the lady was for burning after all.'

He'll soon be toast too, if he did but know it. At least replacing Blimpsky-Korsakov, who has apparently opted for early retirement, will not be his problem. Likewise finding a new Permanent Secretary at the Energy Department. When Snodbury found out Chancer's plans were unravelling fast, he snuck off to Heathrow and defected to North Korea.

Arriving in Pyongyang, he offered his services as Commander-in-Chief of the Korean People's Army, or head of counter-espionage in the Democratic People's Republic. But the Royal Artillery tie didn't cut in that neck of the woods. He's never seen again.

*

Fang's pleased to be back home again, but starving after being stuck up that tree all night. He jumps in a bin in the hope of finding food, but finds instead he can't get out.

Just at the moment Percy fishes him out the Albanian slave also lets the cat out of the bag.

'Busty Blusterham busted.' That's her first tweet. The second is more specific. 'Energy Minister backhander shocker.' Plenty more follow, giving chapter and verse, and very soon the woman's many enemies are retweeting like crazy. Telly's on it in no time.

Spluttering and wheezing like a barrel organ, Biff barges in on Percy, who's working in the Cabinet room because the bullet holes in his office make him twitchy. 'Fecking cow's fecking sunk us! Fecking bitch! Fecking crook as well as smarmy gobshite! I'll mash her fecking kneecaps and make her eat them!'

Having no idea who or what he's on about, Percy wonders for a moment if Biff's as barmy as Brenstorme. Raising one eyebrow, he leans too far back in his chair and tumbles arse over tit.

For once Fang doesn't join in the fun, as he's too busy sharpening his claws on the red leather seats to notice.

CHAPTER NINETEEN

Biff's in such a state he doesn't notice either. Instead he wrings his hands and splatters words like machine-gun fire. 'Fecking Blusterham. Caught red-handed. Paws in till. YouTube footage. Ditch-the-bitch hashtag. Hate mail on Facebook.'

Percy half stumbles to his feet, only to be dragged by the hair to the nearest TV screen. Sky's running it wall to wall. A flick on the remote and there's the Beeb, doing the same.

Their own bowels misbehave as they go through the motions with the media. 'Minister's resignation accepted. Nothing to hide. Full inquiry launched. Nothing to hide. Investigation underway. Nothing to hide. All speculation. Nothing to...'

Nothing to be done, more like. Having got the gizmo off the little spiv on the promise of ten grand, Sleeseby's able to stand up the Albanian woman's allegations in forensic detail. The first edition's held back so none of the others can get it and the paper's sold out in minutes.

But the old saying about today's scoop being tomorrow's fish'n'chip wrapping never rang truer. Nobby will be so miffed he'll even go off Sharon's tits.

Fed up with trying to decode Rodney's ramblings, she found a linguistics expert who could decipher Cornish dialect, even when they're off their faces. What he told her will get her exes through for years.

The daft old git was trying to say he'd been party to a political funding scam and wished he hadn't. 'All my bleddy fault. I put they bleddy Bashars up to it. Bleddy slimy shitheads, they led me right over the garden cliff.'

Sharon's story the following day makes Sleeseby's effort look like a flower show report in the local rag. A junior minister's scalp's tasty, but nothing to Percy's. The Prime Minister's own constituency party taking backhanders? And he hadn't a clue? Oh really?

And his holiday in the sun, would you believe it? The dodgy donors stumped up for that too! Drone footage shows the villa's tacky extravagance, even Mustafa gets his five minutes of fame, mistaking the buzzing flying object for a Mustafa-eating monster and running for his life.

Proves they've got something to hide.

Reverend Charlie Chancer gets a shock when he sees the headline 'Whew, What a Chancer'.

He always thought he was pretty safe with his email address Jay.Hoh'ver@gmail.com, likewise with his web address http// Www.j.hoh'ver666.satanicmills.org. But he'll replace them, just in case.

*

Sharon didn't twig the Chinese stuff on her tape till it tallied with what Sleeseby got out of Blusterham. The Minister got shafted, manner of speaking, but what about the mysterious disappearance of Permanent Secretary Snodbury? It'll make a follow-up.

Over a hasty breakfast next day Percy looks at Viv with infinite sadness. Remembering the Gypsy Rose Lee kid's line about blokes born by caesarean section, he quotes Macbeth's take on it.

'All our yesterdays have lighted fools the way to dusty death.'

Viv's so intent on Sharon's spicily subbed new piece she hardly hears. Nor does she notice she's pouring coffee onto Percy's cornflakes.

Leaning across the table and squeezing his hand, she tries to comfort him with a line from Virginia Woolf. 'How absurd to stay in London, with Cornwall going on.'

Percy finds the thought delicious, unlike his bowl of cereal.

*

Half an hour later Percy realises even Biff's given up when he does what he never does. Says sorry. 'You were right. Should have fessed up. Sod you.' Not exactly graceful, not his style.

'Fecking timing's done for us,' he grumbles. 'Far enough apart, these stories might not have sunk us. But they fecking torpedo us, then do it again before we can plug the hole. Jaysus, the fecking water's cold.'

'Yup. Timing does matter,' Percy seems to be talking to himself. 'Same as in joke telling. Coming out with your best gags the week after the gig. Or the week before. Bad timing.'

Though he and Biff hide in the office for hours they're deluged with questions, accusations and innuendoes. But this horrible day ends eventually. Percy clutches Viv's arm as they head for their separate bedrooms and tries to sound cheerful. 'Tomorrow is another day.'

She recognises the words from the classic movie, grips his cheeks and gives him almost a Vivienne look. 'Frankly my dear, I do give a damn. And don't you forget it, Percy Penislow.'

He tries to do just that as he tots up the uppers and downers stashed in the bedside cabinet and makes sure the bedroom door is tightly closed. The cat's bitten off the buttons on his pink velvet dressing gown, scrunched it up into a nest on the floor and is curled up asleep in it, but so what? Nothing matters any more.

Sitting up in bed he downs half a litre of brandy, straight from the bottle. Some of it spills into his slippers, Fang laps it up and is very quickly very squiffy. Out cold within minutes.

The booze goes some way to soothe the fury and despair Percy can only face head-on now he's alone. But it also skews his judgement, far worse than ever before. He picks up Viv's framed portrait, kisses it goodbye and necks handfuls of drugs. A serious suicide attempt? Or a scream for help?

It's one of those questions that never really get answered. And not as important as Fang's problem. Coming to an hour later, desperate for a pee, he's horrified he can't get out. Only one thing for it. A good yowl, like a baby that's swallowed a mouthful of dog-plop.

A sleepy-looking Viv stumbles out of her room, hastily adjusting her nightie, and takes one look at her husband. Unlike Brenstorme, who would probably have alerted the heads of the BMA, Narcotics Anonymous and Médecins Sans Frontières, she dials 999.

The ambulance is across from St Thomas' hospital in five minutes flat, Percy's stomach is pumped and against considerable odds he makes it through the night. Anyone would say hats off to Fang. Apart from Brenstorme, who'd never risk it for anyone.

*

Gathered in the Cabinet room next day, ministers hope Sir Bernard can help. With Percy out of the way he's risked shedding the body armour, a pleasant feeling. Also he's looking forward to being able to talk without frivolous interruptions. He clears his throat several times.

'Gentlemen,' he begins, forgetting there are ladies present. 'Gentlemen, my exposition on the position may produce propositions, so kindly pay attention.' They do, but already suspect their hopes were misplaced.

'Consider the madness of George the Third,' he continues. 'Seems seamless transfer of power is possible. In this case to his son. Or there's the indisposition, or should I say, ahem, catatonic schizophrenia, of our late King Henry the Sixth. It appears he eventually died of melancholy. A condition approximately approximating to that of our colleague Mr Penislow.'

He carries on in this vein for forty minutes, concluding with a flourish that Vlad the Impaler was not mad, just not a very nice person.

After Sir Bernard swept out of the room looking pleased with himself, the Cabinet does the obvious. A show of hands and boring old Percival Spectacle is elected acting leader. He thought they all hated him. Seems they hate one another even more.

Percy, meanwhile, hasn't said a word to anyone apart from Viv since his supposed suicide attempt. And with her all he's done is sob how sorry he is.

Holding him tight she's told him again and again he's forgiven. It's a while before she really means that, topping oneself being the ultimate rejection of kith and kin. But she does still love him and wishes, illogically, for a baby.

As the days drag on it becomes clear that Percy's having a mental breakdown and isn't returning to his duties. It's equally obvious the Labour government is finished. When it loses a vote of confidence in the Commons, a general election is called and the Tories win it.

*

Ponsomby Tiddledick is tickled pink, but horse-face Fanny hates the thought of being stuck in that pokey rathole in Number Ten again. No joss sticks for a month, then.

This troubles him almost as much as his wafer-thin majority. Public opinion swung during the campaign when papers started suggesting Percy wasn't such a bad bloke after all. A nice new angle. Ernest Shurelynott set the ball rolling with a leader column headed 'More Sinned Against Than Sinning'.

His genteel way of saying the poor sod was taken for a bloody ride.

In addition, turnout is well down as the nation is riveted by a newly exposed indiscretion involving another member of the England squad with his orang-utan. Psephologists will argue for months about whether Tory or Labour voters are more into bestiality.

*

Not that Percy could give a stuff about anything, as one doesn't in a trance. But after thorough psychiatric assessment at the Maudsley he's pronounced fit enough to go home, under proper supervision. Meaning Viv can ship him off to Cornwall, out of harm's way.

At least he's fully conscious now, and the Harley Street shrink who's recently retired to his former holiday home a couple of miles away can't wait to try his analytical skills on Percy. Or his electrodes, he doesn't make this clear.

He's a curious little man, constantly flicking his spotty bow tie with his thumb and forefinger and smiling to himself at some private joke.

Professor Ziggy Froidle was eminent in hypnotic regression, and convinced it isn't money but repressed sexuality that's the root of all evil. One look at Percy and he's rubbing his pearly-white hands together and doing the 'here's the steeple, here's the church' finger game which kids have usually given up on by the time they're four.

Viv half expects his bow tie to start swivelling like the rotor blade on a helicopter.

Between them, they free Percy's soul. A scary New Age

concept, but true in this case. Froidle delicately teases out Percy's repressed recollections of Mummy and the woodshed. Equally delicately, Viv will shortly ease his thingy into her you-know-what.

She's no idea what's been happening on the psychiatrist's couch, such sessions are strictly private. But, sliding her body over Percy's to give him a kiss and cuddle goodnight, she's amazed at what's happening below. The modest single-story dwelling has turned into a quite magnificently throbbing Shard.

Seconds later, after a bit of guidance, it's doing what comes naturally to any self-respecting throbbing Shard.

All the evidence is he's having a glorious time even if he doesn't say much, indeed anything at all. Totally out of it, he's totally in it. Fucking result! Or should that be resulting fuck?

Anyway, he gets the idea, and in the process gets cured.

After the final consultation Ziggy winks at Viv like a naughty gargoyle. 'Dear lady, I only gave directions. Erections were more up your street. Or rather up your, ahem, modesty precludes.'

Blissfully aware of the oozing feeling that would have had her old tutor punching the air with his fist again, Viv blushes scarlet and grins like a schoolgirl.

As the weeks pass Percy becomes his old self again and takes an interest in lots of things, her most of all. They're so on it, and one another, they sometimes forget the cleaning lady, who's shocked at the moans and screams coming from the bedroom. In the middle of the day, too.

After twenty-five years, they do have a bit of catching up to do.

*

Back in Downing Street, Ponsomby Tiddledick almost reshuffles his Cabinet when he discovers the Chancellor of the Exchequer is allergic to cats.

But Fanny has a better idea. Though she loves pussy play she's hated Fang since he punished her for not being Percy. 'Dump the brute on that person who thought he was Prime Minister, Mr Droopy-Willy, or whatever his name was. He lives further west than Kensington, doesn't he? It'll never find its way back, thank god.'

Fanny's finally lowered the joss stick stakes, and Ponsomby's still cross-eyed after last night's aromatherapy session. But he well remembers what the cat left when Fanny tried to get him on her lap.

The puddle on her dress was strikingly smelly, and he mutters something about hell, fury and women scorned, but keeps his voice down.

A lot less effort than rearranging his government, and he'll make a thing of it. The gesture will probably be worth more votes than a million quid donation to Save the Children, and Fanny will reward him as only she knows how. Mmmm, the click of heels and crack of the whip…

CHAPTER TWENTY

It happens the Shadow Cabinet's holding an awayday session in Exeter next day, so the Opposition Leader, Sir Percival Spectacle, can deliver the animal in person. The Chancellor of the Exchequer promises not a word about his allergy, though Fanny can't resist a naughty tweet. 'Ta-ra Tiddles, Fangs for the memory.'

The cameras roll as Sir Percival holds up the cat cage in Downing Street like the Chancellor with his bag on budget day, but he's reckoned without Fang's take on the situation.

This horrid little prison strikes him as an insult after the lovely pink dressing gown, so he spits through the bars at Spectacle. Right in the eye. Tight shots of the Labour leader blinking and looking ridiculous are splashed across the tabloids. Ponsomby can't believe his luck.

*

Things get worse for Spectacle, as Fang makes a racket like fingernails scraped down glass. Now the awayday's over and he's driving on to Percy's he jams the cage behind the passenger seat and covers it with a thick blanket. That and Shostakovich blaring on Radio Three help.

Unsure of the reception he'll receive as Percy hasn't responded to the text messages he's been sending all day, Spectacle almost tiptoes up the garden path and operates the brass bell pull gingerly. It sounds as ancient and rickety as he's feeling.

The quaint little oak door in the quaint little Georgian manor house creaks open, and Percy gawps at him. Having spent the last twenty-four hours in the sack with Viv, to celebrate her second missed period, he's missed all the news and switched off his mobile.

He's friendly, though, in a knackered sort of way, as he's always had a soft spot for dear old Spectacle. Besides, he's curious about what's under that blanket. A hamper of goodies from Harrods Food Hall, perhaps. That'd be nice.

Laying back on a brocade-covered chaise longue, Viv too gives the unexpected visitor a cheery if hazy smile. Sir Percival has the feeling he's looking at two cats who've licked a lake of cream, which reminds him why he's here.

He holds up the cage the same way as in Downing Street, but as he pulls back the blanket and flings open the door the outcome could not be more different. Fang springs out straight at Percy, who wishes he could manage another orgasm.

*

Apart from going through every position in the Kama Sutra he's focussed on convalescing these last months. But getting the brandy out with Sir Percival revives other appetites. Especially when he learns Fleet Street and the publishing world can't wait to sign him up, now he's been more or less rehabilitated.

Not knowing Spectacle isn't in his league as a drinker, he's puzzled on returning from the loo to find the man slumped on the floor. Fang's also looking vacant, but still up for a chinwag.

'Well, my furry friend, guess who's having a baby then?' Fang purrs. A good sign.

'You're going to have to mind your Ps and Qs in a few months. It's not a kitten, you know. You won't be allowed to carry it about by the scruff of the neck.'

Fang seems cool with this, and pads off to the bedroom, presumably to congratulate Viv.

He likes the new sleeping arrangements and their cosy little *ménage à trois*, although when the other two are actually at it he goes for what's left of the pink dressing gown. On a sexual level cats have similarities to rabbits, but he still thinks it's a bit much.

Viv is glad about this. Unlike Fanny Tiddledick, she's a privacy kind of girl, but has never in her life been so happy. And though motherhood looms she's picked up the threads of her market research and polling company.

It's perfectly possible to run it from Cornwall, she discovers, thanks to the digital age and that angel Monty, who's brilliant at everything apart from not falling into swimming pools. When Percy went west Bakyt kept it simple. 'Screw stinky Met, we go Cornwall too.'

She got a research post at a posh university only an hour's drive away, and he became a partner in Viv's company, standing in for her at her office in Mayfair. Opera in the car on the motorway makes up for the Westminster buzz. More civilised than carrying a gun.

Biff misses The Bubble more. Fired when Percy went, he hated the downgrade from Mr Big of Downing Street to Mr Nobody of Nowhere. Worse still a close mate, a rising young Sinn Fein star, died soon after in a road accident. Still, he got selected as replacement candidate and won the by-election. The luck of the Irish…

Sir Roger was so flabbergasted he laid an egg, and had to be rechristened Lady Casement. The hanged martyr he was named after wouldn't have minded, given which way he swung.

But poor Rodney. The booze and the fags finally catch up

with him. The missus tries to look heartbroken, but as she's still got the allotment and the flat in Dolphin Square it's not easy.

Delivering the eulogy from the ornate carved pulpit in the eleventh century parish church, Percy is supremely tactful. He tells how this wonderful fellow once saved his life, and masks how he nearly reversed the process with a handy little quote.

'God giveth, and god taketh away.'

Reverend Chancer, who wouldn't have missed this little shindig for this world or the next, smiles knowingly, but wonders why a cat has just sprung onto his lap.

In spite of his disguise as a disabled blind person, Fang instinctively hates him even more than Fanny. Only this time he goes one better. Sitting up and arching his back, he does a really smelly poo. All over the bastard's trousers.

PART TWO

What Percy Did Next

CHAPTER ONE

Two years have passed. Unlike most political memoirs, which hardly anyone buys and no one reads, Percy's book is a sensation. Punters are curious about how such a basically decent bloke could get so totally screwed, and they like how he laughs at himself.

His opening words set the tone. 'What to do if you're an unlucky leader? Just say bollocks.' And his pay-off line rounds it off nicely. 'All political careers end in failure? Tell me about it!'

Percy's wary of speaking engagements, but writes columns in daily and Sunday newspapers, plus a blog with half a million followers. He turns base metal passed on by old chums into gold. 'I'm a demob-happy squaddie putting one on the fucking sergeant-major,' he mutters.

Viv reminds him there's a child present, but smiles anyway.

Looking up from his computer, perilously perched on the rickety table in the garden, Percy takes in the view. It's lovely, rolling Atlantic waves set off by pretty little blonde, blue-eyed Trudi toddling around with Fang savaging her cuddly toys.

She says her first word later, which sounds like 'kee-ell'. Eventually Mummy and Daddy work out she's trying to say 'fucking hell'. 'Oh dear, where could she have picked that up?' Viv glances sharply at Percy.

He grins sheepishly and studies his watch. 'Good heavens, is that the time?' Viv clocks it, so to speak, stamps playfully but hard on his foot and says he's a bastard.

'Now now, Vivienne, language!' Percy pretends to be cross and wishes he was wearing heavy, protective boots instead of open-toed sandals.

They've calmed down a bit since the early days, more so when she got pregnant. Fourteen times a week does them now, and then mostly at night-time. Still, the cleaning lady might hand in her resignation, because they're getting too much and she's not getting any.

*

Back in The Smoke, Brenstorme's been trying to keep Blusterham's case from coming to court, for fear of smarty-pants silks spotting her department's Permanent Secretary was as corrupt as she was. Politicians don't count, civil servants do.

When Ponsomby Tiddledick realised how difficult the fellow could be, he put Fanny's whip to energetic use. Eighteen lashes later Brenstorme reinstated the body armour and helmet. Clearly the blue ties he'd taken to wearing weren't doing the trick.

As hearings finally get under way at The Bailey, Blusterham's Albanian former slave, now a valued employee of the Foreign Office, seeks out Percy. Of course a little holiday in Cornwall is nice, but there's more to it than that. She wants him to know the fire at the home of the criminal mastermind behind the plot may not have been fatal after all.

'Assumed in Court one not-so-sainted reverend gentleman taken own life because net closing in on him,' she begins.

Percy laughs. 'Rule one in journalism. Never assume anything.'

The Albanian smiles. 'Your mother say she love you? You check it out, right?'

Percy smiles too. 'Proves Blusterham was dumb, not spotting you're smart.'

'Smart, you say? Sure I smart. From racist abuse, kicking, punching, spitting. Now I get revenge. Sweet smell. Not like filthy hag. Concentration camp too good for her.' She trembles and has to put her cup of tea on a small Lloyd Loom table by her chair.

Percy soothes her with an enormous bottle of Albanian raki, which looks like any other brandy but makes non-Albanians think they've swallowed molten lead. Fang has a sip and proves he's not Albanian by twitching, lapping up all the tea and collapsing.

Before Viv can stop her, little Trudi sticks her fingers in Percy's glass and sucks them. She too proves she's not Albanian by screaming 'kee-ell' at the top of her voice.

When order's restored, the visitor gets out a notebook and puts on little round horn-rimmed glasses. Her 180-words-a-minute shorthand meant she got every syllable Blusterham blurted out to get Sleeseby to lay off the story and stop sticking his nasty little cock in her. Handy, as his grunts and groans made the recording indistinct at times.

The most useful bit is an address in Slowden she heard Blusterham mention to Nobby, where Chancer told her to drop off the cash for the chateau. 'In used fivers, sill vouz plate, Madame.'

Maybe a one-off temporary address, or a dead letter box like in the Cold War. Or, just possibly, a clue where to start hunting for Chancer. A job for Monty…

*

'Sounds like the shit's faked his own death again.' Percy grimaces at Viv. 'The bastard will lie low, but not six feet under

155

the ground. In no time he'll squirm up somewhere else. Slowden maybe? Almost feel like warning Tiddledick.'

'So you punish evil woman? Goody gumdrop.' The Albanian speaks better French, German, Italian, Mandarin, Spanish, Dutch and Arabic than English, but she makes herself understood. 'Happiness cup overflow. Good off chest.' Percy and Viv have both noticed she's shapely in that area, and for some reason the glasses make her sexier.

'She'll pay for her crime without any help from me,' Percy murmurs. 'My spies tell me she'll go down for five years.' It ends up as six because she was rude to the man she ordered to OK the nuclear shipments and m'lud places civil servants way above politicians. He was at school with Brenstorme.

The court heard how she'd attempted to manipulate government policy in return for money from the deceased criminal posing as a clergyman. The prosecution case rested on the emails Sleeseby gave the police on the promise they wouldn't mention his interviewing techniques.

'Course not, me old cocker.' The wizened old DCI smirked. 'Don't want any more cock-ups, do we? Or should we say cocks up, eh, eh? Nudge nudge, nod and a wink?'

Sleeseby thanked his lucky stars the light was out in Blusterham's bedroom that night, so the racy footage on YouTube didn't quite identify him as the dirty sod getting his evil way.

The chateau in France has since collapsed and the local *municipalité* snapped up the site for a song under a compulsory purchase order. So Blusterham's kissed goodbye to well over a hundred grand, as well as her career, reputation and liberty.

Handing over her expensively groomed Afghan hound to her sister for safe keeping while she's in jug, she's not happy. 'Feel like I just got a lorry-load of quick-drying cement tipped over the Roller, then found a parking ticket on the windscreen.'

'Yes dear, there is such a thing as a really bad day.' Her sister's dry humour proves they're both as horrible as one another.

When Belinda gets parole in two years she won't be surprised at the matted state of the dog's coat.

Sleeseby's prospects look just as bad. He'd have been checking out that address in Slowden if he hadn't got the sack for trying to knob the editor's wife at a company drinks party. The poor chap's emptying the bins back on his old manor now. Such a shame.

Chancer thought of putting him on the payroll on the grounds psychos like him could be useful, but worried he wouldn't stop at trying it on with the rat. 'You wouldn't like dat, Caligula, nah would ya?' he says, before drowning his old vicarage in eighteen gallons of kerosene, torching it and writing his suicide note. He's rather proud of it.

'*Brethren, I have sinned and yea verily must burn in hell. Do not grieve, god-fearing multitudes in the four corners of the earth, by giving me a Christian burial but cast my bones on stony ground east of Eden. PS: God willing you will not be afflicted by any of my wicked remains.*'

He made good and sure they wouldn't by pinning the scrap of paper containing those words to a charred dog-collar, and scarpering.

Decamping to his former branch office at the disappointing end of Slowden was a risk, but as Sleeseby didn't mention the address in court he imagines only Blusterham knows it. The pic he sends her of an Afghan minus ears captioned 'Mum's da word, Mum' should keep her quiet.

Just for a laugh he adopts her helmet-look hairstyle, set off with a long beard tied in a ponytail, and a black eyepatch. To complete the makeover, he's now Charlie Chancery.

His swanky executive suite is discreetly tucked away behind a dirty book shop which he rather likes. There's a Turkish takeaway on one side that's always getting closed down due to salmonella outbreaks, and on the other is an outlet specialising in stiletto-heeled boots for men. Chancery finds the customers tasty, unlike the kebabs.

Hurtling up the M4 in his souped-up black Beamer at speeds in excess of 120 miles per hour, Monty's trying out the modification he's fitted that beats speed cameras by blurring the number plates. He's glad his mate in the Met let him lift a couple of Sten guns and loads of ammo from the museum by way of a leaving present. The pistol may be handy too.

It's not that he was planning a life of violent crime or terrorist outrages, but he's still a protection officer at heart. And Percy's always been much better at getting into scrapes than out of them.

Time is not actually of the essence, any more than the shooters at this stage, but Monty's discovered he misses the thrill of the chase. Much as he loves his work with Viv, tracking down total bastard villains can be more fun than humdrum hikes to her London office.

As he approaches WH Smut, he gives up counting the mini roundabouts he's driven straight across and connects with his inner poet, adapting a line from John Betjeman. 'Come friendly bombs and fall on Slowden! It isn't fit for humans now.'

The teenager with the sparkly braces on her teeth does not look up as she asks him in a bored tone what he, like, likes. And looks confused when he mentions Milton and Shakespeare. ''Oo? Never 'eard of 'em, innit. Wot they into? Soft? 'Ard? Under the cahnter?'

Monty is discovering how difficult it is to hold a conversation with someone who can't take their eyes off the smartphone that's apparently superglued to their hand. Percy's insistence he doesn't kill anyone at this stage plays on his mind.

He gives his cover story a go. 'I'm looking for my cousin who I haven't seen for twenty years. If his office is behind the shop he must pass through here all the time.'

This gets him nowhere. The dirty macs, defrocked priests and furtive filth all look the same to her. For a start they're ancient, at least twenty-five. And she's never noticed the door tucked between anal group fisting and necrophilia. But suddenly she bursts into peals of laughter.

'Did I say something funny?' Monty is by nature patient and kind, but right now is wondering how Job kept his cool for so long. The kid's totally forgotten his existence.

'I said, did I say something funny?' She doesn't hear him, just carries on giggling at the video her boyfriend's sent her. A trainee chef, he's filmed himself wanking into a tureen of soup he's making for the snobby family that asked for consommé.

*

Monty strides past her and flings open the discreetly positioned door he's just spotted, to be confronted by... a man. After all the havoc the bloke caused, Monty's half expecting a fifty-foot monster with teeth like a brontosaurus. The brute's burly, admittedly, but still just a feller like any other, apart from the weird hairstyle, eyepatch, beard and fingers.

''Ere, wossyour game den?' Charlie's not used to receiving uninvited visitors, and doesn't like the look of this one.

Half-closing his eyes, Monty gets straight to the point. 'I want a word if you please, sir. And I'm having it even if you don't please.'

Caligula twitches his nose uncertainly, and Charlie threatens to call the Old Bill. But Monty spent enough time studying his colleagues in Tottenham to know how to scare people. He toys with his waistband, as though reaching for a Taser gun, and speaks slowly.

'I wouldn't do that if I were you, sir. We don't want any trouble, do we?'

Charlie doesn't. The man's manner has convinced him the pigs have already arrived and he has enough experience of police tactics to know when to come quietly. He remembers being shoved down concrete stairs with hands cuffed behind his back. Once.

It's a relief to find he really might just get away with a little chat.

Sitting down again on his swivel chair, he has to grip the gleaming chrome arms to save himself from falling off when Monty mentions who he is and why he's here.

'Your gaffer's the geezer I worked over, and now you want to join the firm? Well, fuckin' stroll on, you're pullin' me fuckin' plonker.'

'Oh no. The only thing we're going to pull is a stunt. Same as you did on us, but the Tories this time. Change is as good as a rest, eh?'

'Fuck dat for a game o' soldiers.'

'Not keen? Pity.' Monty whips out the Glock 26, points it at the bastard's head and smiles.

'At this range a bullet does truncate a person's social schedule.'

Caligula scurries for cover, Charlie leans as far back as he can and Monty forgives himself for disobeying Percy's instructions about lethal force. The submachine guns are still in the boot, so he's only been a little bit naughty.

They come to terms. Penislow Protection Partnership and Charlie's Angels will sneak the Chinese nuclear garbage into Breezethwaite as originally planned, this time bypassing Whitehall altogether. The Tories wanted to play ball, but their manifesto promise to be even greener than the last greenest government ever was a problem.

Chancery knows Fyok Yu and Hon Ki are running out of patience. 'You'll 'av to meet deez geezers to sort aht da coin.' He's edgy.

'Be a pleasure, dear chap.' Monty means it. He can't believe how this villain coughs when his guard is down. When Caligula crawls out of his hiding place Charlie realises he doesn't need his hands up any more. Useful. Means they can shake on the deal.

Monty's departure interests the teenager no more than his arrival, as she's hysterical at another video on her iPhone. Her boyfriend's filmed the two little girls vomiting into their consommé and told her they all make him sick. Such a witty fellow.

CHAPTER TWO

'Gotcha!' Percy is jubilant next morning when Monty gives him the full rundown. Balances out his setback earlier when the cleaning lady told him today was the last bleddy straw.

It started innocently enough. Birds and bees. Insects buzzing around and pigeons having it away in the trees. Percy grinned as Viv bent to reach home-grown peas. He slipped open his flies, and as she came within range whisked her, still facing away from him, onto his lap.

Her long, loose skirt preserving her modesty, she gave a contented little sigh and wriggled herself comfortable. Unfortunately, little Trudi chose that moment to run away from Nanny to find Mummy, who leapt up in horror. The child didn't see the split-second flash of flesh, but the cleaning lady, peering out of the window as usual, did.

She's so huge it's often hard to tell if she's walking forwards or sideways. Hubby only waddled her down the aisle out of curiosity, but then couldn't find what he was looking for between the layers of fat and decided to stick with what he knew.

He was quite fond of his sheep, actually. And the melons were always a handy standby.

Little wonder the virgin cleaner's obsessed with sex. But

in the pub her dirty Percy story's drowned out by the aliens invading his garden. Everyone at the Wrecker's Arms spits in the sawdust as he's obviously being whipped off to Mars for experiments on his hyperactive penis.

*

Determined not to miss a thing, the villagers give one another leg-ups to peer over the garden wall. As the blokes have had a skinful they drop several ladies, and the cleaning lady breaks her ankle.

'God's way of shielding me bleddy eyes?' she squeals. 'I'll bleddy give Satan a go.'

They're disappointed that the aliens look like humans, the light sabres look machinegun-shaped, while the spacecraft could be mistaken for a helicopter. Worst of all, Percy isn't whisked off in leg-irons. Though the stand-off is proper.

As the chopper descends, Fang almost has a seizure, Nanny stuffs cotton wool in little Trudi's ears and Percy leaps through an open window. When heavily armed men spring out Monty vanishes, but reappears with a Sten gun in each hand and the Glock 26 between his jaws.

Unsure whether Percy would be pleased to see them, the Bashars have taken the precaution of bringing a few heavies along. They're excitable, and it looks like everyone's about to die.

Both Stens jam. And the bodyguards, baffled by the Russian instructions supplied with their guns, can't fire them. They're standing around looking stupid, Monty covering them with the Glock, when the brothers emerge from the helicopter. At that instant Viv appears.

'Gentlemen, a delight to see you again.'

'But dear lady, the pleasure is all ours.'

Monty pops his pistol in his pocket, Percy tries to look like he just popped indoors for a pee, and Fang eyes up the military bootlaces. Everyone's happy, saffron cakes and nice cups of tea all round. The men finally accept this is not an attempt to poison them and tuck in.

Bashar senior thoughtfully dips a cake in his tea. 'Percy old chap, dreadfully sorry about any, ahem, misunderstanding concerning our sincere efforts to give the lads in your local party a hand. No hard feelings and all that? Only meant to help.'

'You're talking bollocks and you know it.' Percy's smiling, but darkly. 'The Tories don't want your oil, eh? So now you're looking for the back door?'

Both Bashars look appalled. At their English public school the back door had a specific meaning and in their neck of the woods the punishment for buggery is death by a thousand cuts. But they eventually cotton on.

'My dear fellow, wouldn't put it quite so crudely, don't you know. But one good turn deserves another, what? We can always supply the jolly old warplanes if you fancy a coup.'

Percy laughs out loud at the thought, but a plan's forming in his head. An air force would be handy, plus an army now that Monty's shown the chaps how to release the safety catches on their guns. They're so pleased they kiss his feet. Fang thinks this is a weird thing to do.

'Combined forces. Penislow Protection. Bashar Battalions. Against Charlie's Angels? Pah! Eagles against sparrows.' Sticking out his stomach, Percy's doing the Churchill voice and gripping the lapel of his jacket. He's disappointed to see Viv raising her eyes skywards.

She steers Monty into the kitchen, to help prepare a monster leek and scrag-end stew. 'Armies always march on their stomachs,' she tells Monty in a Vivienne tone of voice. He gets her drift.

'The sooner this lot get off at the double the better?'

'Precisely.'

The two of them, now the best of buddies, are also

confederates. 'I love him to bits, but Percy can be such a bloody fool. Enemies like himself he needs all the friends he can get.'

Monty knows she's right, and adds another worry. 'He's still a bit fragile after his mental breakdown, isn't that why he avoids speaking engagements?'

Viv nods. 'Of course, the daft 'aporth.' Just occasionally, when she's anxious, Viv's language harks back to the days before her elocution lessons.

*

In the oak-panelled and, to Percy's eye, elegantly spacious living room, the Bashars ask when they're going up to the house.

'But you're in it,' he says, puzzled.

'You're such a wag, old bean. Charming little lodge, but we mean the mansion. Thirty bedrooms and all that.' When Percy finally convinces them this really is it they roar with laughter and wave their silver-topped canes about, same as at Chequers.

'Please don't break my dining room table,' Percy pleads. 'It's quite delicate, and the only one I've got.' They find this even funnier, but useful.

'Tut tut, fellow's strapped,' Bashar senior whispers to his brother. 'But a have-not's a softer target than a have-yacht, what.'

Having always assumed the poor only eat cattle feed, they're astonished to find the stew tastes rather nice. Viv grits her teeth every time Bashar junior stubs out a cigarette in the pureed mashed potato, but against all odds it's rather a fun little party. And when Monty demonstrates unarmed combat techniques the protection men kneel before him and call him Sergeant Superman. They're rather sweet really, giant puppy dogs.

*

On the other side of the wall, the locals are praying it'll end in a hail of bullets. They've erected terraces, like at football matches or public executions. Not a lot happens round these parts, and they love a day out. Blood, gore and death are bleddy proper, but slaughterhouses get a bit samey after a while.

The silver-topped cane routine, clearly visible through the open French doors, convinces them Percy's about to be battered to death. One young man has a spontaneous emission.

They take bets on Monty and his challengers in the combat area, and are fed up that he always wins. By now, no one's in the mood for the bloke with the white van and strange accent.

'Got 'ot paisties, leds. Straight up. Proper, whatever da fuck dat's supposed to mean.'

The guys don't like his tone, or his prices, so they sling him in the river and let his tyres down. As he clambers out they notice he's big and has a knuckleduster, and set the sheepdogs on him. They lick their lips, as in their normal line of work there's a strict no teeth policy.

The cockney drives for his life, without even closing the back doors of the van. When all his pasties tumble out the dogs get over their disappointment at not being able to eat him.

As Monty approaches the gate, around midnight, the locals form a lineout to jeer at his men, who respond by trying out the new techniques they've learned during the evening. In the confusion and darkness the gentle, god-fearing Cornish settle old scores amongst themselves. The dogs bite anything that moves.

Eventually Monty decides to leave them to it and orders his men to fall in.

'By the left, quick... March! Left, right, left, right.' Combat instructors at the Met were often ex-army, and it's Monty's chance to try the silly drill sergeant voice. He can't believe it works.

Shoulders back, heads up, his men stride forth in perfect battle order, sing incomprehensible martial songs and perform long-range spitting. The Cornish lads who're still conscious try and get the knack at the lock-in at the Wrecker's Arms. The landlord is not impressed.

Bakyt's not sorry she was delayed at the university when Monty finally gets home with his bruised and limping troops, one of whom has an arm in a sling. 'Might have been a bit zealous with the jiu-jitsu moves,' he explains. 'And they fought a pitched battle on the way back.'

However, they're all in high good spirits, and delighted at being quartered in a real barn with no shell holes. They're not so sure about the full English breakfast Monty cooks them in the morning, but decide they'd better risk it when Bakyt picks up a broomstick and curses them. 'I put spell on anyone who not eat food on table. Condemn to live forever in bark of cedar tree.'

On the grounds that this doesn't sound very nice they gobble up everything, including far too many baked beans.

Monty thinks of the movie Blazing Saddles, when a bunch of cowboys make the same mistake. Bakyt tries to jam tampons up her nostrils and steps outside for some good clean country air, only to discover the farmer's been spreading pig-shit. Still, smells better than indoors.

The ablutions take a very long time, but Bakyt softens slightly when each man gives her husband a kiss goodbye on both cheeks and a picture of his wives and kids. 'We meet again, proud son of Allah, in this life or next.'

'Better still the one after that,' Monty mutters under his breath.

*

In Percy's elegant little mansion, or dear little kennel depending on your point of view, confidences have been shared.

'For sure I'd like to pay back the bastards who dobbed me in it,' Percy admitted. 'Present company excepted of course.'

'My dear fellow, it's in the bag. Your chappie Monty has

already got the jolly old army tip-top. The air force isn't quite up to par, but the pilots can always create a diversion by blowing one another up.' Bashar senior prides himself on his compassion for the men.

Percy promises to think about their kind offer, and Bashar junior shouts instructions to the helicopter pilot. 'Tally-ho, gung-ho, chocks away.' As the rotor blades turn he remembers the housemaster giving him six of the best for using too many mixed metaphors.

Stepping inside, he has to shout over the din. 'Silly billy will owe us over again. We'll jolly well drown him in oil when he's back in power.'

'He has to give those beastly Conservatives a humdinger of a thrashing first,' his brother reminds him.

Bashar junior, who got three per cent at British Constitution A level, can't see the problem. 'Can't we just pay the wallahs at Buck House to jolly things along? They're the fellows who invite people to become Prime Ministers don't they?'

'Up to a point, Lord Copper,' Bashar senior sighs. He got an A* in English literature A level, as well as in politics, philosophy and economics, so the university snapped him up. His brother's place cost pater a new science block for the campus and a Bentley for the Vice Chancellor.

CHAPTER THREE

As the helicopter gets higher, so does Percy. He's convinced his plan, which now includes the Bashar brigade and fighter planes, can't fail. Viv thinks he may need some more counselling and Monty's glad he's not the only one worried sick.

'All very well entrapping Chancery,' he says, 'but we don't need your so-called buddies.'

'Remember that time on their island when I heard them talking about how they'd teed you up a treat? They framed you twice already, and they'll do it again as soon as look at you.'

'But they're good people at heart,' Percy protests. 'And such fun at parties.' Viv winces at the memory of one in particular.

'Not sure if you're too good for this world, or too bloody gullible,' she hisses.

This irritates Percy. 'I didn't get to be Labour leader and Prime Minister just by being a pretty face, you know.' Spotting her stony expression he tries a winning grin. 'But obviously that helped. Drink, anyone?'

Percy talks like it's all worked out. 'We'll get the bastard clergyman and Chinese turds caught red-handed. It'll make the slaughter of the Romanovs look like an act of clemency.

'This'll be more than a sting, it'll be an uber-sting. A cruise missile with a spear tied to the front.' Bashar junior would have struggled to work out if that was a mixed metaphor or not.

Viv sips her Merlot thoughtfully and watches her husband hitting the brandy. He's still alive, for a start, and looks a lot better than he deserves. But now he's turned fifty-three he might consider growing up a bit.

She's angry with herself, for not just telling him outright not to be so bloody stupid. Especially as she perfectly well knows she's only letting him off because she so lusts after his body.

'First job, bait the trap.' Percy's off again. 'Bakyt's got privileged access to Breezethwaite. Being a nuclear physicist doesn't shorten the queue at Lidl, but has other advantages. Agreed?'

Percy has a knack of selling crazy ideas, by missing out sane objections. Monty thinks of the line about Churchill mobilising the English language when we'd got precious little else to fight the war with, but listens on.

'Can see why they went for Breezethwaite. It's the obvious dumping ground for dodgy nuclear waste, close to Sellafield but a world away.

'For a start the management's not particular about what comes in so long as the price is right. They prefer cheques to checks.'

'Sounds like dancing cheek to cheek,' Monty butts in. 'What are you on about?'

'The security regime's as flaky as a radioactive chocolate bar. Always wanted to close the place down.' Percy sighs. 'But dismantling the Thatcher heritage was a second-term project.'

Viv looks at him with some sympathy. Trudi might have done too, if she weren't snuffling away in her little cot, with Fang splayed out under her head.

'Question is, at what point do we blow the whistle?' Percy continues. 'If we let it go far enough the Tories would look so incompetent they couldn't spot a buffalo in the bedroom. But if we give Tiddledick the nod in the nick of time he can take the credit for tipping off the Bill.

'Who knows? Maybe I get a gong out of it. Sir Percy Penislow? Lord Penis of Percy-Low? Can you imagine that?'

Viv can't. 'And if it all goes wrong do you think you'll get parole in time to see Trudi off to uni?'

'Fie my lord fie, a soldier and afeard? Toodle-pip, Tiddledick? How's that for a headline?'

Viv's not convinced, nor is Monty. 'It's the copper in me. Clink's not exactly a picnic, and where would you go afterwards? The East End? In sackcloth and ashes, like John Profumo?'

Bakyt disagrees. 'Get timing right, pull out in time, we not get in trouble. Like coitus interruptus.' The incident on the Bashars' island flashes through everyone else's mind. Monty has told his wife about it, but spared her the details. He shudders.

Apart from anything else, Viv wasn't even on the pill.

Illogically but humanly this changes the mood. Monty suddenly needs a cuddle and so does Viv. As she blows her guests a kiss goodnight she tweaks Percy's nose, though her brain tells her she's letting herself down. 'Come along, lover-boy, shag me till I scream.'

It's some time before the couple uncouples and the chandelier below the bedroom stops tinkling. The nanny, who gets hopelessly aroused by these performances, sucks her glistening fingertips and falls asleep with a smile on her face.

*

A week later with nothing really resolved to anyone's satisfaction, apart from Nanny's, the men head off to Slowden to meet Chancery and his Chinese chums. Monty's still hoping he can talk Percy into ditching the Bashars and Percy's still saying 'We'll see'. Every parent's way of saying no.

As they hit the outskirts of the town Monty hates it even

more, and Percy is sorry that as Prime Minister he didn't raze it to the ground.

Fyok Yu and Hon Ki assume it was built as a political re-education camp, and as their huge shiny Mercedes glides to a halt outside WH Smut a bunch of youths decide to take it for a joy ride then crash it.

They edge in closer and have a raucous racist laugh at the guys who slither out, but back off when one of them demonstrates skills he's acquired in the karate dojo. The sight of him leaping in the air and giving their top bruv a kick in both eyes strikes them as a bit of a downer, though it earns a round of applause from the Turkish guys next door.

Monty's motor attracts less attention, as black Beamers are the vehicle of choice for all the local drug lords. It's taken as read that the Cornish mud dotted around the bodywork is blobs of dried blood. Respect, like, innit?

*

Remembering what happened during Monty's last visit, Chancery is wearing two Colt 45 revolvers in low-slung holsters and a double bandolier of ammo slung over each shoulder. He's also checked out loads of old Clint Eastwood movies, so he can be quick on the draw.

The teenager with the sparkly braces notices neither the high kicks in the street nor any of the visitors walking into the shop as she's busy wetting herself over her boyfriend's latest video. He's filmed himself on the bog sticking his cock in a jam donut.

Fyok Yu and Hon Ki are shocked at the Western depravity on display in Smut's, but snigger at the sight of their host. Then they spot the bulge under Monty's left armpit as well as the violin case and get the idea.

What baffles them, though, is Percy's calm affability. They're not to know that years spent pretending to enjoy gatherings of the Parliamentary Labour Party make a performance like this relatively easy.

As the meeting gets under way he gets a flashback to that fateful morning in Downing Street nearly three years ago as the same two guys, wearing very similar Armani suits, made pretty much the same pitch.

They're more open about their country's insufficiency of nuclear disposal facilities thanks to earlier experiments with the H-bomb and with more recent rapid expansion of the industry, but that's about it.

However, when they get to the nitty-gritty it's a very different story. No buggering about with phoney Chinese accents now, they look Percy in the eye and give it to him straight.

'Pity to waste our hard-earned money on government officials,' Fyok Yu begins suavely. 'After all, why bribe when you can smuggle?

'And, for the avoidance of racial discrimination, let's cheat our public servants as well as yours. Beijing is providing considerable funds for the, ahem, backhanders. Surely our back pockets would be the better repository.'

Percy's impressed in spite of himself at first at the barefaced cheek of it, less so when Hon Ki follows his friend's lead by taking off his half-glasses and trying Rumpledore's finger to the nose trick. At this point he has to fake a coughing fit to cover his laughter., and wishes he'd brought Fang so he could play at James Bond super-villains.

'Splitting the millions among ourselves will do nicely,' he says. He smiles at the thought of the Bashars' faces if he really did end up with a thirty-bedroom mansion.

Chancery is not smiling, however, as he suspects he's being squeezed out of the action, and his share of the loot. But he cheers up when Fyok Yu and Hon Ki assure him he'll be a busy man, responsible for subverting the bloke who has to wave the shipments through the ports, also he'll be supervising operations at Breezethwaite.

Because his praying days are over now, Chancery settles for scratching his head as Monty chips in, sounding more confident than he feels.

'The trouble and strife will case the joint for you.' Chancery gets that bit at least, though Fyok Yu and Hon Ki have to wait for the translation. Rich though their vocabulary is, they've never moved in Cockney circles.

'My wife is a nuclear physicist, so will be granted full access to Breezethwaite,' Monty explains. 'She will be able to ascertain exactly how many Chinese will be needed, at what level of seniority and what shifts they need to be on.'

This goes down well, as does Percy's promise that Viv too will be able to help. 'She's a polling expert, so can distort surveys if necessary to prove the public thoroughly approves of nuclear leakages contaminating the Irish sea.'

He's amazed they believe a word of it; he certainly doesn't, but presses on anyway.

'She'll prove the Brits think the Irish had no right to independence and deserve to pay the price. Poetic justice if the lobsters turn green.'

Crossing the fingers of his left hand behind his back, Percy shakes on the deal and files out with Monty. In the shop, the teenager's not sounding so happy. Her boyfriend's sent her yet another video, only instead of donuts he's sticking his cock in her best friend.

Percy remembers the line Viv's tattooed friend used all those years back. 'The course of true love never did run smooth, dear lady,' he murmurs.

'Fuck off Granddad,' she screams, then tries to scratch his eyes out.

At this point Percy loses sympathy, Monty gets the Sten out and the girl bolts through the back door, only to face two

Colt 45s. She warns Chancery she'll get her boyfriend on to him, remembers she hasn't got one any more and collapses in a sobbing heap.

*

As the Beamer hurtles along the M4 Percy's anxious. 'If Viv had heard that shit I was talking about her doctoring poll findings she'd have bitten my willy off.'

'Something to think long and hard about, dear,' murmurs Monty, who enjoys camp humour these days. Trying it on anyone in the Met would have got his willy hacked off with a chainsaw.

'But I have to admit Bakyt's getting cold feet about it all,' he adds, slowing down to ninety-five. 'We need some kind of wheeze to square it with both of them. If we can't sell them a clear exit strategy they won't buy any of it. Can't say I blame them, actually.'

Percy takes his point. 'Yup, they're soft and fluffy to look at. Foxes are too, but think what they eat.'

Monty proves he is no chicken as he approaches a bloke sticking to the speed limit while passing half-a-dozen caravanettes doing fifty in the middle lane. He slews across the motorway and undertakes the lot of them.

Percy shuts his eyes tight, thinking about another sort of undertaker.

CHAPTER FOUR

The boys are savvy enough to know their wheeze, consisting of enormous bouquets and insistence that caterers come in with a slap-up meal, may only put Viv and Bakyt on their guard. And Percy's facial scar make-up and funny Donald Pleasence voice is also a bit risky.

Trudi refuses to get into the 007 spirit. She squeals 'kee-ell,' and wees on his lap.

Later, when Nanny's whisked the child off to bed, Mummy and Daddy have kissed her goodnight and Percy's changed his trousers, he kicks off the discussion.

'I know, I know, we could just grass the bastard up and get him sent down. But he'll do a lot more bird if he's actually caught in the act. I've said it before and I say it again, because it's true. Besides, I like to quote myself, it adds spice to my conversation.'

'And you fancy sharing a cell with this dreadful man if you get sucked in too deeply, dear, and it all spins out of control?' House fires and overdoses are flitting through Viv's mind. Also she's finding it hard not to believe in that ridiculous scar, even though it's only painted on.

Fang's fixated on it too, which is why he left Trudi to sleep all on her own just this once. And, another first, he's not distracted even by the sight of unguarded smoked salmon.

'If we set them all up and choose our moment, the Chinese chappies will cop it too. Egg fried rice when they fry. Serves them right. Besides, my protection man here will keep me out of trouble.' Monty sort of nods, wishing he could believe it.

Percy could probably sell ice-cubes to Inuits if he put his mind to it, and little by little everyone gets sucked in. The booze probably helps.

'Of course Fingers and friends will try and drag us down with them, but we'll always be one step in front.'

Bad place to be if the enemy has a dagger, Monty thinks, but doesn't say.

Percy insists the Bashar boys can be kept in check. Viv looks at him and wishes she didn't fancy him so much. Otherwise she'd just lay down the law instead of leaning across and giving his nose that special tweak. Chuffed, he does the sticking out tummy and chin routine.

'We shall fight on the beaches. We shall fight on the landing grounds. In the fields. In the streets. We shall... never... surrender.'

'But as the British army had left everything in Dunkirk Winnie had to admit we'd nothing to fight with but broken beer bottles.' Monty doesn't say this either because he's in a pickle. Viv's right, it's a crazy idea, but Percy's buccaneering spirit appeals. He can be a bit of a boy too.

Sir Bernard Brenstorme does not figure in the conversation, as it never occurs to anyone that he should. Their mistake, as they'll discover in time.

*

Eight bottles of wine later, life is good. 'In shick-steen shicksty-one Schotland had a par'ment called the drunken par'ment,'

Percy slurs. 'They fucked up everything.' Everyone thinks this is very funny, especially Bakyt, who doesn't normally touch a drop. She can't believe it in the morning when Monty tells her what she did.

The rocking to and fro in her seat is followed by hoarse, atonal singing in something profoundly foreign. It doesn't sound at all Eastern European, and could well be a dead language, though this is never established.

Jaws drop when she slips off her shoes, and her dress, to demonstrate traditional Kazakh dancing on the table. By now Percy couldn't care less about the caterers' expensive crockery. In fact, as each twenty-guinea plate smashes to the floor he roars all the louder.

Fang, who's too pissed to worry about the scar, springs up and sends two antique cruet sets flying. Plus a bottle of vintage port and three Dartington Crystal wine goblets.

When the party finally breaks up Monty and Bakyt slump on the sofa. Percy carries Viv upstairs but forgets the way back from the loo and collapses in the walk-in wardrobe. No chandeliers for Nanny then. Such a pity, she'd been so looking forward to it.

*

In the morning Trudi's a merry little soul, unlike everyone else, including Nanny, who made up for her disappointment last night with half a bottle of vodka. Not a lot gets done apart from Percy shelling out vast sums to the caterers, and thanking god at least the table survived.

Bakyt is petite, as well as agile.

The following day she arranges her trip to Breezethwaite and the meetings with workers and management at all levels. When not in a state of mystical delirium she is a scientist commanding the widespread respect she hopes she can hang on to, on sober reflection.

She squares matters with her conscience by giving the bosses a few state-of-the-art insights on radioactive isotopes with a long half-life. She suspects they're not so hot on it. Or maybe too hot, which could be the problem.

'Bad isotopes like nasty shoes,' she confides. 'Never wear out.'

They're much more interested in her looks than her words, but like the sound of her conclusion. 'I give you bare facts. Naked truth.'

There's a sharp intake of breath, and one of them creams his jeans.

*

When Percy plucks up courage to tell Viv what he's said she could do he's relieved at her reaction. 'Dream on, silly sausage. You know as well as I do it'll never come to that.

'Still, unintended consequences have always been your speciality, as well as the old Blair trick of seeming to compromise, but getting it all your own way.'

'My dear, I'm better than that. I shoot first then claim whatever I hit was the target. That's why I never miss.'

Actually, he already has. His plan to keep Chancery in the dark flopped, as the first thing the man did after the Slowden get-together was hack his mobile. Coverage is patchy in Cornwall, so answerphone messages casting doubt on Percy's motives are soon flooding in. Chancery starts oiling his gun barrels every few minutes.

He's taken with the gunslinger look, and often mutters 'Howdy, pardner, whole lotta Injuns out there'. In his cockney accent this is painful, same as when he tries to squat wearing razor-sharp spurs.

It also hurts to hear himself referred to as 'the fuckwit'. Monty's as bad as Percy, but does at least confirm his squeeze has got the lowdown on Breezethwaite. Seems she's worked out they'll need around thirty blokes.

Fyok Yu arranges a factory line of Westernisation plastic surgeons to make the necessary facial adjustments. Some of the guys kick off and demand extra payment and Hon Ki yearns for the good old days, when threatening to cut people's noses off was enough.

*

Percy has a curious sense on the phone to Chancery that he's never telling him much he didn't already know, but pretends to like him. He'd have found this harder if he'd known the fuckwit had taken to pinning up photos of him for target practice.

Chancery's annoyed to discover the Colt 45 is difficult to shoot and not very accurate, feels Clint Eastwood has let him down and gets himself a Tommy gun on the Dark Web. This calls for a new dress code, but happily his broad chest suits the Al Capone look. Perfect for his meeting with the civil servant who OKs nuclear imports for Breezethwaite.

Tracking the man down was easy, as the girl who lifted Blusterham's computer still works in the same office. She has full access to staff files, which include home addresses, phone numbers and past disciplinary issues.

Adolphus Hillter faced a hearing over his relaxed attitude to imported spent nuclear fuel, but no one could disprove his claim he was only obeying orders. 'Tut tut, Nuremberg defence,' the Permanent Secretary muttered. Then he remembered his predecessor vanished in mysterious circumstances and Blusterham went to jail.

Hillter's a curious little man with a small moustache and lock of hair that often hangs over his forehead. He doesn't believe in climate change, has his doubts about the Holocaust, and voted with a heavy heart to leave Europe. His first preference would have been to blow the place up.

The neighbours in his tree-lined cul-de-sac have him down as a pretentious little toe-rag, as well as their idea of a leftie, all things being relative. And the bloke next door really wound him up by painting his half of the drainpipe pink.

But Hillter's convinced he'll show them all when he receives a hand-written letter on posh watermarked paper with a gilded swirl at the top.

'*Dear esteemed and respected Mr Hillter,*' it begins, '*allow me to introduce myself. I am the eminent author and academic Professor Sir Charles Chuffington-Chancery CH, FRS, and I write to crave your indulgence.*'

The little toe-rag reads, rereads and pulls himself up to his full five-foot three. Recognition. About time too.

'*Your valued insights into the finest traditions of the public service will be a beacon to future generations,*' the letter continues. '*I beg you to please grant me the honour of a short interview at your earliest convenience. Your obedient servant, Charles.*'

'*PS: Cough up and you get a gong, all right?*'

That last bit strikes Hillter as a bit odd, but this magnificent document nonetheless gets a place of honour behind glass over the mantelpiece. He's the one being framed, however, as he begins to suspect when he answers the door a week later.

'Wotcha, cock.' Hardly what Hillter expected from someone so refined. Nor is the pink '56 Cadillac that's occupying half the street.

'Tasty little flivver, ain't it?' Chancery's take on this fin-backed, gas-guzzling monster doesn't sound very academic. The wide-lapelled pinstripe suit is also a long way from the corduroy trousers and leather elbow patches Hillter had been expecting. And it gets worse.

As he speaks, Chancery twangs his braces as though they're bowstrings tightening up to slaughter the French cavalry at

Agincourt. This releases endorphins, helps him get over being called 'the fuckwit' again and again and not being able to do anything about it.

Taking his aggression out on this scrawny little worm is zero risk and maximum return. He knows he's on a job, but can still combine business with pleasure.

Doing his best to look like a scar-faced mobster he does his really scary voice. 'Nah cop dis, sunshine. I gonna make you an offer you can't refuse. Right? Right.'

CHAPTER FIVE

Turns out Hillter needs no persuading to get the nuclear shipments in. 'Between you and me, Prof old chap,' he simpers, 'environmental do-gooders are subversive, probably communists, or Muslims.

'Hanging's too good for 'em. Parliament should set up a House Un-British Activities Committee. Prison works, you know.'

'Too right, me old cocker. Country needs more right finkin' folk like you. Gone to da dogs, right? Time to get it back, right?' Politics never did it for Chancery, but even he can't believe what a fascist this man is. He's a greedy snob as well.

'I have an aunt in Cumbria with a fish restaurant in a village close to Breezethwaite and I'm hoping for her continued but not unduly extended success in business. You see old boy I'm her favourite nephew, and, ahem, she's more than once mentioned me in her will.'

'And where dere's a will you wanna be in it, right?'

'I admit I have a vested interest in nuclear waste. If the fish glow in the dark so much the better, saves on electricity, though heaven forfend anything should happen to Auntie. Ahem.

'On the other hand, though I'm pushing sixty I've got what's left of my career to consider. Civil service pensions aren't what they were, but there's still a pot I wouldn't want to lose.'

Chancery twangs his braces again, this time thoughtfully, and does a spot of mental arithmetic.

Generous terms are agreed. Not knowing Chancery's better at making promises than keeping them, Hillter shares his dream of owning a nice little retirement home in Frinton-on-Sea.

'Polite society there, not like the ghastly people round here.'

*

Business concluded, the atmosphere warms. More so when Adolphus switches on one bar of the electric heater before getting out the sherry he was given the Christmas before last.

He shows off his collection of Nazi memorabilia, and Chancery's so taken with the guns he lets on the Caddy's an Eldorado coupe and only set him back fifty grand.

In return, Adolphus gives a rundown on shipping routes used by other exporters of radioactive waste, and ways of keeping prying eyes off the new lot from China.

'The riff-raff working the ports wouldn't know a nuclear flask from a Thermos,' he confides. 'They'd bung their grannies on the trains if it said so on the docket.'

When it's time to say goodbye Hillter gets his guest to lift the bonnet and rev up the Caddy's whopping great engine, to give the neighbours plenty of time to flick back the net curtains. He even tries an awkward man-hug, so everyone can see how important he is.

He has to back off when Chancery runs out of patience and hurtles off in a cloud of blue smoke, almost flattening his feet. But he feels brave enough to stick his tongue out at the old bag opposite and tell her to get back to *EastEnders*.

Once more in his living room he turns off the electric fire, best not count your chickens, lights his pipe and fantasies about

Frinton. *The genteel folk will love me. I'll find a rich widow to nurse through her dotage. With a bit of luck quite a short one.*

*

Thrashing along the motorway, Chancery decides he's earned a little light relief. Now he's got a grip on that mutant's balls he can surely suck a couple of prettier ones in Brighton. *If da Caddy ain't bait in Kemptown da Pope ain't a fuckin' cafflick...*

Just off Marine Parade he's flagged down by a young copper who's fascinated by the car, rather attractive and well up for a shag. *Wot's nice abaht getting' older,* he thinks to himself, *is da filf really does get younger every day.*

Getting home's a downer, however. Instead of Caligula's nose twitching in delight at seeing him he's met by a pert little madam with her feet on his executive desk, filing her nails. She has a mouth like a beaver, but that's no consolation.

Having spent the night sucking the policeman's tasty little helmet, he's holding up the pretty boy's other one like a trophy. He's also carrying the Tommy gun and a spare magazine, but Sharon wouldn't balk at the sight of an invading army mounted on elephants.

'Why hello, big boy, playing cops'n'robbers are we?'

*

Bored at Tiddledick's crowd becoming as suburban as the other lot, the pretty little muckraker's been digging through old files. She always suspected there was more to Sleeseby's botched scoop than ever came out in court, and is convinced of it when she slips something naughty into Ernest Shurelynott's drinks one night over dinner.

He's been a useful contact for Percy in his revived journalistic career, and the traffic is sometimes two-way. So he's picked up something about a fuckwit hanging out behind an odd-sounding shop in Slowden called WH Smut. All in strictest confidence of course.

Actually, Percy only mentioned the bloke for a laugh, and got the response he was hoping for. 'Dirty bookshop? WH Smut? Shurelynott (sic) !!'

However, Ernest was curious, and Percy couldn't resist dropping in Blusterham's name and a few other odds and sods. As gossips go they're as bad as one another. Though, over the odd-tasting port with Sharon in the press restaurant, Shurelynott had no idea what he passed on before passing out. The staff told him next day he was giving the place a bad name.

Slowden's dodgy too, from what Sharon can make out, so she leaves her natty little sports car in the garage and settles for train and minicab. Shame to lose out in the mileage allowance, but better safe than sorry. At least the driver will know where the bloody place is.

Stepping out of the clapped-out Mondeo that smells of stale sick, cheap detergent and vile air freshener she gives the Turkish blokes the finger when they wolf-whistle her, but giggles at the sign outside WH Smut. 'Durtiest booc-shop in Slowwden.'

The teenager's too busy texting death threats to her former best friend to notice her.

When Sharon spots the door at the back of the shop she checks she's not being watched by picking up a book about bestiality with owls and popping it in her pocket. No response. She gets out her set of investigative reporter's must-have skeleton keys, and in no time she's in the swanky executive suite.

Rooting through unlocked drawers and cabinets she's surprised to find a rat in one of them, but doesn't take it out and stamp on it in case the weirdo thinks it's a sign of weakness.

When he does finally show his face she thinks, *What a fuckwit.*

"Oo sed you could fuckin' walk in 'ere, nosey tart. You got

more front dan fuckin' 'Arrods you 'ave. Da last fing I want is to 'urt you, but it's on my list.' That would scare most people, but on Sharon it cuts no more ice than a blunt butter knife on a glacier.

'Tasty hovel you got, apart from da vermin in da cabinet.' She smiles maliciously as she says this, not expecting what comes next.

'Wot? Dat's where da little bleeder's got to? Ta, tart, maybe ya ain't so fuckin' bad after all.' Chancery lunges at the filing cabinet and eases out his hairy pet. 'Dare, dare my little lovely, 'oo bleedin' banged you up? You come to Daddy nah, I'd never let ya dahn.'

'Should hope not, mate. Wouldn't do to rat on a rat, would it?' Sharon is spluttering with laughter, convinced the bloke's soft in the head as well as a fuckwit.

Still, dragged up in the slums same as him, she's cautious. Little by little they reveals bits of their hands, and she clocks he's got more going for him than most, at least in the fingers department.

'Give you an advantage when you're adding up, do they? The extra longers and lingers?' Chancery picks up on the piss-take and fires off a short burst at the ceiling to show they're good for pulling triggers with and all.

'Well, Annie get your gun,' she sniggers, thus hinting she's also spotted he's queer. Just to be annoying she pulls her shoulders down and quivers her breasts at him.

Though this makes him hate her a little bit more Chancery can see she could be useful insurance. If Percy double-crosses him she can drag the bastard through the dirt. For her part, Sharon's astute enough to see the story must go on the back burner for a while.

Chancery gives the impression he's only the facilitator, and won't play any part in the action. That'll be down to Percy and his bunch of incompetents. Sharon doesn't believe him for a moment, but pretends she does.

'No point getting the pigs in before the crims do da job, eh? Gettin' 'em caught red-'anded is a far better tale. I'll be there when dey make the arrests. Make my career and all. Be a bleedin' book in it, see? Ex-PM turns villain? Be a right page-turner.'

Being queen of the Crime Writers' Association appeals, so do the movie rights. She knows she's more digger than wordsmith, but the stuff can easily be ghosted.

Better start a draft now, be ahead of the game, she thinks. *Let's see now, how do you spell 'malfeasance'?*

Chancery promises to drip-feed her titbits, calculating she'll hold back for now. If she doesn't he can always arrange a fatal road accident. 'Couldn't 'appen to a tastier tart,' he tells Caligula as he feeds him a couple of juicy live worms. The rat enjoys this. The worms don't.

The Mondeo's waiting outside, but Sharon can't resist a peek on her way past at the teenager's efforts on the iPhone. *'I'll getcha yer fukin bich scrach yer fukin I's art and mash yer fuckin tits up fukin cah.'*

Even Sharon thinks that's a bit strong. The fuckwit's a psycho and all. That truth dawned when he proved the Tommy gun wasn't a replica by adding to the cluster of bullet holes in the photo of Percy Penislow.

On her way back she calls a few very nasty people, friends since childhood. They could be a handy backstop now that she and Chancery are in this together, like Cain and Abel.

CHAPTER SIX

Next morning Chancery invites himself to Cornwall. Percy begs Viv not to laugh out loud at the sight of him and instructs Fang to mind his manners even though he might want to treat him like the old blind bloke at Rodney's funeral.

'Keep off his lap, there's a good cat. You'll get your reward later. Poo poos on his head? You'd like that, wouldn't you?'

Fang looks as though he would, but bolts when little Trudi gives a stinky demonstration of what Daddy means. At least she's done it in her potty, though Viv wonders whether Stilton and broccoli soup is a bit much at her age.

Bakyt's picked up loads of detailed information from Breezethwaite, and agrees it'll be simpler to share it face to face. She too is warned about how weird the bloke looks, but can't promise to behave herself.

Chancery's journey is uneventful until he hits the Cornish lanes, which he calls alleyways. Some are barely an inch wider than the Cadillac, and the sight of a farmer herding sheep in his path is the last straw.

A blast on his specially modified horn, which sounds like a World War Two air-raid siren, has the dogs running for their lives. The sheep first stampede, then, as they get to an open stretch of pasture, scatter in all directions.

Furious, the farmer jams his tractor into reverse. Chancery warns him off with a long burst from the Tommy gun, fired through the open driver's window. The tractor lurches forward again and the farmer reaches for his twelve-bore repeater.

He soon finds out it's not safe to fire a shotgun backwards while trying to steer forwards. And when the tractor lurches over a ninety-foot cliff, Chancery pulls up and blows the smoke from the barrel of his trusty weapon.

Tilting his Stetson back, he bites the end off a cigar and smiles. 'Shucks, pardner, some buckin' bronco.'

His Buffalo Bill phase is over but he's sentimental about cowboys. As he eases the Eldorado coupe back into gear he gives a couple of confused but ever hopeful old ladies a snatch of 'Back in the Saddle Again' and a quick blast on the siren.

On the beach far below, the farmer hears nothing. As you don't, when you're dead.

Chancery doesn't care about the Stetson not going with his pin-striped gangster suit, any more than the Cuban-heeled boots. The Colt Derringer's a bit Wild West too, and no use against Percy's five-bar gate. Unlike most things in Cornwall, it's seriously sturdy.

Chancery nudges it hard with the Caddy's bumper and sounds the horn. Inside the farmhouse Percy thinks of black and white movies about the Blitz and motions the others to stay still and quiet. Hard to giggle silently, but they try.

An age later Chancery accepts the fucking gate's his problem. It opens outwards, meaning the added humiliation of having to reverse. To cap it all, Percy greets him like an old friend.

Chancery puffs out his chest and tries to sound nonchalant. 'All right, me ole cocker, ev'ry-fing fukin' 'unky-dory?' Viv gasps and grips her chest tightly in a theatrical pretence of terror. Bakyt does too, and Fang bites his boots. Chancery wonders whether he's pitching it wrong.

At least as the business gets underway his attention to detail convinces everyone he's not such a fuckwit as he looks. But he's reckoned without Fang.

Because he's driving straight on to Cumbria, and expects to be there a while, he's brought his pet. Knowing the rat doesn't like being shut in but has to breathe, he's opened the cage door and left a wing window slightly ajar. Fang, who's having fun leaving muddy paw marks all over the roof, picks up Caligula's scent.

Rats aren't strong enough to open hinged windows but cats are, and in no time Fang's in. Caligula hides in a heating duct and fends off probing paws and claws with nasty little bites.

The squeaks and howls are clearly audible indoors, and Percy and Chancery dash out. So do Viv and Bakyt, armed with heavy-duty pink Marigolds and mops. Monty follows, with a Sten.

To Chancery it's an open and shut case. Percy's cat. Percy's fault.

'Dat ain't GBH, dat's attempted fuckin' murder,' he bellows, forgetting what he's just done to the farmer. 'I'll fuckin' string you up for dis. And blow yer fuckin' brains aht an' all.'

'Oh, and which of these death sentences do you plan to execute, pardon the pun, first?'

Percy would have been less calm if he'd noticed the Derringer Chancery's fished out of his pocket. Monty has, and is on it. Anxious not to kill either animal he aims wide and puts a dozen holes in the Caddy's boot.

Chancery leaps over the bonnet and fires back. He misses both times and neither man knows what to do next. The Derringer's out of ammo and Monty would never gun down an unarmed man. Pity, it'd solve so many problems.

Fang, meanwhile, evacuated unseen through the window the second the shots rang out.

Viv and Bakyt approach the two gunmen from behind, poke them with the handles of their mops and tell them to stop being so silly. Chancery turns green, convinced the pink gloves mean a chemical attack is imminent, and opens the Caddy door to say goodbye to Caligula.

'No, you idiot. The gloves are protection against angry animals,' Viv snorts. Chancery has to accept this but can't understand why Caligula's alone in the car.

Acclimatised to gunfire by his master's indoor target practice, he's balanced on his hind legs and dancing in a way that says 'I'm the winner, sod the mog'.

The humans return to the house, the men feeling slightly sheepish, and half an hour later Fang slinks in looking much the same. He was smart enough this time to work out in advance how he'd get down from the tree he hid in, but doesn't feel much of a hero.

Chancery eyes the little brute hatefully as he leaves, wishing looks alone could kill. The Derringer's still unloaded, and the tell-tale bulge under Monty's left armpit is also a problem.

He'd like to but doesn't splat the five-bar gate, and narrowly misses several local lads who've gathered outside it. They were tipped off about a converted missile carrier trundling into Percy's place by his former cleaning lady, who, on top of everything else, is colour-blind.

A bloke driving a baby-pink motor is a shock, but they respond with suggestive gestures involving rapid hand and wrist movements. Chancery can't hear much over the 305 horse-power V-eight engine, but he picks up on 'bleddy woofter arse bandit tosser'.

Annoyingly, the Tommy gun's in the boot, in a bullet-proof box at least. But on the grounds humiliation's a fate worse than death he gives them the tilted-back Stetson treatment and, sprawling in his seat, drives on with one leg on the dashboard. This proves, surely, he's so Mr Cool and the lads so aren't.

Actually, they just think he's a fuckwit.

*

Back at the house the atmosphere's not good. 'Brain and brawn sound almost same to simple foreign cleaning-lady,' Bakyt grumbles at Monty. 'But mean different thing, yes?'

Knowing she's right, he gets on his high horse. 'This individual was armed and dangerous and should not have been approached by members of the public. Mops and Marigolds do not constitute lethal force.'

'But they good to protect against tooth and claw. When man get in way they forget why fighting and try kill him instead.'

'Same as when a policeman intervenes in a domestic dispute and both husband and wife turn on him,' Percy suggests. He raises his hands as though he's trying to shield himself. Monty can't help smiling at the ridiculous expression on his face.

'Isn't it also like good turns?' Viv chips in. 'One loaded gun deserves another?' Bit by bit they all see the funny side. Trudi, who's just come out with her second word, thinks they're laughing at her joke, and says 'Sili-bugga' lots and lots of times.

When they all calm down, Bakyt passes on what she's told Chancery. Breezethwaite employs about ten thousand people, so there's always a hundred or so unfilled posts. However, the 'locals first' recruitment policy won't make it easy to slip the Chinese guys in at all, let alone into the right places at the right times.

A mouse choosing that moment to be in the wrong place at the wrong time helps Fang connect with his inner killer.

'Hope that's not a metaphor for how Chancery's likely to operate,' Viv mutters anxiously.

'Ex-coppers tend to be a bit funny about homicide too,' Monty adds. Bakyt points at the Sten he's still got cradled in his arms and sniggers.

*

Cruising up the M5 at a steady eight-five, Chancery's popped Elvis Country into the CD player he's had fitted. It feels right as

The King had a motor just like his. Besides, some of the tracks chime with his plans for Breezethwaite employees.

'Be a whole lotta shakin' goin' on when I get aluminium tipped into the local water supply. Right, Caligula?'

He's also learned that three of just the right blokes live together in a *ménage à trois* situation.

'Disgusting, but nuffin' a spot of arson won't sort. Tomorrow ain't never going to come for dem.' Caligula's eyes droop. He's getting bored with this conversation.

Chancery's flow is interrupted by a blue light flashing behind him. He pulls over, takes one look at the passable looking young rookies, and looks forward to another sort of pulling.

Two bums for da price of one? Someone say ménage? Well, bonny Bobby Shafto.

Next morning two caps with their white covers are displayed on the back shelf, with the trophy truncheon suggestively positioned between them. Chancery's considerably the worse for wear, but smiling at what his old ma used to say.

'You only get out what you put in, love.'

God rest her bones, she'd have loved the Caddy, same as Elvis's mum when he gave her his. But Chancery was still in his skunk and pill-peddling phase when Ma passed on and she didn't rate the rusty Mustang he thought was the bollocks back then. Said it wasn't respectable, like.

He promised on her deathbed he'd do her proud one day, without explaining how.

As he approaches Cumbria he gives Fyok Yu a ring. 'Da face lifters better get it right, right? Or day don't get a look-in, right?'

Fyok Yu sniffs. 'Concerns noted, Far Quit.' That sounds too much like fuckwit for Chancery's liking, nor is he happy to see his latest conquests' caps no longer have their white covers. Caligula, looking well nourished and not at all guilty, smiles at him sweetly.

CHAPTER SEVEN

Back in Cornwall, the women are getting twitchy about what Chancery may be getting up to up north.

'All very well you saying we can pull out before we get in too deep,' Viv tells Percy. 'But we're already up to our eyeballs, so you've got to check him out.'

'What? Make sure his drive to create vacancies doesn't involve too much slashing and burning?' Percy inquires, half jokingly.

'Precisely,' Viv replies in a Vivienne voice. Monty and Bakyt are on her side, so they win the argument.

Four days later Percy's satisfied the Che Guevara moustache he's growing will prevent the fuckwit from recognising him. 'What with my dark cloak and topper even my own mother wouldn't know me.'

'Would she want to?' Viv sometimes wonders if her dearly beloved really is deranged.

'Fang's boycotting my shoelaces, must be doing something right.' Percy's put out. 'Listen to Trudi. Babes and sucklings and all that.'

The child, who seems to have a natural feel for language, has worked out another new word, especially for Daddy. 'Ugglifukka.'

Because Chancery's already seen the black Beamer, Percy suggests they go in Viv's van. 'It'll take longer, but there's a plus. Citroen insisted a farmer could drive a 2CV over a ploughed field without breaking the bag of eggs on the passenger seat. Smooth ride guaranteed.'

Monty grants this will help prevent the Sten guns accidentally going off, but knows Percy too well. Citroen also stipulated the farmer must be able to ride in comfort while wearing a tall hat.

'You don't suppose the yellow daisies all over the bodywork might make it stand out just a bit?'

Monty's too polite to add 2CV vans stand out a bit anyway because they look like corrugated iron sheds on wheels.

'Be grateful for small mercies,' Percy smiles. 'And sodding great big ones. After a pink Eldorado coupe no one will notice anything, short of an intercontinental ballistic missile.'

Monty strokes his newly acquired stubble, adjusts his dark glasses, and wonders how he's possibly going to manage a four-hundred-mile drive in a forty-year-old left hooker with a glorified lawnmower engine.

He's not too sure about the disguise Bakyt chose for him, but can see the tight jumper, spotty neck scarf and beret combo blends with the motor. Also he likes the way she keeps French-kissing him. Not to mention the 'ooh la la' seeing-to she gives him before he goes.

A couple of hours into the journey they stop at a chemist in Exeter to buy something to counter the strange oily fragrance unique to Citroen 2CVs. Percy insists on a large bottle of Miss Dior for old times' sake.

'Smells like a bloody poofs' parlour,' Monty complains.

'How would you know, dear?'

'OK, OK, it helps. But I still wish we'd bought earplugs while we were there.'

'What?'

'Fuck off, silly sod.' They've travelled a long way, in every sense, since Percy was the flashy big shot and Monty the humble servant.

Three days later they make it to the western Lake District and stop at a garage. The candlestick telephone, ancient till that goes 'Kerchink!' and Bakelite radio with Hilversum, Luxembourg and Lille on the tuning dial convince Percy these people are even more backward than the Cornish.

He's not surprised, therefore, at the weirdness of the answer when he asks the man if he's seen a huge pink car with fins.

'Wossat, wack? Dust mean mordah wit bully halls?'

It happens Monty used to know a young copper from oop north. 'A mordah's a motor car, and bully halls are bullet holes,' he whispers.

'Eh? They see that many '56 Cadillacs here in the arse-end of nowhere you have to specify whether the one you're after's been shot at?'

Actually, the bloke isn't stupid at all. His wife runs an antique stall locally and likes to trial the stock in the garage to make sure it works, and there was a classic American car rally passing through only last week.

He's also quite talkative. 'T'ol fella' served in war and knows a Sten goon bully hall when he sees one.'

Percy starts speaking slowly and loudly, like an English tourist in Paris who can't understand why the frogs insist on speaking French. 'Do... you... know... Toll Feller's... address?'

The garage man looks shocked, but Monty steps in in time. 'Only joking, old chap, of course you know where your father lives.'

He struggles, though, when the bloke mentions the 'watter' making everyone 'queah'. But gets it eventually. The water's making people ill, the authorities are trying to cover it up and Facebook's full of stories about folk going mad. Some say no change there, and this is causing family rows, especially with in-laws.

Percy is horrified. 'Sounds like something that happened in Cornwall when I was a kid. Twenty tons of aluminium sulphate accidentally tipped into the water supply and a lot of local grief. Please, please god Fuckwit didn't do it. Want to strangle him anyway.'

Images of black eye-patches merge in his mind with fedoras and concealed body armour.

His suspicions harden when he reads in the local rag about a suspected arson attack on the home of three Breezethwaite employees. Though again the community is divided, between those who feel sorry for the poor buggers and those who say it's the wrath of a just god.

Trouble at Breezethwaite intensifies as large numbers of people call in sick, claim to be the Holy Ghost, or resign. Adolphus Hillter's aunt fears for her livelihood, then goes off her rocker.

She starts deep-frying crucifixes and renames the chippy 'Cod's Plaice of Worship'. Also she writes to her once-favourite nephew informing him she's cutting him out of her will and leaving every penny to the Church of the Quivering Brethren.

*

Adolphus Hillter immediately takes unpaid leave and shoots up to the western Lake District. As he doesn't touch alcohol he tries to calm his nerves with eight pints of water. Convinced half an hour later he's Genghis Khan with diarrhoea he sends Chancery a strange email.

'Sir. I beg to serve notice you have cheated me out of my inheritance. I demand compensation. One million pounds in used Mongolian banknotes. If monies not instantly received you will hear from the Office for Nuclear Regulation legal department. Also you will have nails driven into your brains through your ears, and your race will be exterminated. I remain, sir, your most humble and obedient servant.'

Chancery reads it several times, not at first connecting it with his little chat with the geezer subcontracted to shift aluminium sulphate around for the water company.

Fifty grand upfront and the deal was done. The self-employed lorry driver would drop the lot where it didn't oughta go and scarper. By the time they worked out it was him he'd be in Marbella. *Hola! Viva Costa Del Crime!*

Chancery found it refreshing, doing business with a fellow cockney wide-boy. Refreshing is not the word the locals would have chosen.

'All dat's water under da bridge, eh, Caligula,' he tells his furry friend. 'But 'ang on a minute, dere's dat bloke again, da one wiv da weird 'at an' cloak, and da mate wiv da surrender monkey bear-et. Am I being stalked? Should I call da Bill?'

The little animal twitches his whiskers uncertainly, looking a bit under the weather. 'Serves you right for gobbling all dat police tackle,' Chancery scolds. He's too anxious to think about pots and kettles. Those traffic cops were right old slags and now it hurts when he pees. They treat him like family already, at the clap clinic...

*

Percy's also getting worried. 'The fuckwit was supposed to ease a few targeted personnel out of the way, not do a King Herod on them. Remember that line of Michael Caine's? "You're only supposed to blow the bloody doors off"?'

'I can hear them saying it already,' Monty confesses.

'Who? What?'

'Viv and Bakyt... I told you so.'

'Shit.'

And there's worse. Percy's discovered Downing Street is also taking an interest. Word has reached the Cabinet Secretary that Breezethwaite appears to be running dangerously low on staff. He's going to investigate the matter personally.

Ernest Shurelynott tipped off Percy about Brenstorme's plan. Waiting for something in the Commons library, he overheard a ruck between a member of staff and a man in a fedora.

Not accustomed to travelling any further north than Islington, the Cabinet Secretary had come to get a railway timetable for Carlisle. Outraged at being asked why he didn't just look it up online like everyone else, he gave the official a severe ticking off.

'Now look here, young man, national security and all that. The Breezethwaite nuclear waste complex is at grave risk. Millions of lives at stake. Have you never heard of Chernobyl?'

'Wot? You mean dat rubbish singer from da dark ages? Cher or sumfing?'

As Brenstorme's idea of popular music is Elizabethan madrigals he's got no idea what this lout is on about.

'Don't you know who I am?'

'Nah.'

The lad couldn't care less about anything other than his bargain basement tat which had gone all itchy and scaly, and was only standing in because one of the library staff called in sick. He wished he had too every time he caught himself in the mirror.

In the end he googled the right pages of the timetable and printed them off, just to get rid of the wanker. Imagining he'd taught the world a bit of respect, Brenstorme marched off satisfied.

Shurleynott banged off a text to Percy.

He's normally a reliable source, but after a couple of days Percy wonders if he might have slipped up this time. 'Surely even Brenstorme could manage to get on a train without closing down the network?'

Monty looks at him meaningfully. 'Anyone who could

almost turn a small fire in Downing Street into all-out war with America…' he begins.

'Bugger and bollocks.' Percy's nervous. 'The Blusterham case left so many questions unanswered it's plausible Brenstorme's half-crazed antennae are still twitching. Just like him to stumble on the right track while heading in the wrong direction.'

Monty thinks about this from a literal point of view. 'We'd have heard by now if he'd stumbled onto a track in front of a train, wouldn't we?'

'If only,' Percy replies with a scowl.

CHAPTER EIGHT

Percy's antennae theory is lamentably accurate, while his belief that Shurelynott might have got his facts wrong is anything but. Brenstorme has a roundabout way of going about things, but he is on his way.

He stumbled on the problem thanks to his secretary, who was giggling at posts a Facebook friend in Cumbria was sending her about everyone going loopy. Wondering how the serious business of government could possibly be funny, he read what was on her screen.

The implications regarding Breezethwaite were obvious, and Brenstorme knew his duty.

'PM's a jolly busy chap so I won't trouble him at this stage,' he told the young woman, who was more interested in the magazine open on her desk. 'But this could be a terror plot by a rogue state trying to obliterate the human race, or, worse, dissident republican activity.

'Can't see how depriving Breezethwaite of its workforce would help the blighters paint more murals on the Shankill Road or put a green flag outside Belfast City Hall, but clearly there might be a clear and present danger.'

'Of course you're right, sir, as always,' the secretary said, marking her place in *Hello!* with one finger before looking up and nodding sympathetically. It didn't occur to Brenstorme to ask her to google timetables for trains to Carlisle.

*

Brenstorme's excited about the trip to Carlisle. Train rides have fascinated him since prep school, when he'd dream the local puffer was the Trans-Siberian Express or Royal Rajasthan on Wheels. Feeling eight years old and whistling a happy tune, he admires St Pancras Renaissance Hotel before heading into the station and jumping aboard.

Feeling less cheerful when the train pulls into Sheffield, he's in no mood to be told he should have set off from Euston.

'Now look here, my man,' he begins, confident his manner will bring the scruffy oik of a ticket inspector to heel. He's wrong.

'If that's your attitude, mate, you can fucking walk to Carlisle.'

Brenstorme stalks off and buys another ticket, but once again doesn't notice the annunciator board. After overnight stops in Cardiff then Glasgow, he reaches his destination several hundred pounds worse off. And pissed off, though he'd never say anything so vulgar.

Branch lines at rush hour. Pushing, shoving, standing room only, and disgusting food. Brenstorme can't believe it.

What's more, the right sort of train could have got him to the Far East in less time than it took this lot to manage a three-and-a-half hour journey.

'Stiff letter to *The Times* in this,' he tells a young man with a rucksack and Mohican hairstyle.

The lad is his country's leading exponent of classical glockenspiel, and would have understood if the man in the strange hat had hummed anything written by Beethoven. But as he doesn't speak English he merely smiles politely. Encouraged, Brenstorme gets his pen out.

'Sir. Stop. British Railways nothing short of British skulduggery. Stop. Privatise forthwith. Stop. All change? TIME for a change! Stop. Deplorable disservice. Stop. Stop at a point? Stop. Past point of no return. Stop. Stop this nonsense. Stop. Signed Brenstorme. B. Stop. CBE. Stop.'

Sir Bernard's rather pleased with this. He feels dashing it off on the back of a postcard in the style of the telegrams he wishes he could still send from the post office proves what a pretty pass things have reached. It's not seen that way at the paper.

The sub in charge of the letters page shows it to the editor with a grin. 'Funniest bit of green biro brigade bollocks ever, don't you think?'

'Sure is,' comes the reply. 'Publish it in full.'

'What?'

'You heard me.'

The editor rubs his hands together. He's convinced this is for real, and will expose Brenstorme for the nincompoop he is. He's been longing for revenge ever since his mate at MI5 let slip who'd caused everyone to go doolally at that drinks party of Percy's three years ago. It's been discreetly mulled over ever since, though no one can agree on the details.

'D'you think the head of the British civil service really never found out the railways were privatised in the nineties? Is that what living in an ivory tower does for you?'

The editor's questions get a sharp response from the earnest young intern with the frizzy hair and nose ring. Though she has no idea the railways were ever in public ownership she takes her politics extremely seriously.

'But that's terrible! How many elephants had to die to create a whole tower made of ivory? The cruelty! The waste of life! How would you like to be murdered, just for your teeth?'

The editor, who has a nasty feeling the root canal treatment he had last week didn't work and he's got another abscess forming finds the idea oddly appealing.

Brenstorme's journey from hell finally comes to an end. Exhausted but desperately grateful the station sign really does say Carlisle, he hobbles into the street and hails a cab.

'Where to, love?' Perfectly normal question, but if Brenstorme had noticed the female driver's skimpy clothing he might have phrased his answer differently.

'I have earned my comfort,' he purrs, 'kindly lead me to it.' The cabbie, who supplements her earnings with far better paid extracurricular activity, takes him at his word.

Whipping him off to a place that rents rooms by the hour, she winks at the receptionist and escorts him upstairs.

'Charming of you, dear lady, sleep is nature's gentle nurse,' Brenstorme says with genuine gratitude.

He's prepared to overlook the none-too-clean pink nylon pillows, cracked sink and dusty plastic flowers on the dressing table, but not what the young lady does next.

Spreading herself provocatively on the bed, she gets down to business. 'Well, Bernie baby, what can I do for you? Fellatio? Cunnilingus? Kissing's extra. So's unprotected.'

Sensing a fiendish blackmail plot, he lashes out with his shooting stick at the hidden cameras he's convinced are everywhere. Both bedside lamps, the overhead light and two glass-fronted display cabinets are shattered before Brenstorme hurls himself out of the closed window.

Lethal shards of glass fly over the tiny balcony onto the pavement below. A pensioner who gets one in the head later dies of septicaemia. The crowd gasps at the sight of a maniac leaping out from the first floor of a seedy boarding house.

For once Brenstorme's in luck. Instead of breaking his neck on the pavement he lands in the back of an open truck carrying soft manure. Police appeals for witness assistance produce no results as no one thought to jot down the truck's number. And, even better, his two-hour ride ends at a village near Breezethwaite.

*

When the driver pulls into the pub car park for his well-earned pint, Brenstorme clambers unnoticed out of the back, slips the fedora under his filthy coat and staggers up to the front door. The AA four-star logo is surely the answer to all his prayers.

'I wandered lonely as a cloud o'er vales and hills, but now I find a host of golden daffodils,' he murmurs at the receptionist, who doesn't understand a word he's saying and has a good mind to tell him to sling his hook. He may sound la-di-da, but he stinks.

Sir Bernard's Amex Corporate card tips the balance. 'Dat'll do dicely sir,' she says, holding a hand over her mouth and gripping her nose. 'Sir will be deeding a roob with a king-sized bathroob?' He nods and totters upstairs. She goes off to be sick.

When Brenstorme awakes, eight good soaks and nineteen dream-free hours later, he makes a to-do list. 1) Scrub fedora with lavatory cleaner. 2) Buy new coat. 3) Get rid of old one. 4) Tell the National Farmers' Union all animal waste must in future be deodorised. Especially if pigs have anything to do with it.

That letter goes in the bin, but the one to *The Times* does get printed, according to the editor's instructions. And when Percy stumbles on it he texts Shurleynott.

'The eejit has landed. Shit.'

He'll find out just how deeply he's in it when he learns the bastard's called in reinforcements. The new MI5 Director General knows Brenstorme's crazier than Kim Yong-un, but daren't ignore the threat of security breaches at Breezethwaite. Once again the operation is so hush-hush the agents must not know about one another.

*

Even before he knew Brenstorme was on his way, Percy was getting jittery. Though he's been trying to give Viv the impression he's not too bothered about Chancery running amok.

'All good this end, apart from Fuckwit doing what fuckwits do,' he tells her. 'Seems to think he can play god with mere mortals. He's got another think coming. Me and Monty will cast him out of his heaven. Bring him down to earth with a bump. On his head if he doesn't behave.'

Viv frowns but doesn't say much. She knows Percy too well to believe a word of it, but lets him prattle on.

'Daresay he thinks he can do what he likes when his Chinese chappies charge up. Well let me tell you – theirs not to reason why, theirs but to do and die.'

'Oh really? You're a sexy guy, Percy Penislow, but so was that dodgy Alan Clark. Remember him? Economical with the *actualité*?'

He squirms, knowing she's right. The call doesn't end happily, and when Viv tells Bakyt all about it she snorts. 'Silly person, Percy, all mouth and trousers sometimes.'

Viv tells her about a cartoon she once saw. 'A mother is holding her little child, who's saying "What will I do when I gwow up, Mummy?" Mummy's thought-bubble says "Don't be silly dear you're a boy, you'll never grow up."'

Bakyt can't help but smile, but both know what the other's thinking. They'll have to go up and see for themselves what exactly is going on. And to make sure the boys don't try and pull the wool over their eyes they'll go in disguise.

'Seems a lot of bother, but I don't see any way round it,' Viv complains. 'At some point we've got to have it out with them face to face. Besides, it's perfectly possible Fuckwit's hacking our phones. Now I've met the man I wouldn't put anything past him.'

'I want put stake in him. And shut in wooden box,' Bakyt answers, baring her teeth and vibrating. 'Kazakhs and Transylvanians natural soulmate, you understand.'

Viv shoots her an anxious glance, remembering that expensive dinner party. Bakyt is the gentlest and cleverest woman she knows, but, as her dear Granny used to say, 'There's nowt as queer as folk'.

Bakyt's eyes focus quite quickly, however, and she sounds normal again. 'I have leave coming at university, so OK to travel. But you?'

Viv worries about Trudi, but is reassured when she broaches the subject and discovers the child has learned yet another new phrase. 'Bug-a-bug-a-bug-a-off, Mummy.' Charming! Still, Fang will teach her some manners, even if Nanny can't.

As the two women barely fill a 32A bra they can easily pass as men. Dungarees will be perfect, with cloth caps to cover their hair. Bakyt thinks this is a hoot. 'We blend perfectly, all country cloddle-hoppies dress so, yes?'

They'll train it up and hire a tractor to get around at the other end. It'll be more or less invisible, and faster than the 2CV.

CHAPTER NINE

The elderly man in Bakyt and Viv's compartment was already in a state about Brenstorme's letter to *The Times*. And when they start practising deep voices and thigh-slapping he'd have got up and pulled the emergency plunger if he hadn't recently had a hip replacement.

He settles for harrumphing several times and spluttering. 'Country's gone to the dogs. Or the bitches. Can't tell 'em apart these days.'

'Boys got balls, girls silly sissies,' Bakyt squeals, giving Viv a manly clap on the shoulder.

The old bloke's grumpiness has cheered her up no end. She gives him a huge smacking kiss and loves how he perks up. 'Must be public school man,' she whispers. 'No way he straight.'

The mood changes when they get out at Carlisle and pick up the local rag. It leads on an epidemic of insanity in the area around Breezethwaite and the suspected arson-related deaths of three of its employees.

'Wish Percy was as good at putting out fires as he is at starting them,' Viv hisses. She sounds fierce, but wants to cry.

At least the hired vehicle is present and correct, and trundling round the village close to Breezethwaite they can't believe their eyes. 'Dear Simone-Sitrouenne,' Viv sighs at the sight of the shed-like vehicle outside the pub/hotel with the AA four-star logo, the Nuclear Arms.

They discuss footie in loud voices as they stride into the bar, slapping their thighs extra hard.

'Evenin' all.' The landlord, a jovial man with a round belly and ruddy face greets all his customers that way, whether he likes the look of them or not. He refers to upright citizens as 'people'. Others are classified as 'individuals'.

The poor chap's never been the same since he got bopped on the head by an individual he was apprehending during a traffic incident that turned nasty. He knows he was once a police officer but is hazy on details, so his dear old dad jogged his memory with a box set he got on Amazon of his favourite TV crime series, *Dixon of Dock Green*.

As a result, ex-PC Ploed is a stickler for the old way of doing things. He isn't sure about the newcomers, but books them in anyway and inquires if they'll be eating in tonight.

'Provided there's Sky Sports in the restaurant,' shouts Viv. She pretends to be furious there isn't. 'You'd better have something with loads of meat and no vegetables.'

Provisionally placing them in the 'individuals' category, Mr Ploed says he'll see what he can do. The sudden influx of visitors is welcome, but he would prefer nice normal families.

The man with the bleached fedora is definitely an individual because he sent the caviar back, complaining the blackberry jam was off. The gent with the topper also blotted his copybook when he read the sign indicating the proprietor was Mr Ploed and said just the wrong thing.

'How do, Mr Plod.'

'I'm of Huguenot descent, my name is Ploed, as in herd.'

'Or as in turd?' Percy couldn't resist the joke, though he had a feeling Mr Whatever-his-name-was wouldn't appreciate it.

He didn't. Any more than Percy's sweeping into the bar and

exposing a stupid kid's toy in his belt. His explanation, that a cloak without a dagger looks ridiculous, was maddening. As was his way of growling at the sight of the freak in the fedora.

*

Anxious not to miss a syllable of their menfolk's conversation, Viv and Bakyt take a table close by and pretend to be fascinated by the décor. A mix of fake Tudor and 1970s kitsch, it's pre-retro but neither vintage nor classical. Actually, it's vile.

Nostalgic images labelled 'Windscale Fire 1957' stand out, because they're so odd. The blaze took place within the reactor. From outside there was nothing to see.

Still, the disaster caused Britain's worst radioactive contamination and some say at least two hundred cancer deaths. Changing the name to Sellafield didn't eradicate the memory and the site's bosses steer clear of the Nuclear Arms, grateful it's not too close by.

Breezethwaite's bosses don't care. They've never heard of Windscale and guess the reference to something going up in smoke commemorates the Great Fire of London, put there to go with the Tudor theme. Being American, they don't know they've got the wrong century.

Percy and Monty hardly notice the pictures, but wonder why the young men close by seem to have their eye on them. They notice these yokels have lily-white hands, and worry about how attractive they are. Percy mutters something about not going there.

The farm boys, meanwhile, would both love to reach across and undo the men's flies under the table. The dark glasses really do it for Bakyt, even though they do look ridiculous indoors.

Keeping a straight face is as hard as keeping up the silly voices, and they so want to ask Percy and Monty to speak up a bit. But they pick up enough to work out what to do next.

Viv plans to crush the pink Caddy with the tractor, if she can bring herself to do such a thing. Bakyt's going to disguise herself as herself and go back to Breezethwaite, to find out whether they've got an influx of new workers.

The men continue talking in hushed tones even after the farm blokes have taken themselves off, though when Brenstorme drops by for a nightcap Percy growls. Monty stamps on his foot, which is annoying.

'You get more like bloody Biff every day,' he snarls.

'Reminds you where the ground is.' Monty does it again but more gently this time.

They agree things are getting out of hand and the sooner they fess up the better. Though when they turn in they're both surprised to read emails from their wives hoping they're being good boys so far from home. Viv also tells Percy pretty young men are all very well, but he's not to go back to his old ways.

Perish the thought, he thinks, though there was something about that lad on the next table that reminded him of someone. He's bloody sexy, in his boyish way. To ease his conscience he takes a photo of the Shard and emails it to Viv, telling her he wishes he could give her one.

He's pleased the little fellow sprung so quickly to life, but horrified that might have something to do with the yokel. His first night with Viv crosses his mind and the Shard shrinks to a bungalow.

Unbeknown to him, Monty's going through much the same process next door.

In the room they're sharing down the passage, Viv and Bakyt howl with laughter and have to cover up their mouths with pillows. They snuggle up together for companionship.

Back in Cornwall the nanny's trying to give herself the time of day without the usual assistance. 'Just not the same,' she grumbles to herself, 'without something to get me started.' She tries playing Rachmaninoff on Viv's piano, but it's no good, tinkling ivories isn't tinkling chandeliers. She switches off the vibrator and the light, in that order.

At least little Trudi is sleeping peacefully. Fang's amused her for hours savaging the bobbly bits round the canopy overhanging her cot and she's knackered.

*

At breakfast next morning Percy and Monty overhear Brenstorme grumbling on the phone at the Director General of MI5. 'Where are my agents? Bit jolly thick of you. Haven't seen hide nor hair of them.'

Because he hasn't got the hang of the mobile he's got it on speakerphone, and the exasperated voice at the other end booms out. 'Wake up, old boy, we employ secret agents here. If you could bloody well see them they wouldn't be bloody secret, would they?'

Brenstorme harrumphs and Percy wants to hold his head in his hands, but can't because of the topper. He also wants to stab Brenstorme with his plastic dagger but can't because Monty gets him in an armlock in time.

Glancing out of the window, they notice one of the farm chappies manoeuvring the tractor out of the car park, giving Simone-Sitrouenne a little nudge in passing. Monty spots the glint in Percy's eye and tells him to bloody well behave himself. It's his guilty conscience speaking.

The two of them are unusually civilised, but still men. Sharing secrets doesn't come naturally. Sharing a bed would have been out of the question.

*

Viv sets off to seek and destroy pink Eldorado coupes with bullet holes in them. Waste of time as Chancery's gone to Carlisle

213

to pick up the first batch of new Breezethwaite recruits. The American boss is expecting them, so when Bakyt shows up he's got all the answers.

'Bin a coupla hits lately, lost a whole heap o' guys, but we back on the doggoned highway now, yee-haw. First three dudes steppin' right thru that door any moment, man. Sure cookin' on gas, lady.'

So Chancery's plan is working out. Bakyt is not happy. Besides, gender bending was already a strain. She could do without this person calling her 'man' and 'lady' in the same breath.

CHAPTER TEN

Bakyt would have been even more unhappy to learn the plan is also working out at the Chinese end. Fyok Yu is overseeing operations and the team of plastic surgeons is proud of its miraculous ability to turn out identikit Westerners.

The operations have psychological effects. Several married men sue for divorce, convinced the new look will make them irresistible to women. The single ones head straight for pick-up joints and nightclubs, but hear the same words again and again, to the effect totally vile.

Fyok Yu finds this hilarious, but Hon Ki insists it's bad for morale, and emphasises his point by giving him a karate chop in the forehead and sticking a finger in each eye. The team at the clinic fit him a new pair in no time, which look all right but aren't very good for actually looking through.

This creates a problem when he gets back to the job of organising a voice coach. Misreading the map, he thinks Breezethwaite is not in the north of England but somewhere at the shitty end of Glasgow.

As a result the guys with the face transplants might as well be Nazi paratroopers when they arrive, though at least the Brits would understand '*Sieg heil mein führer*'. 'That dug vom pure gies me the boke' does not tell Hillter's aunt they don't like her chips.

There's also suspicion deep in the Cumbrian psyche of anything Scottish, thanks to the centuries-old tradition of border raids. They were just as fond of ravaging the Scottish Lowlands, but don't count that bit.

*

For the new arrivals from China the shocks start the moment they get out of the station at Carlisle. They spot the enormous car with fins they've been told to look out for but can't believe the colour. Also the burly man with the eyepatch and pinstriped suit in the driver's seat doesn't even notice them. He's too busy oiling the barrel of a Tommy gun.

Praying the weapon is to save their lives not end them, they tiptoe up to the vehicle and kowtow to its owner. 'Ye'r th' jimmy we're keekin fur. Whit like?'

Chancery releases the safety catch and points the gun at them through the open window. He has no idea they're saying he's the man they're looking for, and how is he?

They try another tack, only to be misheard. 'We ur fae China.'

'Vagina? Wot you fuckin' on abaht? Fuckin' vagina. You fink I'm a fuckin' pimp? You fuckin' watch it.' By now the door's open, he's waving the gun around and the three of them are cowering on the ground, whimpering 'China! China! China!'

The penny drops, and Chancery calms down. 'Oh. China. Right. Why didn't ya fuckin' say so? Get in da fuckin' motor.'

They do, but on their own terms. Because homosexuality was regarded as mental illness back home until it was decriminalised only a few years ago, they insist on hiding in the boot. Chancery shrugs and opens it, thinking at least they'll be able to breathe.

Clambering in, they wonder if all pink cars in England have bullet holes.

Chancery thinks about them on the journey. He can't tell them apart or understand a word they say, but for some reason nicknames them Jock One, Jock Two and Jock Strap. He likes that, and what might lay behind it. Come to think of it, be fun to give them all a go.

For now though the priority's to avoid communication problems when they get to Breezethwaite. He gives them their Brit-friendly CVs, put together by an actual Brit and tells them not to say too much.

The Jocks remember not to bow, but telling the executive interviewing them his establishment is 'well barry' gets them nowhere. Not knowing 'barry' is Scottish slang for 'good', he tells them his name is not Barry but Chuck.

They get the word 'name', forget to not bow and tell him they're called Jimmie, Jummie, and Jemmie. They're proud of how well they've learned their lessons from the voice coach and grin in a way that troubles Chuck.

'Shucks, guys, you limey bastards got me by the nuts,' he announces, reaching for his bottle of Kentucky Straight Bourbon.

Fearing the worst, Chancery intervenes. 'Listen, Chuck, my mates 'ere got all da right qualifications, right? It's all written dahn 'ere. See?'

Though he looks, Chuck does not see. His visual dyslexia causes words to move, change shape and sometimes even to slide off the page. It's bad enough admitting this to his doctor, to colleagues or prospective employees it's a no-no.

Only one thing for it then. He squints at the three complete strangers who could blow Breezethwaite sky high, takes a hefty swig of the Bourbon and hires them.

It's getting dark by the time they leave, so Jimmie, Jummie and Jemmie feel brave enough to ride in the back seat of the Caddy. They're pleased they've now got jobs, less so about the way Chancery's looking at them in the rear view mirror.

Viv gets to the Nuclear Arms minutes after Chancery, and is furious to see the Caddy occupying nearly three spaces in the car park. After a day's hunting there's her quarry just sat there. The cheek of it.

Eight wasted hours in a noisy, smelly tractor can bring on bloodlust as well as a headache. Suddenly she's fearless Toad of Toad Hall. Revving the engine, she prepares to pulverise. There'll be nothing left but the steering wheel she'll still be holding.

Right now she's got no qualms about smashing up the contraption she's hired, but dear little Simone-Sitrouenne is another matter. Because the Caddy's so close it's not possible to take out one without the other. Toad turns into Tantalus, condemned by the gods to never quite get there. Reminds Viv of that first night with Percy.

She's so fed up when she steps into the bar that she forgets the boy bit and asks for a cuddle. Bakyt needs one too after Breezethwaite. By now she's changed back into man's costume, and the three Jocks gawp at the wee laddies with falsetto voices.

Mr Ploed hears them say words to the effect that they don't really approve of homosexuality, any more than he does, incidentally. Though he's not to know the short journey from Breezethwaite to the Nuclear Arms was long enough to convince them they're no more than fresh meat in Chancery's eyes, or, rather, eye.

All day long the ex-clergyman's been wishing he could see more clearly. He originally splashed out for patches to cover both the twenty-twenty left eye and the short-sighted other one, and it was obvious he'd go for the more practical of the two. But Caligula narrowed his options by eating the bloody thing.

This doesn't make driving dangerous as the Eldorado coupe steamrollers all other cars out of the way. But it does prevent Chancery from seeing through Percy and Monty's disguises, even at close range. He assumes there's a fancy dress party going on somewhere, and the bloke in the cloak is going as Dracula.

*

It's a weird evening in the Nuclear Arms. Viv and Bakyt lusting after the men who're feeling guilty and confused about sharing the vibe, Chancery wanting a foursome with his Chinese charges who're praying for the end of Western civilisation, and Mr Ploed thinking it's already arrived.

He's sensed the atmosphere and questions the term 'individual', as most of them seem to want to merge, one way or another. No nice end of episode homily for this lot, then. Hardly standard practice at Dock Green, but he'd like to give them all a good kicking in the cells.

And there's the maniac with the fedora, always grumbling. If it's not the food it's that strange growling sound he claims to hear every time the man in the topper appears. He's also very cross about secret agents, more so when he mistakenly believes he's met them.

'Bit jolly thick of you not to just make yourselves known you know,' he says to the three Jocks, who're clearly agents wearing prosthetic face masks.

'Awa' and bile yer heid.' Jock Strap's answer doesn't tell Brenstorme he'd better boil his head, but his tone does.

'Cabinet Secretaries are a higher civil service grade than spies, I'll have you know. We get carpets in our offices.' Handy for sweeping things under, Brenstorme thinks but doesn't say.

The clones jabber amongst themselves. Brenstorme thinks they might as well be talking Chinese, then realises they are, even though his knowledge of the language is incomplete. He once used what he thought was the correct term for 'gentleman' to describe an ambassador at an embassy reception, only to be told later it translated as 'asshole'. Anglo-Sino relations

219

came under strain and it was decided he was not cut out for diplomacy.

Possibly it's the memory of that humiliation that causes him to lose his temper, or maybe it's simply the cumulative effect of the day. Either way, he's ready to step as far out of character as Viv on her Caddy killing mission.

Removing the fedora, turning it upside down and gripping it in both hands, Brenstorme brings it down on with all his might on Jock Strap's forehead. Three times. Boing! Boing! Boing! Mr Ploed can't believe it as the man slumps to the ground. Nor can Chancery.

Percy takes a liking to the man for the first time. But, humming under his breath 'Oh, oh, oh what a lovely war', Monty half slips the Glock out of its holster and releases the safety catch.

Chancery goes further. Drawing the Derringer and aiming it at the Cabinet Secretary's now unprotected head, he shouts in his best Texan drawl, 'Reach for the sky.' When Brenstorme does as he's told, Jocks One and Two headbutt him in the chest.

Because normal people in English hotels tend not to wear body armour, they won't realise their mistake until they black out. Knowing Brenstorme's secret, Monty makes a mental note never to headbutt a brick wall.

As a woman, Viv's more interested in the immediate and practical than the hypothetical and unlikely. She positions herself between Chancery and Percy in the way Monty would have done to protect the Prime Minister. In the event Chancery's so astonished he drops his gun.

And Bakyt? For all her education and sophistication, there lurks in her DNA the Kazakh warrior instinct from the days of the Mongol Empire. And the sight of all this violence and weaponry unleashes urges. Of a different kind from those she's already displayed.

Everyone stands amazed, apart from those lying on the floor, obviously, when the farmer rips off his cap to reveal a neatly coiffed black bob and leaps onto a table. She's bellowing like a chained bear.

The war dance is nuttier than the guttural lowing at Percy's dinner party, and the shepherd's crook she's been carrying around for days doubles up as a spear. She doesn't throw it, but Chancery and Brenstorme duck every time she looks like she's about to.

Monty can't believe such a small person can make such a large noise. But, police training kicking in again, he sneaks up on Chancery and whacks him over the head with the butt of his pistol. After dragging the bodies outside, he brushes his palms together and bobs up and down, toes pointing outwards.

Giving the half-salute policemen used to when they only had bikes and whistles, he does the Central Casting bobby-on-the-beat voice. 'All in a day's work, sir.'

That does it. Instead of an individual, he becomes a person, with a new fan.

CHAPTER ELEVEN

Mr Ploed's so delighted to meet a fellow Met vet he's prepared to overlook the altered sleeping arrangements and the racket the couples make. The other guests will have to lump it.

After an exhausting night the couples flirt outrageously over breakfast, despite the women becoming men again. Brenstorme, whose sleep was constantly interrupted by an apparent succession of earthquakes, can't understand why Mr Ploed keeps winking at him knowingly, instead of showing him the door for what he did last night.

The transgender agricultural person with the demented tendencies, he notes, is still there, along with the other country yokel. Why they've suddenly struck up such a friendship with the two men in fancy dress is beyond him.

He also wonders what happened to the gunman with the peculiar hairstyle and the three rude spies. To help him concentrate he asks the waitress for six fried eggs, three sunny side up and the others down, served with strawberries and tartare sauce.

Normally that order would have been a chucking out offence. But not today. Specially for Monty Mr Ploed's put on his favourite muzak, the *Dock Green* theme song. 'Maybe it's because I'm a

Londoner' repeats endlessly on a long cassette tape. It's fuzzy because the player's so old, so he turns it up louder than usual.

As a result Brenstorme can't hear a word the foursome on the table opposite are saying. He's cross about this. They aren't.

Exasperating though this tune becomes after the eighteenth replay, they find it convenient. Especially Viv, who got an email during the night telling her the Bashars really haven't given up on the oil contracts they were trying to blackmail Percy into signing off.

Though it's Tiddledick's turn now, their means are as close to identical as their ends.

After Percy and Monty have demolished their full English and their wives have finished toying with their smoked salmon and scrambled eggs, Viv dabs her elegant little mouth and starts talking. Within seconds Percy's gripped. He wonders how anyone that courageous can also be so clever, not to mention horny.

He slips his hand under the table to seek out her flies. Annoyingly, these bloody dungarees don't seem to have any, but she gets the message and winks at him.

Once again it's the girlie heart-to-heart thing that's done the trick. Percy thinks about his gossipy chatter with Shurelynott. It's often indiscreet, but not intimate, unlike Viv's correspondence with Belinda Blusterham's Albanian former slave.

In his last email to her he promised all the help he could give after what she'd done for him. She couldn't think of anything offhand, but stayed in touch with Viv because she needed sound advice about a young man who'd caught her eye.

Thanks to her Eastern European language skills and instinct for black propaganda she's brilliant at teasing out the real meaning of titbits passed on from GCHQ. The Foreign Office minister she's answerable to has been boasting about her, largely to annoy colleagues, and nicknamed her Miss Moneypenny.

The chap she fancies comes under a different minister, but

when they had a watery coffee together in the canteen, he told her he was 'fwightfully pwoud' to meet her. Viv smiles as she quotes the message as spelt. His speech defect is highly noticeable.

'Don't tell me, he's a Middle Eastern specialist?' Percy can see where this might be leading. He gives up on his second attempt at locating the flies and sits up, all attention.

'Who's a clever boy, then?' Viv still enjoys her husband's mental agility, though in recent times the bodily bit's had the edge.

'Seems Miss Moneypenny's found her man. She says she finds his dropped Rs as sweet as his tight arse, I quote. They knew they'd fallen in love when he didn't mind her saying he was "wavishingly pwetty". He told her she'd got "glorwious bweasts".'

Percy and Monty snigger. Bakyt looks puzzled, but smiles when Monty reaches under the table and pinches her bottom.

'So different sections of the Foreign Office are actually talking to one another? Has to be a first time for everything.' Percy's thinking about how often he wanted to reshuffle the chronically uninformed Foreign Secretary, ideally to somewhere like Bergen-Belsen.

'Well,' she continues, 'Miss Moneypenny was so grateful to me for telling her to go for it she ignored the Official Secrets Act, and tipped me off about intel the wavishingly pwetty boy had, concerning the Bashars.

'Ever since he failed to spot in advance the brothers were coming to Chequers for that little shindig of yours, Percy, he's kept a sharp lookout for them. Apparently he thinks having to say "fwightfully sowwy" to two successive Pwime Ministers would destwoy his caweer.'

Viv smiles at the reaction this provokes. Cruelty is not in her nature, but she has an impish sense of humour.

'He told her the Bashars have been offewwing pwivate island bweaks to the Chancellor of the Exchequer and his Permanent Secwetawwy. And they're twying the party funding twick too.'

Percy snorts, but shuts up when his wife tells of another email conversation she's been having, with, of all people, Tiddledick's wife. It started when Fanny courteously congratulated her on the birth of little Trudi, but added a second line.

'She said the baby should be taught at the earliest opportunity to hunt its own food, starting perhaps with the cat. So I advised her to house-train Ponsomby by putting a clothes peg on his willy. One outrageous suggestion deserves another.'

'And?' At Prime Minister's questions Percy used to calm his nerves by picturing Tiddledick heaving and straining on the lavatory. This is so much better.

'Next day she told me the experiment was a great success as she never realised she had such hidden depths.'

Bakyt squirms. So do Percy and Monty, for different but related reasons.

'Time was I wouldn't have found Fanny funny. But I've opened up now.' Viv smirks at Percy.

'When I asked how Ponsomby kept it on while getting it off, Fanny said "K Y do you ask? Always room for one more up the aisle."'

'That did it. We've opened a kind of back channel, which I'm glad isn't your bag any more, Percy dear.' He winces at the thought of his near miss with the farmer's boy who's talking to him now. But she carries on before he has time to deny anything.

'I told her Ponsomby needs to watch his behind or find the Bashars rooting round there.'

Percy gapes at his wife. Bakyt's unexpected qualities have nothing on hers. It's like discovering she's had polygamous relationships with an entire pod of dolphins.

He sits back and puts his fingers together in a gesture Biff would have recognised. 'You know, Viv, you should have been Prime Minister instead of me. We'd still be in Number Ten.'

'Certainly wouldn't be in the bloody mess we are now.' Her voice has suddenly got an edge to it. 'Anyway, role reversal wouldn't have worked because I can do numbers. You, you have to take your boots off to count past three.'

'We could have run the show together, like William and Mary.' Percy's on the defensive now.

'Or Pinky and Perky,' Monty chips in, anxious to keep things sweet.

Percy's irritation goes as quickly as it came. A pause, and he speaks softly. 'When we first met I thought your forehead was a trifle high. It needed to be, to fit in such a big brain.'

Viv blushes. Yes, actually blushes. She didn't think Percy could make her do that after all these years, but it seems he can. Once in a while. She strokes his hand under the table and tries to sound calm and collected.

'I think you'll all accept it was the best thing to tip off Tiddledick, now we know what the Bashars are up to. And the sooner we can get them off our backs the better. Agreed?'

Percy and Bakyt nod, but Monty clears his throat. Noisily, several times.

'Well?' Viv raises an eyebrow. 'What is it?'

'Er, how can I put this? You see, the fact is the Bashars asked if I'd give their guys some extra training. And now we know there's loads more Chinese fellers on the way I thought... that's to say...'

'Oh Jesus,' Percy mutters. 'Don't tell me...'

'Afraid so. They're arriving tonight.'

*

By the time Jocks One, Two and Strap regain consciousness, Chancery's already come to. He drove them away in the Caddy, and a mile or so down the road commandeered an agricultural building by smashing his way in. Even with the patch he couldn't miss a barn door.

Licking their wounds and worrying they'll be licked all over, his happily married unhappy band of brothers set up a rota to keep him at bay.

Come the morning, thanks to a bruised ego as well as severe contusions to the skull, Chancery was not polite to the farmer who owned the barn.

'Go fuck yer mother, yerself, yer granny, and yer pigs.' This didn't go down well, but after a dozen rounds from the Tommy gun the man put down his pitchfork, piled up the twelve dead chickens and started fixing the door.

When Chancery learned Jocks Four to Thirty were already on the plane, the famer, whose name is Giles, mentioned his cousin's business offering country getaway holidays in gypsy caravans. Unusually, he swore on his mother's grave, some were available right now. Sorted.

Chancery's also taken with the gay rights posters everywhere, even covering the pot of roadkill the man lives on. Unusually for a farmer, Giles is a big willy in the local LGBT community.

When Chancery offers a hundred quid a day for sole use of the farmhouse the two become bum chums. A shag pile carpet seems fitting for the first time. The chicken sandwiches they share afterwards are nice, apart from the crunchy fucking bullets.

*

Unaware he's got problems up the road, Monty's grateful for a tip-off he gets from Mr Ploed.

The call he overheard was delayed as Brenstorme didn't realise the phone with buttons A and B was only for decoration. Pressing button B got him four old-style pennies, but putting them in the slot did not get him a line. Nothing for it but the mobile, still on speakerphone.

'Now look here, old boy, that rabble of spies your chaps sent were jolly rude. Two of them tried to kill me. Also there's an armed maniac on the loose, and a deranged woman with a spear.'

Three hundred miles away in Marsham Street SW1, the Home Secretary sighed with an infinite weariness. 'All right, all right, I'll get the Flying Squad on the case, if I must.'

Monty doesn't admit a bunch of self-important plain-clothed dicks is the last thing he needs, as Mr Ploed is clearly fonder of the force more than he is. 'Thank god for the thin blue line,' he announces, wishing he could rub it out altogether.

At least the Bashar beat-up boys will soon be here. Best get them on the jiu-jitsu mat pronto. When he mentions this to Mr Ploed he spots a gleam in his eye and hopes he isn't cooking something up.

The reunion is tearful, at least on the Bashar side, and rather touching. Competing to be first to put their arms round Monty, they proudly show him pictures of their wives and kids. Mr Ploed eyes them suspiciously as they lumber about in their heavy military boots. But when he spots how fond they are of Monty he reclassifies them as 'persons'.

He books all ten of them in, with a few curt words for punters who'd already got the rooms. 'Scarper if you know what's good for you.' When he threatens them with a clip round the ear they decide he's as loopy as everyone else round here and they're better off out of it.

Mr Ploed promises Monty a nice little surprise tonight, and puts a large sign outside the bar. 'Private function. Everyone else can hop it.'

To soften the blow he scribbles at the bottom 'Evenin' all', leaving the ladies who'd planned their hen party at the Nuclear Arms anxious as well as confused. The male stripper they've booked for tonight is very difficult to get hold of, more's the pity, most of them think.

CHAPTER TWELVE

Mr Ploed is satisfied with this evening's arrangements. The judo club was happy to lend him their mat in return for free booze for a month. The gesture's not as generous as it sounds because they're all fitness freaks and only drink tap water.

He's inclined to refuse admittance to the three individuals who arrive separately wearing identical trilby hats. But when they each produce identical pistols and suggest he changes his tune he does so. Hardware like that? Must be friends of Monty's.

Later he gets the same treatment from a gaggle of guys with loud mouths and large feet. But, spotting the tell-tale bulges under their left armpits, he gives one of his knowing winks and lets them in too.

Carlisle airport has never had so many helicopters showing up on the same day, or seen so many shifty-looking characters getting out of them. But the control tower staff think it's fun darting out and taking selfies with them. There are several fatal accidents.

After dinner everyone awaits Monty's martial display. By now the men in trilbies have sidled up to Brenstorme separately, shown their MI5 ID and warned him not to trust other men in trilbies. He's also had the Detective Chief Inspector in charge of the Flying Squad team telling him not to approach suspicious individuals and to keep his head down.

All Brenstorme cares about is keeping it covered, but he's vaguely reassured. No one's tried to kill him, yet, though the lunatic in dark glasses looks like he could with one flick of his wrist.

He looks vaguely like some chappie lurking in Number Ten years ago, but thanks to his civil service training Brenstorme is better on names than faces. If anyone had said the words 'Sergeant White' to him he'd have reeled off record of service, qualifications, marital status, address, vaccinations and date of birth.

The Bashar boys take their bashing bravely, even the one whose arm's only just out of plaster. Bakyt starts rocking back and forth ominously, but controls herself with an effort when Viv places a towel on her head. Years ago it was the best way to shut the budgie up.

Mr Ploed is not happy to see the men who should be setting an example to the public placing bets on the contestants and squabbling about odds. He thinks police officers should behave with decorum, even in plain clothes.

The secret agents try to mingle with the cops, but their posh accents and way of not looking at one another mark them out. Percy pulls Viv's sleeve, points at them and gives them a wave. They scowl at him and pretend not to notice, a self-cancelling tactic.

*

Suddenly it's as though the building's evaporated and god's just stepped out of the sky. Everyone's transfixed by the hunk in sequins striding majestically through the door and pressing a button on the miniature sound system attached to his G-string.

Distracted by the opening bars of 'The Stripper', Monty

takes his only hit of the evening. Bakyt rises to her feet, rips off her cloth cap and flings her head back. It's not clear whether she plans to enter the spirit of the dance or avenge her man.

She has no time to do either, as the unexpected visitor sees she's a woman dressed as a man and assumes everyone else is as well. Sticking his cock in the Detective Chief Inspector's face does not go down well with the lads, or the Bashar boys.

The secret agents, all public school men, are more understanding. For the first and last time they're a team. Drawing their pistols, they command everyone to back off or die.

But the Bashar boys whip out neat little folding stock AK-47's from under their fatigues and take surprisingly steady aim. Monty's impressed. So are the MI5 men, judging by how quickly they dive for cover.

With the first volley Mr Ploed produces his notebook, licks the end of his pencil, and begins a tally of breakages. He's not sure who to bill for the smashed bottles of brandy, whisky, gin and sherry, plus assorted Toby jugs, as all combatants are friends of Monty's. That'll be worked out in the morning, assuming he lives long enough to see it.

Monty makes sure he does by leaping on the bar and bellowing in his best Regimental Sergeant Major voice. 'Squad... Cease... firing! Squad... Shoulder... Umms!' He's pleased it works as he's in the direct line of fire. Not that there'd have been any pain, at six hundred rounds per minute per gun.

To calm the men down he gives them twenty minutes' close order drill, concluding with barked instruction. 'Stand at... Ease! Stand easy, lads.' The Flying Squad guys, mesmerised, forget all about the stripper cowering under a table.

When Monty leads him out they hear the squawking in the Half Life free house next door and guess that's where the hen party went. The hunk girds his loincloth for another go, but is so traumatised he can't get it up.

The bride-to-be sets out to cure his erectile dysfunction.

Several breathless hours later she sends her fiancé a text. 'Wedding's off, darling, I found love. Mmmm.'

There's a happy ending for the MI5 men too. While Monty was taming his troops they stole away, separately, to a nearby farmhouse, where they stumbled on an orgy.

Chancery gave his new recruits the eye, best he could do, and the unmarried ones were so relieved anyone would still look at him they discovered their inner slut. He remembered a line from the Three Musketeers movie. 'All for one and one for all.' Yesss…

Farmer Giles was put out as he's a sensitive soul and thought he and Chancery had something special. The MI5 men too are troubled, in case these guys are the enemy. They get over it.

*

The Flying Squad guys enjoy hunting out chambermaids to proposition, while the Bashar boys lay out sleeping bags on their bedroom floors. Viv and Bakyt have more fun on their husbands.

In the morning Mr Ploed quizzes Bakyt about her husband's chums and is so taken aback by her obviously low opinion of them that he feels it his duty to investigate their rooms. But the Kalashnikovs convince him not to take her advice and spit on them.

The shagged-out couples hold a council of war over breakfast. 'On two fronts? Always a dangerous proposition,' Percy suspects. It's decided Monty's muscle is needed here, while he and Viv head south and do something about the Bashar brothers. They're not clear what.

Bouncing along the M6, they opt for a small and carefully targeted survey about attitudes to party funding, unexpected approaches to constituency offices and the law. Only local Conservative Party chairpersons are being polled.

Their calculation is that Tiddledick probably will have acted on the warning Viv passed on to Fanny about the Bashars meddling with ministers, but not the party funding problem. Cabinet colleagues are easily sorted, but he wouldn't take on the grassroots without proof.

Viv's London office gets the questionnaires out immediately, and by the time Simone-Sitrouenne finally ambles back to Cornwall there's a sprinkling of surprisingly frank responses.

Offers of support to Conservative associations usually stop at promises to serve the cucumber sandwiches at garden parties, but not now. 'Something fishy going on,' Percy mutters. 'The Bashars are casting the net wide, as well as tickling the trout.'

He'll drop in on these guys as himself, a journalist seeking truth about hard-pressed political parties surviving at grassroots level. Some may be surprised to receive a visit from a former Prime Minister, but many won't even recognise him.

The Tories took Percy's seat at the election and the party chair is willing to talk. Viv asks Percy to pop into the supermarket on the way, and Nanny glances up at the chandelier and wonders if he wouldn't mind awfully picking up some K-Y jelly.

She and Fang have been wonderful pretend parents this last week or so. Every time little Trudi escaped the cat pretended she was a giant mouse and captured her. The child loved it when Nanny got scared. She'd cheer her up by licking her face and calling her 'silli-bludi-moo'.

Clutching his shopping list from Viv and Nanny's heavily underlined add-on, Percy wonders how professional he looks in Simone-Sitrouenne, and in the end parks it round the corner from the Con club. Colonel Huffington-Splutterage isn't big on laughs, a Tory chairman thing.

His ruddy complexion says as much about blood pressure as years of service in the Orient, and the red and blue Royal Artillery tie clashes perfectly with his green and orange checked suit, as does the yellow and white striped shirt.

Percy tries to introduce himself to the peppery old bastard but is immediately interrupted.

'Now see here, reporter chappie, we didn't win the war to have scruffy oiks like you messing the place up. Scribbling and scrabbling and poking your nose in where you're not wanted.'

The impression that Colonel Huffington-Splutterage is not from the party's liberal wing is confirmed by the rant that follows, aimed at anyone not of pure English yeoman stock. He concludes with a salvo directed at whoever it was who's recently written to offer financial assistance. 'Some Johnny Foreigner or other', to use his words.

Stomping off, presumably to get another snifter, he leaves Percy to find his own way out. Also, in his careless and sodden way, he's left the offending letter on his desk. It's beautifully Bashar.

'Dear fine and loyal servant to the jolly old crown,

Our Ponsomby's a corker of a fellow and deserves a gay old time running the sceptred isle. Dashed difficult keeping the worker down. Wouldn't know their place if it were served up in their beastly humble pies. Nil desperandum, Gurkha gold to the rescue, what?'

Percy isn't surprised to learn an identical pitch has been made to loads of other local parties, and that quite a few have taken up the offer.

He's no idea if Huffington-Splutterage even knew overseas donations happen to be illegal. Or whether the man had the faintest who he was.

CHAPTER THIRTEEN

Percy returns to a hero's welcome. Nanny's frightfully glad he's remembered her shopping and little Trudi's so pleased he's home she runs up the grassy path to greet him.

Her display of filial affection was thwarted by Fang springing out of a lavender bush and bringing her to the ground in a catty rugby tackle. But the thought was there.

Viv is pleased Percy's got his entire conversation with Huffington-Splutterage on tape, as it tallies with other responses she's received. Several confirm there's a new revenue stream, but add it's all pukka so would she kindly mind minding her own business.

Though Percy isn't a double-crossing kind of guy he is tempted to keep shtum for a while to see if the Bashars can possibly bring down the Tories and give Labour another crack of the whip. But Viv puts her foot down.

'They'll never get away with it. Fanny's told me Tiddledick's already acted on what I told her about the Bashars' pop at the Treasury.'

Turning on the computer and trying to look serious, Viv reads out loud.

'*Guess what, darling, old Poncey really put his foot down over the tacky beach huts!*

Ghastly man at number eleven in such a snit! Said wifey would do the D-word on him! My dear, he's the ugliest man in London! He's screwed. Except, he isn't!'

'What the hell did you say to that?'

'*Penetrating analysis, dear. D'you think a clothes peg might cheer her up?*' Viv glances up, and quotes Fanny's answer from memory. '*Don't suppose he's got one to put it on, darling!*'

Further correspondence revealed the girlfriend of the Permanent Secretary at the Treasury reacted in the opposite way. So pleased that she didn't have to go on holiday to some dangerous hot foreign place after all, she promised to marry the man.

'You'll like what she says about that,' Viv grins. '*Darling, they can live happily ever after somewhere nasty in Essex and shop till they drop at Aldi's!*'

Percy guffaws, though he knows he shouldn't. 'Never knew stuck-up Tory snobs had a sense of humour. If there's a joke in it she'd probably deny the Holocaust.'

'Daresay she thinks Auschwitz is a Swiss ski resort and Golders Green is a garden centre in Chelsea,' Viv says thoughtfully.

Percy too is suddenly pensive. Perhaps it's his deep-seated sense he's not quite the ticket that makes it hard to warm to people born with silver spoons in their mouths. But there it is, he is. He seeks out Fang and pours him a saucer of Courvoisier.

'Westminster's supposed to be dog eats dog, isn't it?' Fang's eyes narrow, and Percy starts again. 'When I say dog eats dog, I mean cat eats rat.' Maybe it's just the cognac, but Fang claws his way onto his chest and bites his nose quite gently. He's coming round.

'Have I got it wrong all these years? Is there a world out there where swords really do turn into ploughshares? Where claws turn into soft fluffy bits?'

Fang looks doubtful, but leaves it at that.

Percy knows he's only really talking to himself and is pleased when Viv slips into the room and interrupts. But he doesn't like what she has to say to him.

'Breezethwaite is spinning out of control. And Bakyt's convinced Monty's having problems with those wretched men he's supposed to be in charge of.'

Determined to protect the honour of the hotel chambermaids, they upped the prenuptial nookie offers to four camels and a bison, only to discover the detectives had beaten them to it. In their fury and humiliation they marched out of the Nuclear Arms, whistling an angry tune and spitting.

Monty's exasperated he's got to hunt for his bloody army, but at least the tractor will come in handy. They're bound to have holed up somewhere impossible.

So they have, though the camp camouflage is pointless, as they've set up roadblocks on all nearby lanes and taken pot-shots at anything driving along them.

In their way they're only obeying orders. Bashar senior told them to fight the good fight to the last man standing, and Bashar junior went further at their farewell briefing. 'Hold the jolly old line, lads, or you'll regret it for the rest of your life. All five minutes of it.'

They suspected the brothers were drunk but aren't taking any chances.

Luckily for Monty, they fire a warning volley over the tractor instead of blowing it up with an anti-tank rocket. Leaping out without thinking to put the brake on, he screams at them to behave.

They lay down the bazooka, so far so good, but the tractor's rolling down a gentle slope towards a ditch. Monty orders them to stop it and nine of them stand smartly to attention when they do.

The tenth, who stuck his foot out to halt it, won't be standing at all for a while without crutches.

Monty goes with them to their fortified makeshift barracks, which has a stencilled sign at the entrance. GSMWBHQ. It stands for Glorious Sergeant Monty White Brigade Headquarters. He's rather touched, in spite of himself.

*

Bakyt has news when he gets back. 'Percy and Viv on their way. Be good, have another sensible woman around.'

'Too right. I should have been firmer with Percy,' Monty agrees. 'If I'd only told him to include me out of his bloody hare-brained scheme he might just have seen reason. Maybe.

'Trouble is he's so sodding persuasive. Whatever he says sounds plausible at the time. A Labour leader years ago, name of Kinnock, they used to compare his speeches to Chinese meals. Taste brilliant at the time, only you're hungry again an hour or so later.

'But Percy's more like Churchill. All that screw you Adolf stuff in 1940? Germany could have walked all over us, and he knew it.

'So here we are. Manacled to the bastards who're more or less committing treason. Again.

'That way we catch the rats red-handed? Thanks, Percy. We're the ones in the bloody trap.'

Bakyt's eyes moisten, partly in relief her husband's at last facing the facts, partly in despair there's no escaping them. 'We get out of this somehow,' she murmurs. 'We burn entrails of evil spirits and eat mothers.'

Monty laughs, forgets where he is and kisses her on the lips. The detectives stiffen, and when all Mr Ploed does is wink at them they tell him they're off to shag his chambermaids. Because they're straight up and down geezers.

Brenstorme's appalled. After trying and failing once more to get the heritage phone to work, he shouts into the iPhone. Monty whispers a commentary in Bakyt's ear.

'Does the Cabinet Secretary really expect the Home Office to supply a better class of detective? Surely he doesn't really believe they still have deerstalkers and magnifying glasses? Can any government employee above the rank of toilet cleaner be that stupid?'

Bakyt has to stuff a hankie in his mouth when the exasperated voice at the other end shouts back at him. 'Why aren't you in Downing Street messing things up as usual?'

'That's a bit bloody thick coming from you.' Brenstorme swearing? Blimey! 'At least I'm not inviting in millions of terrorists and drowning the country in drugs.' Monty has to leave the bar, clutching his sides.

*

There's less laughter when the Penislows set off from Cornwall. Viv doesn't like it when little Trudi gives her a V sign. Fang goes off in a sulk, while Nanny looks forlornly at the chandelier and checks for an expiry date on the K-Y jelly.

Crawling along the M5, Percy and Viv are overtaken by several hearses and a 1920 Vauxhall driven by a white-haired man wearing goggles. It's comforting being out of kilter with the world.

They wonder what planet Fanny's on too, when they stop for fuel and read her latest email. It's her take on extra detail Viv's passed on about the Bashars' dodgy donations.

Darling, no idea how Poncey's going to cope! Can't find the funny little country anywhere! Somewhere near Tanganyika? One for bonkers Brenstorme, but he's gone AWOL! Smack his botty if you see him!'

'Tanganyika ceased to exist as a sovereign state in 1964,'

Percy murmurs. 'Wonder if Fanny's noticed Daddy's atlas is a bit out of date.'

'She probably likes it because of the pink bits,' Viv replies, then bangs off a reply.

'*Radar scanning for Brenstorme buttocks. Silly arse. Poncey better have a word with the Foreign Office, the funny looking place across the road, they know where everywhere is.*'

Seconds later there's a one-word answer. '*Right-oh.*'

'She'd probably say the same if someone suggested nuking Moscow,' Percy snorts. But he's pleased the woman's on the case. If the Foreign Office does manage to scare the Bashars off it might make life simpler for him. Or, rather, less complicated.

'Smacking Brenstorme's botty would be good,' he adds, 'preferably with a baseball bat.'

'I wonder how yours would look if you got the punishment you've been asking for, dear.' He doesn't reply to that. Doesn't need to.

*

Simone-Sitrouenne finally splutters into the now familiar gravelled car park, and Percy and Viv head for the bar. The fake pot plants and soft easy listening music convey a tacky air of calm, but Monty's words don't.

'The fuckwit's still winning.'

Bakyt's been back to Breezethwaite on the pretext of checking a couple of details and learned masses more Jocks have been recruited. The first few batches are expected any day now.

'And talking of recruits,' Monty sighs, 'the Bashar boys are getting worse.'

As he feared, they've repeatedly disobeyed orders to dismantle the roadblocks. When law-abiding citizens have reported armed men in military uniforms demanding to see their papers they've been written off as loony victims of the water poisoning. But the situation can't last.

One coffee follows another. Then the aperitif. Percy slips out for several smokes. Dinner is announced. They're too busy trying to figure out an exit strategy to even look at the menu. Tonight's special will do, whatever it is.

'Maybe the Bashar boys can terrorise Chancery's mob into fleeing the country, preferably without filling the local morgues in the process,' Percy suggests. 'Psychological warfare. We've got enough military hardware to give an army the shits.'

He's suddenly sympathetic, however, when he glances down at the food that's just arrived. Meat madras and mashed artichoke, garnished with sweet and sour prawns, Yorkshire pudding and apple sauce.

Monty looks at him despairingly and mutters 'Bon appetit, Snafu'.

'Sir? Naff? Oo? What that?' Bakyt wonders.

'Military acronym,' Monty tells her. 'Situation Normal, All Fucked Up.'

CHAPTER FOURTEEN

About a mile from the Nuclear Arms, Chancery is on top of the situation, but not Farmer Giles, who can't forgive him for his infidelity. He's not consoled by the claim that the Scottish sluts are members of a cell of gay rights activists, currently on leave.

The MI5 men actually are on holiday, from reality. They feel they're back at prep school, discovering wanking's only the beginning. Who cares their new fuck-buddies are talking gibberish? They don't need to say much anyway.

Brenstorme's grumbles left them none the wiser about what they're supposed to be doing, so they settle for keeping these guys under close surveillance. Blissfully close.

There's a bonus for Chancery too. Fully briefed on how dangerous life is in the West, his lovely boys have picked up a bump stock assault rifle each from the Chinese Embassy. So he's got a private army, same as Monty, as well as a harem.

His only problem is the hail of bullets he faces every time he takes the Caddy out. Opting for maximum security, the Officer Commanding Bashar Ground Forces has ordered all motorised vehicles be repulsed on sight. A pink Eldorado coupe is hard not to notice.

The farmhouse is primitive, but rather grand in its

ramshackle way, The oak-beamed dining area's rotating roasting spit and open log fire suggest a mediaeval castle's great hall.

Chancery worries his troops' expensive new faces are going to waste in a foggy farmhouse in the middle of nowhere. But, when the gypsy getaway people start delivering reinforcements to Breezethwaite, via the farmhouse, luck is on his side.

The Bashar boys long ago topped up their Muslim faith with the ancient cult of horse-worship, so whenever the caravans appear they put their guns down and get the prayer mats out. Meaning the Chinese contingent can get in, and out, with relative ease.

After a while the Civil Nuclear Constabulary stop cocking their sub-machineguns at the sight of weird-looking contraptions clip-clopping up the road. The guys jumping out of them and saying things they don't understand seem to be there by invitation.

*

One of the many flaws in Percy's plan to terrorise Chancery's mob is he doesn't know where they are. Monty would have done if the Bashar boys had thought fit to mention the monster vehicle they'd been blasting away at, only they didn't because they weren't supposed to be shooting anything.

So instead he's reduced to bumping along unmade roads and criss-crossing fields in the tractor, all the time wondering why.

Percy's his friend. He's thrown in his lot with him and would defend him to the death. But now he really is struggling with the man's Walter Mitty craziness.

A chink of pink brings him back to reality. A barn door in the distance opens a crack and there, surely, is a fin! In trying to rub his eyes he knocks the shades off and they go under the bloody tractor wheels. But at least he can see properly now.

He begins slowly driving round the building as though it's a circle of covered wagons. Normally every bit as sensible as Viv, he can also relate to Bakyt's lapses. And right now the grown-up former police officer is a kid playing cowboys and Indians.

Of course he can't carry on pretending he's ploughing fields when he's not towing anything. Nor can he move in for the kill without so much as a stone-headed axe. The windows might start spitting lead anytime, and instead of Sitting Bull he'd be Sitting Target.

Monty flips the reins and swings his hoss away from the juicy scalps in the wagons, then tells himself to stop being so ridiculous. It's a Massey Ferguson, not a bloody Palomino, with a steering wheel, not a pair of reins. Plus he's not in a saddle, it's a seat.

Back at GSMWBHQ he gets another rush of blood to the head and refers to Charlie Chancery as General Custer, making the chaps wonder if Sergeant Superman has been on the funny fags. But they're happy to stake out the hideout.

Their preparation for bivouacking round the farm is impressive. The circle of slit trenches looks nice and intimidating. Monty vetoes bazookas, but suspects they'll sneak back for them anyway.

As a token of good faith, the men hand him an ancient-looking walkie-talkie, explaining the batteries on their iPhones are all dead. Monty only hopes it works, as they really mustn't launch a pre-emptive strike. Even round here mass murder would take some explaining.

He gets the first call, over dinner, between the cold crudités and spam fritters with Peshwari naan. And the second between the mild or mature cheddar cheeseboard and Nescafé.

As the thing gurgles and hisses a group of old ladies from the flower-arranging and macramé association cross themselves and Mr Ploed turns up Mantovani orchestra's 'Golden Strings'.

Things get worse when Monty accidentally turns the volume knob the wrong way and an excited voice blares out in broken

English words to the effect that the enemy's been sighted and needs his throat cut. Also bombs, bayonets and mustard gas might be the way forward.

Monty's reply is drowned out by the scraping of chairs on the polished parquet floor. The old ladies run for their lives, and the sweet young thing on the next table is so sure this is her horrible date's idea of a joke she flounces off, telling him to go fuck himself.

The men head for the Massey Ferguson. The women, close behind, fling open Simone-Sitrouenne's doors. Viv turns the key and Bakyt squeals 'Follow that tractor'.

It's a moonless night. Pitch black. Somewhere in the middle distance an owl screeches. They all start, but continue their cautious approach towards the farmhouse. The radio has fallen silent. Suddenly a light starts flashing from the ploughed field dead ahead.

'Looks like Morse code,' Monty mutters. 'Can't read that. Are they saying another yard and they'll blow us up? Or if we identify ourselves by edging forward they won't blow us up?'

'Maybe they don't know the fucking dit-dit-dit dah-dah-dah bollocks either, and are just flashing because they like playing with their new toy,' Percy suggests.

When Monty hears the distinctive sound of cocking AK-47s he slams on the brakes. Simone-Sitrouenne smashes into the back of the tractor and the bumper falls off as it was only held on with gaffer tape. Another inconvenience, on top of the fifty-fifty chance of instant death.

Bakyt leaps out of the car brandishing one of the Stens, and Monty's terrified she's planning a suicide attack.

She's only out to protect her man, but it's not clear from what. Peculiar noises are emanating from the trenches now, followed by globules of liquid raining down on them. At this point Viv emerges with more useful technology than the gun.

The umbrella, she explains, is the solution to the Bashars'

new mode of communication. Ballistic spitting's obviously the boys' way of saying 'Welcome, comrades-at-arms'.

They stumble forward, all huddled behind the one not very big brolly. Whispering in a Drill Sergeant's voice is tricky but Monty gives it a go.

'Squad! Squad… cease… gobbing!' The boys don't know the word but recognise the voice. The sky dries.

When he finally makes out the grinning blacked-up faces and helmets camouflaged with undergrowth he hisses at them 'What the hell's been going on?'

Turns out it was a false alarm. In the darkness they'd confused an Aberdeen Angus for a human with two bendy spears, but slaughtered it anyway. It'll feed them for days.

'At least you're a cheap date,' Monty concedes, wishing yet again Percy had never won that bloody election.

'Why did Maggie defend islands full of sheep halfway across the globe, and Tony take the nation to war over, excuse me, what weapons of mass destruction? Are all leaders distant descendants of Genghis Khan?' Monty's musings are nothing if not eclectic.

He's distracted by signs of a party going on barely fifty yards away. Christmas 1914 crosses his mind. Imagine, these guys you've been trying to kill for months, suddenly you hear them singing carols. Their trenches are that close.

'It so happens the Huns went for '*Stille nacht, heilige nacht, alles schlaft,*' to which the Tommies responded in their own way with 'On Sunday after supper I had the fucker up her, corblimey…'

Though Chancery wouldn't spot a historical reference if it licked his eyeballs, he proves he's a patriot by opting for 'The hairs of her dicky di-do hung down to her knees'.

Farmer Giles tries to raise the tone with 'So many men, so little time', but as a door opens and light floods on the pair, Chancery can be clearly seen whipping his trousers down and trying to lick his balls.

Giles takes a swipe at him. But the boys stiffen and cock their guns again. Monty exerts his authority in the nick of time. 'Squad... Wait for it... Squad... Present... Umms!' He knows it's impossible to shoot anything from the present arms position, apart from UFOs.

On the way back, Monty senses Percy's hatching a plot. A bad sign, from past experience. But he can do no more than sit and watch as the silly sod slithers out of the tractor, whips out his phone and has a long talk with someone.

Afterwards Percy's thoughtful but doesn't let on, even to Viv. Another man thing, if you're doing something your wife won't like you try not to tell. She'll really hate this.

During his time in Downing Street Biff became his only confidant. Viv was jealous in a way, and the sensation hasn't all gone. Same as a glass of gone-off milk accidentally necked as a kid. There are things you don't forget.

Percy's hope is that with things spinning so dangerously out of control Biff just might be the man to come up with something. Because he's a relatively respectable Member of Parliament these days, threatening to blow people's fecking kneecaps off is off the agenda. Or should be.

CHAPTER FIFTEEN

As bad luck would have it, Biff is squiffy and swashbuckling when he takes the call. So's Sir Roger, squawking and warbling in he background about drums and republican guns. Percy can picture the creature hopping from one foot to the other with his feathers fluffed up.

He wonders if some parrots really do hate Brits.

In his present mood Biff certainly hates anyone giving Percy a problem. 'I got a mucker from the old days who could blow these fecking eejits to hell and back,' he growls. This is the last thing Percy was looking for, but he's programmed to take Biff's advice. And before he's had time to say 'never', he's agreed to hook up with Chopper McMurphy.

Actually, Chopper was brought up in South London, starting life as Blobby Steele. Fat and ugly, he never made it as a rock star with girls throwing their knickers at him. Still determined to be special, he adopted his Irish mother's maiden name and headed for the Falls Road.

By the time he got to Belfast the peace process was spoiling everyone's fun, so he gave up on liberating his people and settled for drug dealing and running a protection racket. At least he was good at it, having gone to the right school. The same one as Monty and Chancery, as it happens.

Much like Eton, it was stuffed full of eager young thugs with a sense of entitlement. The difference being its graduates are more likely to rob banks than own them.

Of course it had its dropouts. Lord Lucan damaged the old boys' brand, so did Monty when he joined the filth. When Chopper's Bentley swishes into the car park at the Nuclear Arms, scattering gravel everywhere, the reunion is not cordial.

'Haven't lost any weight I see.' Monty's more honest than friendly when he sees through the blubber and recognises the wart between the waddling duck's eyes.

'Still full of shagging shite, then.' Chopper's way of saying 'nice to see you too'. It irritates him that, grey hairs or not, Monty looks better than he did when he was eighteen. Bastard.

The atmosphere in the restaurant that night is toxic. Percy had admitted he'd called in an expert, but left it at that. The combination of this psycho and the look on Monty's face leaves Viv in doubt about one thing only. Is her husband a bit loopy or totally raving?

However, they accept they may need reinforcements. Whether a bunch of ex-IRA guys who fancy a punch-up for the craic will be more dependable than the Bashars' boisterous babies is open to question. Monty makes the mistake of mentioning Chancery.

Screwed-up alpha males, Chopper and Chancery spent their school years vying to be top dog. A blood feud, no forgiving and no forgetting. Hard to tell which of the two was worse, though Chopper's elephantine capacity for hanging on to a grievance took some beating. Aged sixteen, he blew up his infants' school because Miss had once told him not to nail another kid's head to a desk.

So yet again Percy's broken the golden rule of politics that says stop digging when you're in a hole. And, alone with him in bed, Viv finally snaps. No shouting, it's not her style. Instead her delivery is low-key, steely, and menacing.

'You remember that film, my dear, *The Italian Job*? Right at the end the coach is hanging over the side of the mountain, and the gang leader tells the lads to hang on a minute because he's got a great idea?'

Percy instinctively reaches under the beige paisley-patterned duvet and cradles his balls. He can tell he's in for a bollocking but doesn't want it to hurt more than it has to.

'Yes of course. Great pay-off line.'

'The ultimate cliffhanger, in every sense,' she snarls. 'Fine in fiction, rubbish in reality. You do not have a great idea, do you?' Viv is beyond Vivienne. She's vicious.

'All you have is one ridiculous idea after another. Don't know who I hate more, you for dreaming them up or me for going along with them. But that's your lot, chum. Count me out.'

With that she turns away from him, flicks off the light and does not turn back. Percy can only hope he can talk her round, but is not confident.

In the morning he's so all sweetness and light he'd have had the Sugar Plum Fairy reaching for the sick bag. But the dark shadows under Viv's eyes remind him she's not a woman to be fobbed off with a cheery smile and a nice cup of tea.

'You're a father. And a husband. And you're behaving like a six-year-old. See the end of your nose?'

Percy squints, in a vain attempt at humour.

'It's not bloody funny. There's a world in front of that finely chiselled hooter of yours. And something in it for you to take. It's called responsibility.'

Percy sits on the uncomfortable armchair by the bed and squirms. He looks at the green uncut moquette cushion covers and wishes he could hide between the stitches. Viv only swears at him when she really hates him, like at the end of that party they'd both sooner forget.

'It's snakes and ladders, only the fun and laughter with

Fanny wasn't a game, it got you close to the top of the board. Now you're right back at square one.

'Suppose I could try and have you sectioned,' she says after a moment's thought. 'The new Broadmoor's not as horrible as the old one. But we might never get you out. Well? What have you got to say for yourself?'

For once there's no get-out clause, no room for manoeuvre. When your back's against the wall what can you do? Snarl back? Won't solve anything, but you do it anyway.

'These bastards shafted me. All those years fighting my way to the top. And they ripped my fucking legs off. OK, I wasn't looking for revenge, but when it was handed to me on a fucking plate what did you expect me to do? I'm not Jesus fucking Christ, you know.'

He's trembling. So much suppressed anger. And such a welter of self-blame after what seemed like poetic justice, and a bit of a lark, has turned so nasty. He feels like a kid in America playing with the family gun collection who accidentally shoots the dog in the head, then in panic fatally wounds Mom and Pop as well.

His eyes well up. It's not self-pity, more a primal scream. As a child he wanted to do things, possibly great things, but felt held back by being just Percy. The boy from nowhere who knew nothing. He wishes he had Fang on hand for a heart-to-heart, and wonders if he really is insane, wanting a fucking cat to solve his fucking problems.

Viv usually melts when Percy cries. Not this time. He remembers when he accidentally broke almost the entire bag of eggs he'd been trusted to bring back from the shop. Mum was so cross he really believed she didn't love him. Same feeling now.

If only he could just click his fingers and magic himself back to Cornwall, playing with Fang and dear little Trudi and writing witty and insightful things about other peoples' idiotic behaviour, instead of reaping his own whirlwind…

But no, he's stuck with the tried and tested formula of keeping the show on the road by pretending to be a super-hero. Did the trick for Churchill, he thinks. And Ronald Reagan had class, acting the stout-hearted cowboy when he'd just taken a would-be assassin's bullet.

Knowing the state Percy's in, Viv is impressed in spite of herself when he swaggers up to the breakfast table as though he hasn't a care in the world. Feeling sucked in, she thinks back to uni and how he played King Lear going loopy. He's too good at making the switch.

*

Far from sharing jolly reminiscences about what a lark it was at the old school, Monty and Chopper are finding they hate one another even more than back then. But, with the boys of the old brigade due to be flying into Britain within hours, they need a war strategy.

Roosevelt, Churchill and Stalin beat a common enemy though they mistrusted one another almost as much as De Gaulle, but Percy knows he's not in that league. Maybe Brenstorme should get the Flying Squad to march him off to The Tower. Be his sanest act in years.

Eventually they agree to a recce round the battlefield. Percy and Viv in the tractor, the other three in Simone-Sitrouenne. Chopper breaks wind every time the overloaded little van struggles over a bump. Horrible noise. Horrible smell.

At the farm they can't believe their eyes. The Bashar bivouacs have turned into a circular trench, complete with mud wall, firing step, machine gun posts and periscopes. A wise precaution, given there's another mud wall clearly visible, with rifle barrels pointing outwards.

Monty scratches his head. He's not to know his boys have decided lying flat on the ground every time they see a horse is

252

a less than sure-fire way of sealing off the enemy position. A circular trench, by contrast, can't fail to work.

Still clinging on to a vague hope that this isn't really happening, Monty removes his beret, places it on a pole and raises it above the mud wall.

Four shots ring out and the hat flies back with four neat little holes in it. Bakyt is mortified, and insists Monty carries on wearing what's left of the gift that made him look so sexy.

Seconds later pineapple-shaped objects are lobbed at them. The grenades explode short of their target, but the point is made. The Bashar boys take aim with their bazookas.

'Being in a ship full of loose cannon gives me a sinking feeling,' Monty mutters. Percy giggles nervously. They both suspect telling the men to hold their fire is as pointless as telling a turtle to sit up and beg.

In the inner trench, Chancery's having problems too. Everyone's had everyone now and his natives are getting restless, likewise the MI5 men. And Farmer Giles is fretting at missing two market days in a row. Bugger Chancery. Or, rather, don't bugger him. He's not worth it.

To cap it all, the phone never stops ringing. Breezethwaite's increasingly irritated Director of Personnel wants to know why the newly hired employees aren't turning up for work, and why they're all on the same number.

Chancery explains he's the proprietor of the hotel where they're staying, and there's been an outbreak of bacillary dysentery. He thinks it sounds infectious enough to buy himself time with this bumhole, not realising the disease can be spread through sexual activity involving that part of the anatomy.

Malaria, lung cancer or bubonic plague would have been fine. The man would have prayed for the unfortunate souls. But bacillary dysentery is the devil's work, like AIDS, syphilis and hepatitis. All that matters is keeping the sinner alive, so he's conscious while being roasted in hell.

Bible belters from the American South keep their faith simple. Love god, hate faggots. So much for Chancery's attempt at protecting his boys' backsides.

Though they're good on Scottish slang, they can't read English. When the sacking emails zap into their inboxes Chancery improvises, explaining they're get-well-soon greetings. He never could tell the difference between little white lies and dirty great whoppers. Never cared, either.

What Fyok Yu and Hon Ki will do about it is another matter. He daren't risk more fibs in case his nose grows. For all he knows they might cut it off.

Suddenly, and he may be the first person in history to experience this, he loves Slowden. Even the moronic teenager has her charms. He promises himself, if he gets out of this alive, he'll marry the bitch. There are ways of having fun, even with a girl.

CHAPTER SIXTEEN

Ponsomby Tiddledick has got off lightly lately. A few cross words with the Treasury chaps after Fanny tipped him off over those foreign rats and the jiggery-pokery over their holidays and no more need be said. As for that funny business over local party funding, he didn't see what he could do without a bit more detail.

He did try to probe Fanny's sources, but when she started rummaging around in her joss sticks drawer he lost interest in anything other than handcuffs and pink fluffy whips.

Apart from that, the economy is no more shambolic than at any other time in the post-Brexit and post-pandemic era, and the opposition leader's too much of a gentleman at the despatch box to give him a hard time. So he has the energy for the nicer sort with Fanny.

It can be so for quite long periods in politics, not much happens. The hyperactive hacks scribble away as usual, but most of it wouldn't get the birds out of the trees for a peck.

Tiddledick has no ambition to go down in history as a great reforming Prime Minister. Survival will do, and Brenstorme's disappearance is a great help. The civil service is so much more efficient without a nutter running it.

But it seems the good times are over when Tiddledick hears

a specific ringtone on his iPhone. It indicates that far from obliging the world by falling out of an aeroplane and landing in a volcano, his Cabinet Secretary can still key in a number.

'Why, Brenstorme dear chap, joy to hear from you after such a relatively protracted absence.' More a sigh of disappointment that it might soon come to an end than a good ticking off.

'Now look here, Prime Minister, there's a revolution brewing up here.' As ever, Brenstorme isn't exactly making himself clear, and Tiddledick's exasperated already.

'Up here eh? Top of the London Eye? Dark side of the moon? And, pray, what revolution? A seismic geopolitical event or a better way of playing conkers?'

Brenstorme harrumphs and starts again, at the beginning this time. 'I've been on a secret mission close to the Scottish border, and found evidence of severe racial tension and a plot against the stability of the realm.

'In addition, the police force has been infiltrated by swaggering sex maniacs with appalling manners. A bit jolly thick if you ask me.'

Tiddledick turns the telly down, struggles to make sense of any of it and eventually gives up.

'Take all the time you need on this one,' he tells Brenstorme. Forever would do nicely. He crosses his fingers Her Pervy Ladyship knows something.

Indeed she does, thanks to Viv, who's been really getting into her stride in her correspondence with Fanny.

'*Can you believe it? Batty Brenstorme's done something useful! Still wearing the silly hat, but opened his eyes for once! Such a bore, ghastly details! All in this thingamajig! Pass it on to Poncey! Suck me off if it doesn't put lead in his pencil!*'

Fanny's initial '*Right-oh*' is followed by a postscript. '*Darling, sobbing at your news! In the jim-jams at bed's end every night, praying he was dead! Take him home, would you, get the cat to give him rabies!*'

Viv can't imagine Fanny praying or wearing anything other than a mask and stilettos at bedtime. But she's pretty sure the Word document she attached to the email will be passed on. And quite certain Tiddledick will take a great deal of notice.

Like any good pollster, Viv is clever with words. Hazy about causes, detailed about effects. As she hoped, Tiddledick decides it's all Brenstorme's fault, again. He's careful to pass on to the Ministry of Defence the outlines of the problem, and the grid references.

A brace of Brigadiers is discreetly admitted to Downing Street via the Whitehall entrance, sidestepping COBRA. That always gets the media frothing, and Tiddledick can't be arsed with answers when the punters don't even know there's a question.

As the tanks trundle up the M6 on their transporters, morale is high. Even the officers are buzzing with excitement.

'Haven't had so much fun since that nitwit Penis-hoojamaflip tried to destroy Downing Street,' the CO tells his batman.

'And that was a washout, the cad couldn't even set himself on fire, let alone anything much else. Damned Trotskyites. Worthless people.'

*

The Trotskyites in question at the Nuclear Arms are feeling extremely damned, and worthless. They've managed to order breakfast, but haven't the foggiest what to do when they've eaten it.

Percy overhears Brenstorme grumbling that the porridge is a bit thick. 'Spot on, for once,' he mutters. 'Hope it chokes him.' Monty nods, so do Bakyt and Viv.

The only cheerful person at the table is Chopper McMurphy. He's so sure his boys will arrive any minute he's picking his nose in anticipation. This puts everyone off their food.

Hearing a disorderly whooping in the car park, he leaps to his feet like a heavily pregnant beached whale. For the first time in days Percy and Viv share a meaningful glance, albeit only one of shared distress.

Chopper reappears with his motley crew. It's nine-thirty in the morning, but they're all pissed. Because this shower arrived in a minibus that's driven off in a hurry the Flying Squad guys can't do anyone for being drunk in charge of a motor vehicle. They're furious.

So's Mr Ploed. He's proud of the apron he's had personalised with a 1950s-style policeman's helmet and crossed truncheons, but ashamed he's not arresting any of these appalling people.

Chopper's not totally dumb. The boys need to get their heads down before he gets them out there with their sacks of what he takes to be grenades, so he's got to book them in. Mr Ploed is not happy, even though Monty's given him the nod.

Viv glances at Percy. 'Gets worse, doesn't it, stupid sod?' Not exactly 'I love you to distraction, man of my dreams', but it breaks the ice.

Percy's response is equally cautious. 'Fubar, my dear.' When she raises an eyebrow he risks looking her in the eye.

'Army term. Fucked Up Beyond All Recognition.' The sheepish grin clinches it. Crisis over.

Should they fling themselves on Tiddledick's mercy? Fanny may think it hilarious, but Ponsomby couldn't just let them off, even if he wanted to. Or should they sneak back to Cornwall and hope no one notices? Like in the good old days of smuggling and wrecking?

No, not in the digital age. Percy's eyes start leaking again, but this time Viv reaches across under the table and caresses his hand. This only makes him worse. Viv knows he'd never cope with a long prison sentence, unable to watch little Trudi growing up, or Fang learning he can't trip her over any more.

For a long moment they gaze at one another, and on some

imperceptible cue slip upstairs. The upside of really beastly rows is the kissing and making up that often follows. Odd they should choose now to feel horny, when they're perched on the edge of a precipice.

'They may give us separate cells, but at least we're in it together,' Percy murmurs much later when he gets his breath back. Viv sighs, and kisses the lobe of his ear.

Now the situation's out of their hands they're suddenly calm. Passengers in a plane grappling with turbulence. The pilot's doing all he can, while they needn't even bother praying when god's already got the situation sewn up.

Still, baling out feels increasingly attractive, even though the parachutes probably won't do the job. Standing by the reproduction Victorian brass bed, looking down at his wife and doing up his flies, Percy comes to a decision.

'We stick around for a bit, then slither off?' Viv toys with the moisture curdling between her thighs, smiles and quotes Fanny. 'Right-oh.'

In reality, events are moving so fast there's barely time to breathe, let alone share Zen moments. The Belfast Brigade only need a day to sober up, and they're in a hurry. Can't risk showing up on the battlefield only to discover the other side's wussed out. Typical Brit trick, like when they blew up half of Dublin then snuck off home.

McMurphy has paid a visit to the local dairy, threatened its owner with death by a thousand kneecappings and got use of a small convoy of electric-powered milk floats. Not exactly a fleet of Ferraris, but faster than Simone-Sitrouenne.

The only sounds on the battlefield that starry, moonlit night are the soft whirring of the milk floats' motors and the occasional crack of sniper fire. No defiant songs about glorious Irish defeats, and from the inner trench none of the laments about failed Jacobite risings the Chinese guys learned before leaving Beijing.

Chopper confers with the troops in authoritative tones, and Percy and Monty feel like children who've started a fire in the kitchen and now have to stand by helplessly while the grown-ups put it out.

The sky's suddenly lit by a flare fired from the inner trench, swiftly followed by sustained bursts of small arms fire, and the Bashar boys hit back with the AK-47s. But no one leaps out of either trench and attempts to charge across no man's land.

The incoming force is not pining for the jihadists' seventy-two virgins of paradise, the defenders reckon Mother Mary has plenty to be going on with, and Chancery and his chaps would prefer a life of shagging to the life eternal.

So the battle is all sound, no fury. Defences breached? Nope. Casualties? None. Advantage gained? Zero, on either side. Percy and Monty cross their fingers. Wars of attrition can simply drag on till the combatants finally lose interest. It took tanks to sort the problem in 1918, but there aren't any here. Yet.

CHAPTER SEVENTEEN

Though the war's been inconclusive up to now, the Bashar boys know they can tip the balance with their secret weapon, only a phone call away. The BAF, they tell Chopper, is armed, primed, and as good as airborne.

'What's the shagging BAF when it's at home then?'

'The Bashar Air Force,' the boys cry out in unison. 'World's best Brylcreem boys. Bar none.'

Because Ireland remained neutral in World War Two, Chopper refuses to recognise the reference to the Royal Air Force, but he picks up on the word 'bar' and inwardly shudders.

He's good on the Potato Famine and the 1798 Wicklow Rising, but can't bear Guinness. A problem, as necking anything else on the Falls Road is a mortal sin. The first thing he always does in pubs is check out where he can tip the fecking stuff when no one's looking.

Eventually, however, he admits airborne attacks have their uses. 'We have our share of shits in Norn Iron too,' he growls. 'Proddie bastards.' The Bashar boys nod knowingly, though they've no idea he's talking about Northern Ireland and Protestants.

'We kill anyone not friend of great and glorious Chopper.'

Again they're shouting in unison. And, again, they mean it. In theory at least.

Hearing this, Percy sums up the situation as only a mature political strategist knows how.

'Piss.'

Having learned the lingo in Downing Street, Monty responds in kind.

'Shit.'

The game's up, then. Bouncing back to the Nuclear Arms in Simone-Sitrouenne they confess to their wives it's not a matter of if but when they're off to the slammer. But like cancer patients in the terminal ward of life, they're learning to love every second they've got left.

So dinner is surprisingly festive. The dated pine panelling in the restaurant takes on a seductive glow. The prints on the walls, even those of Windscale, feel comforting. And Percy, bubbling with graveyard humour, is almost his old self again.

The dining room gradually clears. Waiting outside the ladies' before she remembers she's supposed to go to the gents', Viv earwigs the old blokes at the next table.

Turns out they're members of the local pigeon racing and whippet fanciers' society, bent on sharing highly confidential insights. She suddenly craves the excitement, all things being relative, of the speaking clock.

But they clear off eventually and the serious talk begins. Or would have done, but for Percy's mission to prove booze sharpens the brain. The Belfast boys are next door proving it doesn't, as they empty the Fallout and Bunker of Guinness. Chopper's only proving he's a tosser.

His dead little piggy eyes look like inflated condoms as Percy outlines a strategy based on key conflicts of the twentieth century. Using cutlery, crockery and his plastic dagger as scene-setting props, he starts with the Schlieffen plan, which let the Germans down and ends with the atom bomb that blew the Japanese up.

Viv clocks Percy's winding Chopper up and joins in.

'But my dear, what if the Nuclear Arms is fresh out of nuclear arms?'

'Perfectly straightforward,' he replies without a flicker of a smile. 'We'll hack into the Kremlin computer system and get the Ruskies to do the job.'

Chopper yawns and waddles off to bed. He's had enough.

*

The second the fat fucker's gone Percy and Monty snatch up the gold lame Liberace-style jacket he's left on the back of his chair, whip into the loo and wee all over it. They return to their ladies feeling much better.

All four of them would have felt better still if they'd known help was so close at hand.

It'd have been there already if the army hadn't got lost on the way, ending up in the grounds of a care home for oldies whose families will pay anything never to see them again. The owner chains all new arrivals to their beds and forces them to watch Monty Python movies back to back for a month. This guarantees they go barmy and he gets rich.

Colonel Humphrey 'Huffie' Shrapnelle-Sidebotham, the commanding officer, sensed a problem when the naked civilian he asked for directions told him he wasn't the messiah, just a very naughty boy. Also he's a lumberjack, like his dear mama.

Guessing the driver of the lead vehicle had set the satnav incorrectly, Huffie poured a jerrycan of petrol over him and ordered a horrified lance corporal to 'torch the blighter'.

When the convoy gets to the western Lake District the noisy military vehicles worry the sheep to a point their tails might fall off, but the locals are unperturbed. As their idea of world events is the British National Ploughing Championships, they assume England's won a war somewhere and this is a victory parade.

Pretty ladies are out in force to welcome the heroes, kissing the fellers astride the tanks and popping flowers up their noses and phone numbers down their trousers. The grinning squaddies look forward to getting laid.

But everything changes when planes start swooping around, apparently dropping bombs. Old men mutter darkly about the Luftwaffe and young women wonder if the local adult learning centre does courses in German. The squaddies are well pissed off.

Colonel Shrapnelle-Sidebotham is distantly related to Brenstorme and his behaviour suggests certain mental conditions run in families. He hits NCOs with his swagger stick and issues orders out of the side of his mouth. 'We get the hell out of here. Sitting targets, dammit.'

A mile up the road he spots a plane directly above and tries to shoot it down with his pistol. Pathetic, but he's convinced he's about to be crushed by an all-powerful enemy.

Little does he know the excitable young BAF pilot with the handlebar moustache and Brylcreemed hair thinks the same. 'Major ground force deployed. Over. British bad people. Over. They execute us as spies. Over. It's over. Over.'

The Bashar brothers are scared. Planes and personnel are expendable, but the Brits' crazy invasion of the Falklands proves they'll stop at nothing. The operation's called off.

In their enthusiasm to obey orders the airmen all disperse in exactly the same direction. Two of the jets collide mid-air and vanish without trace in the Irish Sea. The BAF Wing Commander reports back they died heroically in action fighting overwhelming odds.

Their infantry colleagues use their initiative when they get the order to retreat. First they spike Chopper's glass of Dubonnet with half a bottle of crushed Diazepam tablets, then flit away at dead of night. The promise of a lorryload of Guinness each to persuade the IRA guys to go with them was a lucky guess, but it worked.

There are also developments at the farmhouse. The MI5 blokes have been spying on Chancery, a habit thing. Seems he's told Fyok Yu the infiltration of Breezethwaite has gone wrong, and The China Nuclear Engineering Group Corporation's aborted the mission.

When they share this intelligence with their multiple lovers they're impressed by the response. These guys would prefer to risk a bullet now than be tortured to death later by the Chinese Ministry of State Security.

After gangbanging Chancery into a coma, more than he deserves but needs must, they slither over the top and crawl across no man's land. Hurling themselves into the outer trench they discover there's no one there apart from Chopper, snoring on an unsurprisingly camp camp bed.

Always confusing, life expectancy revised upwards from fifteen seconds to around fifty years.

The MI5 blokes lead them towards Scotland, hoping there at least these freaks will be able to make themselves understood. Handy for ordering plane tickets, and something to eat.

*

Not much happening down the farm then. When he regains consciousness Chancery tells his ex to do one and staggers up to the barn. Grabbing the Tommy gun from the Caddy's boot he revs her up. Chopper does the same, with Bentley and bazooka.

Both planned to go, but at the sight of one another they become knights in shining armour, their powerful cars doubling up as warhorses. The first charge goes nowhere as Chancery finds he can't fire accurately while driving on a ploughed field. Chopper has problems too, as you need both hands to operate a bazooka.

A hundred yards up the field they handbrake-swerve round to give it another go, only this time it's bonnet to bonnet. Steam gushes out of both mangled radiators, but both drivers manage to stumble out before the cars blow up in a pall of smoke.

Nothing for it, then, but a punch-up. Only, there's a problem. Always handy with anything that's got a blade or a trigger, neither of them has the bottle to put their fists up. So they run for it, both of them, in opposite directions.

Farmer Giles finds it hilarious. Less so when the bit of roof he's been trying to fix gives way under him and he tumbles first through the loft and then the bedroom ceiling, rupturing his spleen somewhere on the way down.

When his mum asks him in hospital if it hurts he replies truthfully. 'Only when I laugh.'

CHAPTER EIGHTEEN

Later that day Percy and Viv head for the farmhouse with Monty and Bakyt, and can't figure out why the outer trench is deserted and why the beret on a stick doesn't get shot at. Then they notice the wrecked cars. So the pall of smoke they saw earlier wasn't a tornado after all.

Percy scratches his head. 'Curiouser and curiouser,' he mutters as he examines what looks like a piece of sweet and sour pork. 'D'you think if I eat this I'll suddenly become huge? Or tiny? Or get my head chopped off by the Queen of Hearts?'

The release of tension is too much for Viv. After weeks facing the imminent end of life as she knows it she collapses in a flood of tears, but still manages to pick up on the Alice gag. 'Was it all just a ghastly dream?' She gulps. 'Is it possible to just wake up? And everything's fine?'

Percy kneels at her feet, kisses her hands and begs forgiveness. She looks down at him, not caring what a mess she must be looking, and strokes his forehead with the back of her hand. Because she's feeling exactly the same, Bakyt also starts to weep uncontrollably.

Monty finds himself welling up, reminds himself blokes don't blub, but wishes he could anyway.

The men leave their wives to their girlie stuff for a minute and take stock. Percy speaks first.

'Think the girls are jumping the gun a bit, pardon the language. All we've got is a stay of execution. Major criminal enterprise. Vulnerable strategic industry threatened. Havoc wreaked in small community. Dozens dead. All my fault. How's that for a charge sheet?'

For some reason, he's no idea why, Monty's feeling more optimistic. 'All those crazies always were on a hiding to nothing. Maybe they really have seen the light and gone. And the army nutters. Those fucking fuckers have fucking fucked off too.'

Though the F-word isn't Monty's style he can see Percy needs cheering up. He's right in thinking the turn of phrase would make him smile, but wrong to believe the army's gone.

*

The two men issue tissues to their wives, after having a sneaky dab at their own eyes, and try to decide whether to advance and be damned, or call in the Bill.

'Let's just take a chance.' Though the silence is eerie, menacing even, Monty's pretty confident the place is empty. Percy isn't. 'Got away with one suicide attempt, remember. A second go would be pushing it.'

Bakyt has other ideas. She fiddles around in the back of Simone-Sitrouenne, utters a fiendish guttural moan and charges back, waving the starting handle like a battle hammer.

'God help us, it's the Kazakh thing again.' Monty braces himself to stop her but she's too quick for him. Giving a demented scream she hurls herself across no man's land, leaps into the air, clearing the inner trench in a single bound, and flings herself head-first at the farmhouse door.

Monty's there in no time. Clasping her prostrate form in his arms he really does weep like a baby.

'Stupid, crazy, wonderful goddess,' he murmurs over and over again, too distressed even to feel her pulse. Though Viv gets there last, she's the first to do anything sensible.

After holding Bakyt's wrist for a few seconds she opens the farmhouse door by turning the handle, a bit boring but it works, then disappears inside and hunts out the freezer. Returning with a bulky green plastic bag, she orders the men to lay the unconscious woman on the ground and gently places the frozen peas on her severely bruising forehead.

Though she's built like a gazelle Bakyt has the constitution of an ox. Minutes later she's come to and is already wiping the tears from her husband's face.

'Silly sausage,' she whispers. Then she slips one hand in her trousers and invites him to kiss the love-juice on her fingertips.

Monty sucks them softly, cries a little more and feels like he did that night they first fell in love. He wonders whether now might be a good moment to suggest she goes off the pill. Any fruit of those loins will direct empires from the cradle.

On second thoughts, best leave it till he knows whether his next stop is Cornwall or Belmarsh.

On the way back he shoots a glance at Percy, who does the same at Viv. Then they both look questioningly at Bakyt, trying not to laugh at her two black eyes. She senses what they're asking and once again settles the matter.

'We bunk, comrade fellows, naughty burglars by light of silvery moon.' Normally her English is better than that, but she's still groggy. Anyway, it's sorted. They'll slip away, like thieves in the night.

Of course they'll pay Mr Ploed first. After all they're law-abiding citizens, except when they're planning lethal acts of terrorism, treason and subversion.

Monty and Percy half expect to find Chopper propping up the bar at the Nuclear Arms, large as life and still wearing his stinky Liberace jacket. But there's no sign of him. Also, joy of joys, Brenstorme seems to be gracing the place with his absence.

In recent days he's felt outnumbered. The peculiar person with the top hat and his psychopathic sidekick with the beret full of holes, the two farming types of questionable sex and those frightful policemen who think of nothing else. It's too much, he's going home.

True to form, however, he gets on the wrong platform at Carlisle station, spends several days and nights on various forms of public transport, and ends up in the Outer Hebrides.

At this point he gives up and joins a monastery. A comfort to be surrounded by men as bonkers and bald as himself. No point telling the Prime Minister, he won't mind. On this at least, Brenstorme's as spot on as he was about the porridge.

He's like a stopped clock. Twice a day it gives the correct time.

*

The journey back also takes an unexpected turn for the Bashar boys. After the batteries on the milk floats die on them, they leave the IRA guys at a bus stop and yomp to the airport cross-country, then try to hijack a helicopter.

The only one big enough to carry them all is in for repair and the boys don't notice it's got no rotor blades. It's even less airworthy when they respond to the squad cars screaming up the tarmac by smashing the windows and firing their Kalashnikovs through them.

Too agitated to aim properly, they're out of ammo in no time. And they stick their hands up when the Police Inspector warns the English punishment for resisting arrest is hanging, drawing and quartering. Struggling to keep a straight face, a constable gets out his penknife. Probably wouldn't be quite up to the job, but it's better than nothing.

The boys are held for a spell in an immigration removal centre, for decency's sake, then quietly deported on a troop transporter.

Back in the heaving bosoms of their families, the returning heroes splash out the money they've saved with the free ride home on a slap-up meal out for their wives. They've never done it before, probably never will again. But, tonight, it'll be the full monty. Or at least the full mezze, plus a glass of real, drinkable, tap water each. The ladies love them.

Bashars Major and Minor don't. Any delay getting those confounded oil contracts means the extra palaces and Bentleys they've set their hearts on will also have to wait. And the boys haven't exactly speeded things up.

*

Chancery's pretty chuffed, however. Slowden is indeed the loveliest place on earth, no accounting for taste, and the teenager readily agrees to be his blushing bride. She's been through several boyfriends in his absence and they all turned out to be wankers.

Young men, she's discovered, always promise more than they can deliver. Either humping her frenziedly and trying to swallow her tits or slamming doors and telling her she's ruined their lives. At least Chancery is consistently surly, and there's room on his moped for two.

Chopper's pleased to be home as well. At least in Belfast you know your enemies are a safe distance away, in Liverpool. If you get a problem on the Falls Road, you always know just the right person to break the shagging eejit's legs for him.

He celebrates the return of his deserters with a ceilidh at a pub that has plant pots everywhere, which solves his Guinness problem nicely. No one spoils the fun by mentioning their expedition. Drug running, protection rackets and the occasional spot of torture are obviously the better option for peaceable folk like them.

Tiddledick, meanwhile, has already cracked open the champagne to celebrate Brenstorme's failure to turn the incident into all-out nuclear war. In fact, it looks like the bugger's buggered off for good.

Fanny's so pleased she bursts into a full Cabinet meeting in her S and M outfit.

*

When the returning Chinese heroes finally hit Beijing they're not sure whether to expect a row of medals personally bestowed by the President of the People's Republic, or something not quite so pleasant.

In the event they're met by a shabbily dressed Fyok Yu, who presents the married guys with divorce papers from their wives. An equally ropey looking Hon Ki hands them whopping great bills from the plastic surgeons. And several pretty young women who've been staring at them suffer an extreme bout of projectile vomiting.

Only one thing for it, then. They get on the first flight back to Edinburgh, open a Chinese food emporium with a built-in brothel and live happily ever after.

Fyok Yu and Hon Ki, whose standing with the standing committee of the politburo is clearly never going to recover, join them. Though they still don't exactly feel they're among friends, as they're immediately set to work dishwashing. Fourteen-hour shifts, Monday through Sunday and a subsistence diet.

*

Adolphus Hillter gets luckier. When his aunt mistakes a sizzling deep fat fryer for a font and tries to baptise herself in it he overturns her latest new will, on the grounds the World Earwig and Worm Protection Society doesn't exist. And the estate doesn't run to ten million.

Codicil twenty, leaving Buckingham Palace to Bonnie Prince Charlie, clinched it. 'Sound mind? Sounds potty to me.' Hillter's solicitor puts things in a lawyerly way.

*

Things also work out perfectly for Colonel Shrapnelle-Sidebotham, in that he survives, unlike the potty lady.

When he saw the BAF plane circling directly above, convincing him death was at hand, he proved his time at Sandhurst wasn't wasted. In a dashing display of military genius he saved his and his men's lives by besieging and overrunning the Norman castle he'd spotted through his binoculars.

That phase of the operation wasn't too difficult as the drawbridge was down, the portcullis up, and the sole defender the grizzled old duke who owned the place. Huffie had the battlements fortified with razor wire and improvised anti-aircraft guns mounted on each tower.

In his rage the duke tried to bag him with a twelve-bore. Aged ninety-three and so riddled with gout he could hardly stand, however, he found his aim lacked the required precision.

The poor man had been in failing health for years. And when he saw his ornamental lawns and Elizabethan kitchen garden transformed into a minefield he died of a heart attack.

Huffie tactfully classified this as collateral damage, and ventured out two days later when GCHQ assured him there were no hostile forces deployed anywhere this side of Pyongyang.

The stand-down was sounded by a lone piper in a ceremony bristling with military precision. The band played 'The White Cliffs of Dover' and 'Rule Britannia', and the NCOs looked embarrassed at what a fucking farce it'd been.

Returning to the area where the bombs looked as if they'd been dropping, they found nothing more than a couple of circular ditches round a farmhouse with a hole in the roof. The duckponds dotted around were all exactly the same size, but Huffie saw nothing odd about this. Mission accomplished then.

So, twenty-four hours after Monty surmised the fucking fuckers had fucking fucked off the fucking fuckers did indeed fucking fuck off.

CHAPTER NINETEEN

The morning after they decided to disappear like thieves in the night, Percy, Viv, Monty and Bakyt set off, appropriately, before daybreak. The Beamer would have been a better getaway car, but at least Simone-Sitrouenne's missing front bumper makes her lighter.

She goes even less slowly when the headlamps fall off as well. Fortunately, this happens after dawn has broken.

Knackered as they are, they're all buzzing with ideas about how they can turn the tables on everyone, now they've broken loose.

Percy takes off his topper, claiming he's always hated the bloody thing, and scratches his head. 'Maybe Guy Fawkes was onto something,' he says thoughtfully.

'You're quite tall enough as it is without being stretched on the rack, you dozy hare-brained twat.' Monty's not in the mood for jokes. That's if it was one.

Viv has a better idea. Swerving into a motorway service area, she boxes Percy on his now exposed ear, whips out her iPhone and bangs off an email to Miss Moneypenny.

An hour or so later, hallelujah, her wildest expectations are exceeded by miles. GCHQ has got a sniff of the Chinese plot to sneak nuclear waste into Breezethwaite. The intelligence is incomplete, but there's been enough digital traffic to build up a picture.

And there's more. Viv reads Miss Moneypenny's email out loud.

'*My lovely man is "fwightfully sowwy" to learn the Bashar "bwothers'" efforts at "cowwupting" the Tory party have been more successful than they first seemed. Loads of local associations are suspected of soaking up illegal donations, naughty people.*

'Even naughtier Tiddledick,' she adds, 'not checking more thoroughly in the first place.'

There's a silence, broken by Percy. 'I can guess the rest. The Foreign Secretary's hated Tiddledick since they were at Eton together. Thought he was a slacker, which he is, by the way. This is his big chance to get the lazy sod out of Downing Street and himself in it.'

Viv's impressed. 'Got it in one, lover. Miss Moneypenny says the list of dishonest Conservative associations has been sitting on the Foreign Secretary's desk for ages. She and Fwightfully Sowwy are convinced the man's just waiting for the right moment before leaking the news.'

Percy's brain is whirring. 'Obviously the party would get a good kicking. All the more reason for a new broom, namely that slimebag, to come in and clean up its act. Westminster sucks, no?'

Monty's always thought so, but never wanted to hurt Percy's feelings by admitting it. 'OK, if you're right, why hasn't Fwightfully Sowwy tipped off Tiddledick?'

'Miss Moneypenny says he knows too many stories about messengers getting shot,' says Viv. 'But she thinks he's being weedy. That's why she's got no problem passing on the full list of dodgy donees to me. Besides, after the appalling way she was treated by that cow Blusterham she loves whistleblowing. Launched her career, remember.'

'Hmmm.' Percy's brain is whirring faster than ever. 'Play it right and I can revive Tiddledick's faltering fortunes. And do myself one big fat favour into the bargain.'

Bakyt remembers the Kazakh way of doing politics, chucking failed leaders out of aeroplanes or shooting them with howitzers, and doesn't follow his logic.

'Simple,' Percy explains. 'If Tiddledick knows nothing till he reads about it in the papers he'll be neck deep in doo-doo. But if I tip him off and he flushes out the culprits he'll be a decisive leader. OK, of a tarnished brand. But at least he'll be safe. And boy will he owe me.'

By now they've pulled in to yet another service area, queued for lunch and sat down. Percy hacks up his greasy sausages into remarkably tiny pieces. Monty remembers how much he always hated Blusterham and half expects him to chuck the fragments on the floor and jump up and down on them. Percy would, only he's hungry.

Ten minutes later he's about to slip out for a ciggie, but doesn't when Bakyt's phone pings. It's an email from Breezethwaite management stating a recent recruitment drive had to be abandoned when a tranche of newly hired engineers failed to turn up for work.

She shares the next bit slowly as she doesn't understand a word of it.

'*These limeys were doggone filthy critters and would have been plugged for less in Murka.*'

'What is limey? What is doggone filthy critter? Where is Murka? Explain please, someone.'

'Americans have smaller brains, they can't help it,' Monty says soothingly. Bakyt is still not satisfied, but agrees the rest of it tallies with an update Viv's received from Miss Moneypenny, stating GCHQ is now confident the Chinese have called off their nuclear waste project.

*

All that's needed now is written proof there definitely was a plot and Percy definitely wasn't behind it. This could be tricky, but it's decided it might be worth Monty dropping by on Slowden on the off chance, bringing the Sten guns with him.

To save time, he completes the journey to Cornwall on the train then screeches up the motorway in the Beamer. He barges through WH Smut into Chancery's office and finds him there, still fiddling with his executive toys. No sign of anything having happened apart from a little gold ring on his left hand.

Monty can't believe a bloke like him would have got married, but recognises the evidence is inconclusive. When there's one too many of them it's hard to work out which is the correct finger for a wedding ring,

Chancery, by contrast, has no problem working out the correct response to two sub-machine guns pointing at his head. Putting his hands up, he curses the Tommy gun getting blown up along with the Caddy.

He will replace it, but even in Slowden you can't just pick one up in the corner shop.

Hugely enjoying himself, Monty gives him the full bad cop routine and is amazed how well it works. Within an hour the confession's typed and signed. And it's agreed Chancery can reinvent himself yet again, anywhere, no questions asked.

So sad to leave his lovely home, but for some reason his bride adores Canvey Island. He hopes it'll be nearly as nice.

*

'Boy, have I got news for you.' Monty's normally calm, but he's been wanting to punch the air with his fist from the second he sauntered calmly and quite slowly out of Chancery's office. Maddeningly, he had to wait to call Percy till he'd driven a couple of miles up the road.

He's irritated at Percy's jaunty response. 'Oh, really? I've got news for you too. But yours first.'

'No, yours. I insist,' Monty explodes. Percy changes tack, saying he won't divulge anything till he's heard the whole story. When he does the poor old air gets another wallop.

'You wait ages for a bus then two come along at once. The dodgy donors cop it. And now, thanks to you, the China shit's shuffled off as well.'

'Quite,' says Monty, mollified. 'But you were saying, you have news for me too?'

'News for you? Did I say that? Suppose I might.' Percy's being wicked, and he knows it. 'Remember Shurelynott? That dear old queen who gives me tittle-tattle from the lobby?'

'Yes yes yes, get on with it. What's he told you this time?'

'Well. You're not going to believe this. Not sure I ought to tell you, really. Another time, perhaps.'

Now he really is being exasperating. Although she's driving the car Viv reaches across with her right hand and tweaks the end of his willy. He takes the hint.

'OK, here goes. Shurleynott's paper has got a sniff of the illegal donations to the Tory party and the Foreign Secretary's slimy little ploy. And that little digger Sharon, who's now chief investigative reporter, is on the case.'

'And I'm on my way,' Monty replies sharply. 'You're going to need the written confession PDQ if you're going to head her off in time.'

Belter the Beamer and slowcoach Simone-Sitrouenne hook up near Bristol. Monty, Bakyt and Viv's material is enough to button up the nuclear case. Sharon will see at a glance it's watertight.

She needn't know the sources of the story, or how come Percy's got it. His call is short, but perfectly phrased.

'My dear, got a bit of titty-tickling tittle-tattle that might just goggle your gondola.'

She recognises his voice on the phone immediately and is very happy to head straight to Bristol. Especially as it gets her out of lunch with a sleazy old peer who always wants to swop government secrets for an inside track on her knickers. Fat chance, fat slob.

Percy's a different matter. She rummages in her drawer for the see-through bra she keeps there for special occasions, pops by Shurelynott's office and winks.

'Off to see Penislow, dear, may have something juicy for me. May have something juicy for him too.'

Shurelynott tries not to look surprised about the meeting, but is astonished at the girlie giggle. He's never heard it before. 'Have fun, dear lady. Percy does have his charms.'

Sharon clocks the wistful tone and promises herself she'll spike his drinks again one of these evenings. Not out of malice, just curiosity. She guesses a quarter of a century ago Shurelynott was quite pretty, but hopes for once she's got it all wrong.

Three hours later, Percy receives her graciously at the Bristol City Centre Premier Inn.

'Afraid it's not quite the Dorchester,' he says with that self-effacing grin that's served him so well in the past. Sharon tries to be abrasive and pert at the same time. It doesn't work.

'Well, what can you do me for?' In her flustered state she's not sure that came out right, nor is Percy. He notices her blush and decides to keep her guessing for the moment.

'How can I phrase this? Mutual satisfaction beckons? We can put a smile on one another's face?' He's speaking professionally, she takes it personally. If the fat slob had said that he'd have got a fat lip by now.

As it is, the only lips that are swelling are Sharon's, though no one's to know as she's still got her knickers on. She's fancied Percy for years, but reminds herself she's on a job. Not the job. That might come later, as she hopes will she. Several times, if he fancies making a night of it…

To allow time to let her breathing settle down, Percy asks her how much she knows about the Tory party funding scam people are whispering about. If the tale's pretty much sewn up he's wasting his time, but if it's still only chaff in the rumour mill she may be tempted by his offer.

Remembering all the tricks of his old trade, including the one about soft drinks when you're playing hardball, Percy eventually gets her to admit she can't yet stand the story up.

Throughout the meal he keeps her wine regularly topped up, and gets her sniggering at saucy tales from his days in media and at Number Ten. He's a legend in Fleet Street, and she loves the way he's opening up to her. She's so aching to do the same with her legs she forgets how much gossip she really shouldn't be sharing about her own bosses.

Everything he tells her is in his book, probably why it sold so well, but Percy's pretty sure she's never even looked at it. He guesses on holiday she visits historic buildings only so she can take selfies next to them. That she's a now kind of girl, razor sharp but deeply shallow.

Over the coffee and brandy he finally puts it to her straight.

'In this dossier I have chapter and verse on an international conspiracy. It'll open the floodgates.' He produces a wad of papers from his inside jacket pocket and lets her read chunks of it.

Doing so, Sharon smiles at the aptness of Percy's turn of phrase. Some journalists actually get a sexual thrill out of a cracking good yarn, and this is as good as they get. She discreetly checks her crotch and is relieved her trousers aren't giving anything away.

'And in return? You want something from me, surely?' Her pupils are dilated, her hands are trembling and she doesn't care about her jeans. She'll be whipping them off soon enough.

'Yes my dear. I do want something from you. I want it a lot.' Sharon leans forwards. She's almost panting.

'Well?'

'I want you to drop that party funding crap. In return this stuff is all yours. You've seen enough to know it stands up.'

'And there's me thinking you wanted me to drop my drawers and wait for something even nicer to stand up.' Sharon's attempt to make a joke of her misunderstanding flops miserably. She's quite close to tears.

In spite of everything Percy feels sorry for her. He relates to a kid from the wrong side of the tracks fighting to break through barriers. Also he thinks of Viv on that first night, desperately wanting something he won't give.

'So sorry, dear lady, I know the only way to overcome temptation is to yield to it, but I couldn't bring myself to betray my wife.'

Reaching across and pressing her hand, he hopes he's letting her down gently enough.

Annoyingly, such loyalty only makes him more attractive in her eyes. It's so charmingly old-fashioned, so not what she's used to in men. But the story's blinding, and watertight. Self-preservation is kicking in.

'But why? Why would you look out for that Tory tosser? I don't get it.' As she knows she isn't going to in either sense, Sharon's thinking logically. Percy's answer sounds like sense too, in its convoluted way. It's also designed to throw her right off the track.

'You know the saying my enemy's enemy is my friend? Well if this bastard's the bastard I think it is he's not my friend, he's the bastard that did me over in the same way. So I hate the bastard. Get my drift? He's a cult, spelt with an N.'

CHAPTER TWENTY

Percy blows Sharon a kiss as the doors swish closed on the lift whisking her up to the room she's booked. Too bad it's a suite when she only needed a single. Still, she's satisfied in one way. His reason for wanting to shaft the dodgy donor rings true. Can't argue with hatred.

She thinks of what she used to call Nobby Sleeseby, something like a cult but without the delicate spelling, and compares him not very favourably with most of the paper's execs. Part of her hopes she wasn't too indiscreet about them.

Percy's glad she was. Her every word is loud and clear on the miniature tape recorder he had in his breast pocket throughout the dinner. The scumbag editor lunging at anything with tits? Wouldn't be safe in a taxi with a lactating cow? And the proprietor's tax evasion? No getting round that one.

He's ashamed of having tricked her like this, but desperate times and all that. The nuclear material he's handed over will keep her busy for a while, and she's promised to lay off the dodgy donations. If she changes her mind later the tape will change it back for her.

When he returns to his peculiarly purple room at the inn, Percy gives Viv a huge hug. 'The reptile's off the case, so Tiddledick's all ours. When I tip him off he'll be so bloody grateful maybe he really will give me a peerage.'

'Why not pop the question, dear? You'll get the chance sooner than you think.' Viv smiles. 'Remember, he and Fanny like little breaks in Cornwall. There's one coming up, and they're on their way.'

'Bloody hell. Good thing I didn't fuck up with the hack. What exactly are you cooking up?' Percy didn't mean this literally, more fool him.

'You know, I can't decide whether to go for nouvelle or traditional.'

'Sorry, you're losing me.'

Without a word, Viv motions Percy to the computer, opens her emails and starts slowly scrolling down. He can hardly believe what he's reading.

'Darling Fannykins! Know Poncey will hate it! So will Percy! You simply must come for din-dins at ours! They'll both poo themselves, silly boys! Promise?'

'Right-oh.'

Percy snorts at Fanny's postscript.

'Be a hoot, darling! Tiaras at tea-time! We can eat the cat!'

*

The final leg of the journey home is fraught with tension, as Simone-Sitrouenne has clearly had too much excitement lately and keeps coming over all unnecessary. Intermittent bursts of hissing and farting from the engine are followed by puffs of smoke wafting from under the dashboard.

But when they do finally teeter up the drive, the welcome makes up for it all. Little Trudi's so pleased they're back she has a little accident. Nanny's eyes light up at the three tubes of K-Y jelly they got her and Percy's shoes get the treatment.

He thinks about getting some Chelsea boots, just to be annoying.

After prising the animal off his feet he gets an extra hard bite on the nose followed by loads of licking. It seems he's no right to be away so long but is forgiven, just this once.

'It's surreal,' Percy begins, over a nice cup of tea. 'In the old days when the telly zoned out a card appeared saying "Normal service will be resumed as soon as possible". It just has, as though it's never even been interrupted.

'Reminds me of a story about a guy who fought his way through World War One and somehow survived. When he finally returned to work at his old factory, you know what the foreman said?'

'No, tell,' murmurs Viv.

'He said "Haven't seen you for a while. Been on nights, have you?"'

Viv smiles, but adds a caveat.

'Of course there could be a knock on the door at any moment. The police, telling us we don't have to say anything, but whatever we do say may be taken down in evidence and used against us.'

Still, the chandelier tinkles that night, Nanny gets so worked up she does a little tinkle too. And in the morning Percy sits at his rickety table in the garden to write a coruscating piece about modern politicians' foolish tendency to act in haste.

'And if they repent at leisure they've no one to blame but themselves.' He's quite pleased with that line, though Viv thinks it's a bit rich and tells him so.

He knows, but to get her back pinches her bum, hard. Little Trudi finds her squeal so funny she doesn't stop giggling till Fang springs forward and savages her foot. He's annoyed little girl bootees have the wrong sort of laces.

Viv takes her cue from the cat. Leaning over Percy as if to kiss his ear, she bites it. He grimaces then grins, taking his punishment like a man. He wishes it was all as everyday as it seems. Stepping purposefully back into the house, she's thinking the same.

In her office, Viv checks her survey's final tally of local Tory chairmen against the names Miss Moneypenny has supplied. Those most emphatically telling her company to mind its own business are those with the best reasons to mind anyone wanting to know their business.

She snaps shut the lid of her elegant little Queen Anne bureau. Its polished mahogany surface reminds her how far she's travelled in life. Her childhood desk was pretty enough, but did come from a charity shop.

Looking out of the window at the sun's rays caressing the Atlantic and the pink and pastel blue hydrangeas skirting the garden, she sighs. The illusion of calm serenity is heightened by the call of gulls in the middle distance.

Fixing a date for the dinner party, she promises Fanny a comfortable bed and a night to remember. *'Know how you've missed the cat, darling! Any serving suggestions? Slow roast? On a spit?'*

Seconds later comes the reply. *'On a hot tin roof, darling!'*

The two women have never actually met, and Viv can but hope she can keep up the banter while Percy and Poncey have their little talk. Monty and Bakyt will help break the ice, and if there's a Kazakh episode Fanny's bound to find it funny.

There's a good chance Nanny will enjoy the ride later, judging by gossip Monty's picked up from the lads about goings-on at Number Ten. There are two chandeliers in the living room, one under each bedroom. Viv decides to get her another tube of K-Y, just to be safe.

*

The appointed day dawns bright and clear. Sharon's exclusive about the Chinese radioactive imports appeared yesterday, under the snappy headline 'Nuclear Attack Thwacked!' A Breezethwaite spokesperson claimed the conspirators would never have got away with it, which Fleet Street took to mean the company got lucky and bloody knows it.

Trying to enjoy his holiday in Cornwall, Tiddledick notes the Office for Nuclear Regulation has launched an inquiry, and hopes that'll keep the pack off his back. Probably, as it's essentially a crime story involving a private company. He'll congratulate Percy tonight on his piece entitled 'No Nukes is Good Nukes', which seemed to set the tone.

Viv thought Percy should have steered well clear of that subject, and wasn't impressed when he said chutzpah can be fun.

'Yes, dear, but what about the boy who murders his parents then demands clemency from the court because he's an orphan? Isn't that chutzpah too?'

Percy frowns, and for the millionth time worries about Sharon suddenly blowing the gaff on the party-funding scandal.

'I should've told her about that bloody tape. Warned her if she published she'd be damned. And buggered. And down the jobcentre pronto.'

'You trusted your instinct, dear. Beats dishonour among thieves any day.'

Percy thinks about this, picks up little Trudi and tickles her face with his hair. She giggles and says 'daddisabusted'. He's not sure busted was quite what the child meant, but hopes he won't be.

Minutes before his guests are due to arrive, the postman shows up with a bulky, expensive-looking envelope Percy has to sign for. He guesses the coronet printed on the top left-hand corner means it's something boring from the Lord Lieutenant, wanting him to show up at the Royal Cornwall Show or open a bloody fete somewhere. It can wait.

Tiddledick can't wait to get it all over with as he drives through Percy's gate, and is irritated when his bodyguard grumbles at being told he's got to wait in the second vehicle outside the high brick wall.

'For god's sake, that chap Chalky White will be there. Knowing the Met, the fellow's probably still got his gun.'

Though that last bit was meant as a joke, the policeman's forced laugh sets him straight. He'll be well protected then.

Still, cruising slowly up the drive, he's nervous.

'Last time I saw Penislow we were shouting insults at one another across the chamber. Feels weird having to be nice to him.'

'He's probably a sweetie really, if Viv's anything to go by, darling.' Fanny reaches across and jiggles her husband's balls.

Ponsomby almost hits an ancient elm tree.

'Save that for beddy-byes for god's sake,' he splutters.

Fanny smiles, and manages to combine soothing kindliness with waspish irony.

'Temper temper, lover boy.'

Pulling up outside the front door, Tiddledick clambers out with the fixed smile and outstretched hand he uses on ghastly grassroots Tories.

Too late he remembers he hasn't opened the passenger door for Fanny, but Viv's beaten him to it. The women share a mwah mwah mwah embrace, thus looking after one another's make-up as well as starting as they mean to go on. Memsahibs' masonry, never fails.

Ponsomby feels Tony Blair's pain, wanting to be sick before Prime Minister's Questions. He's been telling himself not to be patronising about Percy's pebble-dashed council house, and is taken aback at the sight of the rustic chic manor house, much cosier than a Palladian mansion.

He's thrown further off his stride by Percy's greeting.

'Why, it's been ages. Delighted to receive you at last, and your delicately exquisite wife.'

Turning his gaze on her, he ceremoniously bows his head.

'So pleased, dear lady, to begin our acquaintance with a compliment. Certain to turn into a lasting friendship, it starts in the right manner.'

Fanny sniggers, already briefed by Viv on Percy's theatrical ways. It takes Ponsomby several martinis and half a bottle of Bollinger to loosen up, but he gets there in the end, what with Percy's bonhomie and Monty's armed but disarming presence.

Bakyt helps things along with reassurances about Sharon's scoop. Much needed, as the nuclear industry's rather a mystery to Ponsomby, surprise, surprise.

'Waste imports from China? No problem for government. I investigate verse. And chapter. Official checks, balances? Perfectly in place.'

'Goody goody,' Tiddledick mutters, then wishes he'd sounded a bit more prime ministerial. He relaxes when Percy tops up his glass, winks and tells him it's all bollocks anyway.

Same as on his night with Sharon, Percy's been careful not to get too pissed till the business is out of the way. He also makes a point of keeping an eye on Ponsomby's intake. No use coming to an agreement only to find the silly sod can't remember any of it in the morning.

When he mentioned his strategy to Viv earlier she snorted. 'Kettles and pots, Percy?'

'Watch yourself, or I'll scratch your eyes out.' Percy was only playing, but Fang's tail twitched. Claws are for cats, not humans.

CHAPTER TWENTY-ONE

By eleven the chandeliers are turned off but reflect the candle light, giving the dining room an intimate glimmer. Viv turns the weird music up, Bakyt springs lightly onto the table, Fanny thinks of whips and tassels and Percy discreetly invites Ponsomby to step into his office.

It's beautifully choreographed, and Monty's been careful to leave them a large flask of something brown and wet.

To his own amazement, Percy's taken a liking to Ponsomby, clocking he's no Tory fundamentalist and perfectly easy-going, provided no one's getting on his tits. Still, there's a job to be done.

'Dear fellow, thought you might like a gander at this,' he says, opening a Word document listing dozens of local party chairmen. Ponsomby wonders who cares about these swivel-eyed Neanderthals and wishes he was still in the dining room. Bakyt's dead sexy, much more interesting than these dreary old farts.

Then he registers the charges against them, and his body language changes. He takes a huge slurp of what turns out to be weapons-grade coffee, sits up straight and clamps on his glasses.

'What? What? What the hell's this?' It's his first profanity of the evening, which suggests he's getting it.

'Sanctimonious turds, always banging on at me how to run the country. Couldn't run a brothel at Cheltenham Ladies' College.'

Percy smiles at the thought, and notes Ponsomby's normally pink complexion has turned puce. Another good sign.

'How long's the Foreign Secretary known about this? Why wasn't I told? I'll have that bugger's guts for garters.'

'Delighted to hear it,' Percy murmurs. 'Yours would have been ripe for ripping out if he'd done his worst. We both know what I mean. Hate to mention it, but further inquiries on your part might have been advisable when the first allegations surfaced.'

Tiddledick glances round the room, takes in the Victorian pine bookcases stuffed full of leather-bound classical works which look well thumbed, and finally focuses on Percy.

'Won't ask how you got this, but why are you showing to me? You of all people?'

Normally he's quick at summing up a situation at a glance, but right now he's stumped.

Percy tactfully paraphrases Viv's line about dishonour among thieves. 'Been there myself, dear chap. Never quite got over it. The pain of betrayal. Wouldn't wish it on anyone, not even you.' His smile, like the Mona Lisa's, can be read several ways.

Ponsomby pauses for thought. Eventually he gestures towards the printer. 'Would you mind? Be awfully obliged, old boy.'

As Percy presses the button he hopes his grin isn't too, well, crooked.

It isn't. Ponsomby's mind has been racing. He thinks back to Fanny's handy insights into the attempts to entrap top Treasury people, and the few dodgy donations he did manage to sort out. Also he's noticed her obvious camaraderie with Viv. Everything falls into place.

Stuffing the papers in his inside pocket he rejoins the party. By now Bakyt, still dancing on the table, is stark bollock naked. The performance is chaste and aesthetic, well, relatively, but for some reason everyone's up for bed. In no time the house is full of Eastern promise.

At first Nanny's puzzled by the smell of joss-sticks. But with the opening bars of Symphony for Two Chandeliers she grasps the point of the extra K-Y, and several other things. When Percy and Viv were away she more than once thanked god Ann Summers had a sale on.

An hour later she really can't keep her eyes or anything else open any longer. She falls asleep with a contented sigh. A bit sore, but none the worse for that.

*

In the morning Ponsomby's itching to get away, for reasons he doesn't specify. But as well as a handshake Percy gets a man-hug, and a glance of gratitude and respect.

Waving the car off, Percy winks at Viv. 'Put not thy trust in princes?'

In response, she tweaks first his nose, then his willy. He waits till the car is safely out of sight before he turns and snogs her, vehemently.

Nanny averts little Trudi's fascinated gaze, recognises tell-tale signs and blushes scarlet. She can but hope the unmistakeable moisture isn't showing.

Two days later criminal charges are brought against thirty-three local Tory chairmen, and Ponsomby announces he's adopted a zero-tolerance policy on corruption. Seems he's been busy, what with that and the Cabinet reshuffle after the Foreign Secretary's sudden resignation.

Percy's impressed. 'Talk about the front foot, this bloke could sprint a marathon in leg irons,' he tells Viv. 'But if he's that ruthless, why stop there? Why not take out take out poor Fwightfully Sowwy while he's at it? And Miss Moneypenny? And...'

And... a police car is nosing its way up the drive. Percy goes white and curses himself for the fool that he is. So much for buying favours. Anyway, Ponsomby's the Prime Minister, not Director of Public Prosecutions. There is such a thing in England as the rule of law.

As the Chief Inspector steps out of the vehicle, flanked by two burly sergeants, Percy stands up, head hanging low. Viv squeezes his wrist while Fang arches his back and hisses.

'Are you Doctor Percy Penislow PC, former Member of Parliament?' The tone says it all. Public humiliation, mockery, vilification and years behind bars. Maybe a bit knocked off for good behaviour. Best he can hope for. It's not as if he didn't have it coming to him.

Percy gently disengages Viv's grip and stretches out his arms for the cuffs, closing his eyes in despair. Which is why he doesn't see one of the coppers winking at Monty, who'd been gripping his pistol in its holster in case these guys are imposters.

The Chief Inspector takes Percy's hands, turns them over, and places on his palms an envelope. OK, arrest isn't imminent. This'll be a summons to appear somewhere for questioning. Percy thinks of ancient torture methods, the slower the better, it sharpens the pain.

He opens the letter, which, astonishingly, has the Number Ten logo. Has Ponsomby taken leave of his senses? He can't just get people put away any more than he can just let them off. This is ridiculous. Still, better look at the bloody thing, learn the worst.

It's a scrawly hand-written note.

'*Sorry about the hoo-hah, rozzers and all that, wanted to be sure this was delivered to you personally, dear boy. Did me a great service, never forget it. Saved my bacon. Can't think how to repay you. Fancy a peerage? Yours if you want it. Sincerely, Poncey. PS: Fanny says Bakyt's got great little titties. Toodle-pip.*'

The policemen salute and return to the car, the Chief Inspector shaking the demented cat off his boot with some difficulty. Percy sits down and bursts into tears, but Fang and little Trudi carry on licking his face till he starts laughing instead.

His face crumpled, his voice cracking, he glances up at Viv. 'Lord Penis of Percy-Low it is then?'

'Just settle for Penis, penis-brain.'

*

Of course he'll gratefully accept. He's always had a soft spot for the red benches because the lords' chamber is so screaming camp. Besides, it'll give him a platform if he wants to sound off in person instead of just in print.

'And the three-hundred and something a day attendance allowance is better than a kick in the *cojones*, don't you think?'

Viv smiles. 'Life after death? And the good life at that. More than you deserve.'

Percy lowers his eyes in an insincere display of humility. But the ancient traditions of the House of Lords remind him of that letter with the coronet on it that he'd forgotten all about.

Sliding open his Victorian roll-top desk, which contrasts nicely with the wobbly 1970s chair he's sitting on, Percy holds the bulky envelope close to his face. To find out how the other half smells.

He feels insulated from his appalling misdemeanours by Tiddledick's note. The Lord Lieutenant can do his worst. The Royal Cornwall Show's a breeze, now he's got a future.

But when he prises open the envelope, seems a shame to tear it, Percy discovers he doesn't have a past. At least not the one he thought he had. It's the biggest shock of his life.

The letter heading bears the names Messrs Ffilch, Ffitch and Ffilth, Solicitors.

'Dear Percy Penislow,' it begins, *'I beg to inform you that you are no longer Percy Penislow. You are Lord Trelooney, last descendant of the ancient Normandy family of Trèsfou, which came to Britain with the Conqueror, and anglicised its name after the battle of Agincourt.*

'You were domiciled in childhood with one Peter Penislow (decd.), espoused to Pearl Penislow (of unsound mind) according to the wishes of your father, the late Lord Trelooney. Peter Penislow (decd.), hitherto in the service of the late Lord Trelooney, acceded to the care and maintenance of his infant son, your aforementioned self.

'Adoption papers were presented to his lordship at intervals deemed fit, but never received his written imprimatur. Ergo on his regrettable demise, which took place on the 15th inst., you inherited his title. Insuper et statum, according to the terms of his last will and testament, you are also sole owner of Trelooney Hall, an hereditament of limited pecuniary value.'

Percy scratches his head and tries to translate.

'Mum and Dad weren't really Mum and Dad,' he tells Fang, who doesn't look bothered either way. 'And now my real dad, Lord fucking bonkers or whatever, has left me his title and his gaff. Well, stone the fucking crows.'

Fang perks up at the thought of loads of birds landing lifeless in front of him but doesn't say anything. Not a cat thing, talking.

'Viv! Viv!' Percy calls out then remembers she's gone shopping. Nanny's disappeared somewhere, to change her skirt, as it happens, but Trudi wanders in. Not an ideal confidante, but he feels the need to tell someone. Anyone, really.

'You're going to be a lady one day, young lady. What do you say to that?'

'Fucking hell.'

Trudi has no idea what he's talking about or the meaning of what she's just said, though her pronunciation skills, Percy notes, have come on leaps and bounds. But now Nanny reappears and whisks the dear little girl away, leaving Percy free to wonder who he is.

Leafing through the bits of paper and crinkly parchment, he finds the birth certificate that confirms the pompous twat was telling the truth in his maddening way. He also finds the deeds of the ancient family home that's now apparently his. And there's more…

*

It's a handwritten letter, written in a shaky hand, though the style suggests it once belonged to a forceful personality.

> *'Well m'boy, time to say goodbye,'* it begins. *'Bit overdue, but you know how it is. Your loving mater copped it having you and what could I do? Never was one for the old pater patter. Dear Peter Penislow, god rest him, head footman in the jolly old household. Obvious choice.*
>
> *'Couldn't keep him around the place, what with you in tow and all that, but I bought him ovens. So he could feed the poor. And you dear boy. Good soul, that Peter, took good care of that silly filly Pearl too.*
>
> *'Little minx that one, after he'd shuffled off I had her meself once or twice, then got the sawbones to give her the chop. Stumped up for the op, naturally. Best service I ever did anyone. Would have so many children her fanny would've fallen off.*
>
> *'Bit of a let-down as a mother on her lonesome, I*

understand. Try to forgive her, couldn't help herself helping herself. Must admit sis Nora didn't do much for me, but she stepped into the breach. Did gallant service. Boring old bag, but just the ticket for you, what?

'Should have got to know you better. But distractions, you know. The ladies, and tax and other awkward things. Didn't dare show up in Blighty. Not sure the house is shipshape these days, but kept an eye out for you. Got a roof over Nora's head. Humble, but these council wallahs see they don't leak.

'You seemed a brainy-box, no need for Eton and all that, but invested in health insurance. Cost a dashed fortune, but the old family has its foibles. Had a feeling you'd be nesting in the Priory now and then. Should've popped by but always preferred monocles to manacles.

'Must dash, got an appointment with the jolly old maker. Best not keep him waiting. Stiff upper lip old chap. Your ever-loving pater.'

CHAPTER TWENTY-TWO

Percy sits back, pulls Fang onto his lap and absent-mindedly caresses him in just the wrong way. Though the punishment makes his hand bleed he doesn't notice. His head feels like a hamster cage with a rhinoceros stuffed into it. To distract himself he googles Trelooney Hall.

It's now a ruin, he discovers, so overgrown it isn't even open to the public. Aha. For 'limited pecuniary value' read diddly-squat. Who cares?

Dazed and numb, he wonders vaguely if Trudi would like to elaborate on her earlier statement, then decides fucking hell summed up the situation nicely.

In the absence of Viv he reaches for the broad-based brandy decanter. Fang looks more forgiving when they both have a tipple. Though Percy's is more of a torrent it does help unclog his brain, so he scoops the animal up to resume their conversation of a few years back.

'I'm not a village oik, I'll have you know.' Fang's eyes do not open wide in wonderment. All he does is purr, in a slurry sort of way, as he doesn't hold his drink as well as he really should by now.

Percy presses on regardless. 'I didn't go to the Sistine Chapel as a kid, and didn't feel like I went to school with the Medici brothers. But I should have done, because I'm a blue-blooded toff. The chapel up the road? The bloke in the Post Office? Not for my sort, me old china.'

Fang blinks, but only because he's getting bored now and fancies a kip. No matter, Percy's talking to himself really. Joking, more like, to protect himself from cascading grief.

He never was like Mum and Dad, but that's who they were. They changed his nappies. Put up with him whinging. Played with him. Sat up with him all night when he got ill. Loved him. Same as Auntie Nora, through his adolescence, right up till she died.

Now, out of nowhere, there's this 'ever-loving pater' he never met. Aristocratic, irresponsible, slightly crazy, riddled with snobbery, emotionally strangulated and a womaniser. Even had it off with the mummy who accidentally fucked up his sexuality for decades.

*

Viv gets a shock when she gets back from Waitrose, not forgetting Boots, with Nanny in mind. For sure, her husband does like a tipple when the sun's over the yardarm. But it isn't every day she finds him slumped on the floor, gripping the decanter like a battle hammer.

'Gesh what, darling, Auntie Nora'sh not my auntie.' Percy's expression is as haggard as his news is unexpected. Putting down her bags, Viv kneels beside him and cradles his stooping head in her arms.

'What is it, lover? Comedy? Tragedy? Tragicomedy? For god's take tell, crazy man.'

'That'sh jusht it. Shink I am going crazy.' Percy's eyes are tightly closed as he's fighting back tears. 'Pershy Penishlow doeshn't exisht. Never did. It'sh all in there. Read for yourshelf. Been shumshing of a shock. At least I can shtill shay shock.'

With a tormented giggle he gestures wildly in the direction of the pile of papers on his desk and passes out.

Viv gets Nanny to help manhandle him into bed, tucks him up, then returns to the office.

He'd said he really must sort out letters lying around. Boring, routine stuff. But he'd mentioned one with a coronet on the envelope. They have no secrets, and anyway she's reading by invitation.

The pages are so muddled it takes a while to work out which go with which. But eventually she gets everything in order, on the desk if not in her head. Halfway through the ever-loving pater letter she pads softly out of the room, returning with a small glass of sherry.

Like Percy, she struggles to grasp the enormity of it all. But unlike Percy she's not traumatised. A lot of what she's reading makes pieces of the jigsaw puzzle of a man she married a quarter of a century ago finally fit into place.

Then she remembers something Fanny said about why she felt connected to Cornwall, when Bakyt was doing her stuff and the men were out of earshot. She bangs off an email, not expecting a reply for a while. Past gin o'clock, the computer is not what Fanny likes to open.

*

In the morning, after a fitful night's sleep, Viv googles Trelooney, on the off-chance, and is amazed how much comes up.

She's particularly intrigued by a blog written by an amateur historian. It claims the first notable Trèsfou was the illegitimate son of a blacksmith, granted a dukedom by another bastard, Guillaume Le Conquérant, for his heroism at the Battle of Hastings.

According to this account, Trèsfou slaughtered eight of King Harold's bodyguards with a specially sharpened horseshoe then stuck an anvil in his eye. The arrow depicted in the Bayeux tapestry, it claims, was the result of a mistranslation, but William liked the idea of life following art.

In the English Civil War, the blog continues, Trelooney, as he'd now become, sided with the crown. Trelooney Hall changed hands several times during the conflict, and at one point the poor man had to fire cannon at his own home. On the royal restoration King Charles the Second graciously paid for the broken windows.

More recently, and, Viv hopes, more plausibly, Percy's grandfather got the Victoria Cross for valour in the second battle of Ypres, and his father picked up a Distinguished Service Order for gallantry in Burma.

Reading how he earned the decoration, taking on an entire Japanese platoon armed only with a ballpoint pen, Viv isn't sure gallantry is the word she'd have used.

Still, she decides, it's very Percy. And when he finally stumbles into the room in his dressing gown, rumple-headed and bleary-eyed, he looks like he's also taken on an entire Japanese platoon, but lost.

'Good morning, dear,' Viv says cheerfully.

'Good? That what you call it?' His croaking voice is distinctly less cheerful. 'Looking for a pointed stick, so I can deflate my skull.'

'Wouldn't do that, you might need it for later. And a stiff upper lip, now you're a peer, dear.'

Percy grips his forehead with both hands, wishes he hadn't as it begins pounding all the harder, and his eyes gradually come into focus.

'Shit. Wasn't a dream then? God help me.'

He slumps down onto the little pastel green brocade-covered chaise longue that Viv's particularly fond of. Its delicate Victorian frame creaks. The noise feels like a drill through Percy's head.

Viv leans over him briefly, kisses his hands, promises to return with the best medicine in the world, glides into the kitchen and fires up the rocket espresso coffee machine.

The entire household picks up on Percy's mood. As Viv leaves the room little Trudi trots in, climbs onto his stomach, gives him her special look of wide-eyed innocence, and quotes herself. 'Fucking hell.'

She hasn't learned overnight what the expression means, but he seemed pleased last time she used it.

Nanny smiles at the sight of Percy perking up a bit. He and Viv let her down badly last night, and hope springs eternal in her needy little breasts.

Fang joins the party, grabs Trudi's bare feet, and bites them playfully but hard. 'Fuck off bluddimoggie,' she squeals. At this Percy can't help but laugh, and be impressed how quickly the tiny child's getting the hang of Anglo-Saxon.

Viv returns with the steaming jug, Percy's favourite half-litre mug and a delicate little white bone-china cup and saucer for herself, and shoos the others out.

'Admit it, you knew you were a misfit all along,' she begins. 'But Pearl and Peter will always be your family in your heart. Same as Auntie Nora. No one can change that, not even that old screwball who gave you his genes. He got a military decoration in Burma, by the way, for being as insane as you.'

For the first time Percy's half-closed eyes register a flicker of interest. 'You sure about that? Be nice to know the old sod did something more than roger ladies and dodge taxmen.'

Viv turns to the computer. She's a whiz at research and pretty soon she's got verification both of the decoration, and how old Trelooney got it. Percy's astonished at what he's reading.

'Good god, the guy really was as nutty as I am. Can't believe I was even born.'

Maybe because he was, against the odds stacked up by a platoon of Japanese soldiers, or maybe it's down to Viv's kindness, or the coffee. For whatever reason, he's feeling better.

'So I'm a chip off the old suicidally manic block, and descendant of centuries' worth of remarkable people. Shits,

I expect, mostly, but remarkably shitty. And there's me, a blue blood, devoting an entire career to bringing down my own kind. Whatever next?'

'Funny you should ask that,' says Viv as her computer pings and she sees it's an email from Fanny. 'Perhaps you'd better read this for yourself.'

'Darling!! Had the hots for Percy, naughty me, smacky botty!! He's my third cousin twice removed!! Sobs!! Must be a law against getting it off with rellies!!

'Tell him from me to piddle on the proles and join the Carlton Club!! Totally Tory!! Poncey can get him in anytime!! Bit stuffy, though!! Fancy a night out with me, darling? Torture Garden's much more fun!! Bring Bakyt!! She's horny too!!

'PS: Cat still alive? Yes? Pity!!'

A long silence. Broken eventually by Percy. 'Don't know if I want to kill the woman or kiss her. But surely we aren't related? Tell me she's not serious.'

'Only about two things. Sex and the family tree. She told me it's pinned up in the walk-in wardrobe at home where she keeps her fetish gear. Becoming a duchess is her dream, only it'd mean killing hundreds of relations first. Plus some of them live in Brighton, well Hove actually, she says, and crossing the river's against her religion.'

'Fucking hell.' Just as Percy says this little Trudi barges in and claps her little hands.

'Clever-daddi,' she cries, impressed that he too is getting to grips with Anglo-Saxon. As Nanny whisks her out again Percy clamps one arm round Viv and uses his free hand to pick up the phone and key in Monty's number.

'Now hear this, lower-class person, I am a peer of the realm. You are not. So show respect if you wish to avoid groaning under yoke of servitude or screaming under torture to death.'

Monty knows Percy well enough to spot when he's messing around, but the late-night call he got from Viv last night helps explain what it's all about, and he plays along magnificently.

'Oh lord and master, honoured to be at your service in however humble a capacity. Privilege to lick the underside of your boots, or of your person if you prefer. And my dutiful lady wife, one Bakyt of this parish, respects the *droit du seigneur*. In sooth she's gagging for it.'

Charlie Chaplin's line, 'A day without laughter is a wasted day', crosses Percy's mind as he puts the receiver down. Suddenly he's still Percy, still alive and blessed with a family and a future. And a cat, for better or for worse.

He looks out of the window. The waves are crashing on the beach as they have for millions of years and will for millions more. He'll try and do his little bit in the House of Lords, all thanks to Poncey and none to Trelooney as that's so last century, and he smiles at Viv.

'All is for the best in the best of all possible worlds, darling?'

'Let's hope so, dear. With you anything's possible.'

For no apparent reason Fang chooses this moment to attack Percy's left hand, causing a destructive reflex action. The Apple Mac does not rate the coffee that's just been tipped into it. A whole week's work is lost forever, and, by the looks of it, the computer as well.

This does not make Viv's day. '*Autre jour, même merde,*' she mutters.

Percy understands her complaint, that he's always messing things up, but pretends he doesn't.

'Is that French for you lust after me passionately and always will?' He's cocked his head on one side like a puppy that's puzzled by a funny noise, but his face is laughing.

Viv's expression is a mixture of exasperation, despair and desire. Mostly desire, actually. Leaning down so her forehead is almost touching his, she grips his cheeks and stares at him intently. 'I'll give you French, bastard,' she whispers.

With that she kisses him so deeply his eyes nearly pop out. For one so petite, Viv has a surprisingly long tongue.